HER
PERFECT
REVENGE

BOOKS BY LESLEY SANDERSON

HER PERFECT REVENGE

LESLEY SANDERSON

bookouture

Published by Bookouture in 2023

An imprint of Storyfire Ltd.
Carmelite House
50 Victoria Embankment
London EC4Y 0DZ
United Kingdom

www.bookouture.com

ISBN: 978-1-83790-342-9
eBook ISBN: 978-1-83790-337-5

To Nariece, my swimming buddy

PROLOGUE

The swimmer stands in the sea, waves lapping at waist height, before diving under the water and emerging with a gasp, confronted by the first shock of the cold. The reflexive recoil, then the composure. Deep breathing, relaxing. Strong arms reach forward, hands tucking back down, curving under the sea, dragging the water backwards to propel the body forward. Feet straight and flipping up and down, toes pointed, like a ballet dancer, the swimmer a thing of beauty. The others in the sea pay no attention, focusing on their own swims, encountering the cold temperature in their individual ways, moving fast or slow, finding their own pace. Nobody sees the swimmer travel out too far, getting slower, fighting for breath. Nobody sees them look frantically around for anyone, anything that might help; nobody hears the desperate moans; and nobody witnesses them swallowing huge gulps of salty water before sinking under the waves.

Nobody sees the swimmer disappear. Only one person knew it was going to happen.

ONE

PRESENT

The ceremony took place at the local registry office, thirty people, all fitting neatly into the small room where they said their vows. Yellow rose sprigs in their lapels, Alex's sister, Caroline, one witness, Felicity's mother, Sheila, the other. Colleagues from the university where both Felicity and Alex worked, their friends from the swimming group, other family members and a couple of old friends. They'd wanted to keep it small. It had been a curious feeling for Felicity, standing there saying her vows to Alex, part of her still incredulous that this was really happening. Tania's inappropriately loud whoop at the first kiss made her jump. Her hand shook as she signed the register, and the touch of Alex's gentle yet firm hand on her back was reassuring. After came the short drive to the sea-front hotel chosen for the venue, a familiar building they swam past every morning with their swimming group, whatever the weather. The sun was high in the sky on arrival, the sea breeze causing hair to dance and the women to clutch at their hats. The meal of fish fresh from the nearby seas smelled delicious and tasted even more so, and the white wine chosen to accompany the meal slipped down easily. Felicity's initial anxiety at the seating together of her softly spoken mother with Alex's gregarious family, who were meeting for the first time, was unnecessary; the three parents chatted incessantly, so much so that Alex had almost shattered the glass he was banging on to get their attention. Conversation only stopped when Caroline stood up and bellowed, 'Speech time, everybody!'

Alex jumped to his feet, smoothing down his suit, looking poised and not showing a sign of the nerves he'd confessed to feeling whenever he'd mentioned his speech beforehand. 'Lecturing is a different kind of skill, and the speech... well, obviously it's a bit of a sensitive subject,' he'd said. 'It's important to get the tone right.'

He needn't have worried.

'Before my lovely sister and best woman, Caroline, gives you her speech, where she will do her utmost to embarrass me with stories which I can tell you now are utter fabrication—' here everyone tittered '—I'd like to thank you all for coming today; it means so much to my...' He hesitated. 'My *wife* and I...' The stress on the word 'wife' provoked more laughter. 'We are so grateful for all your good wishes, all the cards and presents, but above all for being here today to witness our marriage. As you all know, my first wedding couldn't take place...' Here he reached for his water and took a long drink as a murmur of sympathy ran through the gathering, and Felicity placed a hand on his arm. 'I'll never forget Beth, and the precious time we shared, and before we celebrate this new life I've been gifted, I'd like to raise a glass to Beth, much loved and never forgotten, before we toast Felicity, for helping me get through the most painful experience of my life. To Beth.' This time he picked up his champagne glass, and everyone did the same.

'To Beth.'

Felicity wasn't the only one in the room with tears in her eyes. Despite Alex's concern about the appropriate amount of time to wait before embarking on a new relationship after losing his fiancée, the reception in the room was warm. These were their friends and as usual he'd got the tone exactly right.

'See,' she whispered as Caroline got stuck into her speech. 'I said you'd smash it and you were fabulous. You pitched it just right.' She took his hand, the sparkling diamond on her left finger catching both their attention.

'We did it,' he said. 'We're married.'

He held her tight during the first dance, before spinning her to and fro, both of them in time with the music and smiling into one another's faces, Alex lapping up the attention of the crowd. After, they stood at the bar getting their breath back. 'Four hours to go,' Alex reminded her, 'don't forget to pace yourself.' As if to hammer home the point, he ordered them both a glass of sparkling water. That was the last time they had a chance to snatch a moment together as the wedding took over, guests vying for their attention, and some serious dancing got under-way. Caroline invited Felicity to meet Alex's aunt and uncle and he was commandeered by his friends from the sailing club.

Tania and Miranda from the swimming group appeared in front of Felicity, both breathing heavily and Tania wiping sweat from her forehead. She sparkled in her dress, so different to the swimwear she was used to seeing her in.

'Come and dance,' she said, not giving her much choice as they took hold of an arm each, dragging Felicity to join them.

'It's fantastic,' Tania yelled to make herself heard over the pounding music and the buzz of conversation. 'And the DJ is seriously hot. Is he single?'

'No idea.' Felicity grinned. 'You'll have to ask him.'

Tania laughed. 'Try and stop me.'

Felicity stopped after a couple of tracks, wanting some air, and stepped outside onto the terrace. Tables were spread out over the large decking area with only a wooden fence separating the end of the terrace from the beach. A cool breeze blew on her shoulders and the music faded as she made her way to the fence, drawn by the lure of the sea. White fairy lights were threaded through the trees surrounding the outside area and a half moon was throwing light onto the sea, but it was too dark to make out where the sand ended and the sea began. The sound of lapping waves told Felicity the tide wasn't far out and she checked her watch. Not long to go now. She'd cooled down and was aware the sweat she'd worked up on the dance floor was cloying on her back. She stared out at the infinite blackness, her skin cooling rapidly, overcome by the immensity of the ocean. She shivered. Was what they were about to do foolhardy?

'What are you doing on your own out here?'

Caroline's voice made her jump.

'I was hot after dancing but now I'm getting cold.' Felicity threaded her arm through Caroline's. 'Let's go back inside. We'll all be getting cold enough shortly.'

'I'm having a fabulous time. Were you having second thoughts back there?' Caroline nodded back towards the sea.

'No, not really. Alex is so determined.'

'I know,' she said. 'I told myself I wasn't going to drink and I've just had a large gin and lemon. Oh well, as long as I'm in control of my faculties I should be alright. Talking of which, I'd better go and check on Aunty Margaret. She keeps forgetting where she is and wandering into the hotel foyer. The receptionist is very patient.'

Felicity went in search of her mother and found her chatting to some of their swimming friends. When she'd first arrived in the area she hadn't expected the notice she'd posted on Facebook and in the library and a few local shops to garner much response. *Anyone fancy a swim?* A flurry of friendly messages confirmed she'd made the right decision to move to the coast. A pool of around eight of them swam regularly; Alex and Beth had joined them too when they'd moved into the area.

The swimming group had a good number of members now and most of them were here tonight. A hardcore few swam early every morning; Felicity took part as often as she could as it was an energising start to her day. A surprising number of guests had said they were going to swim, although no doubt a significant number would drop out when it actually came to it.

'I've been trying to get your mother to join the swim,' Annabelle said, 'but she's having none of it.' Annabelle had been the first local to join Felicity's swimming group; recently retired, she'd been wanting to swim for a while, but was hesitant about swimming alone. The two women had quickly become friends.

'I'll be helping you all when you come out freezing cold and trying to find your clothes,' Felicity's mother said. 'Honestly, it's a ridiculous idea. I've been trying to talk them out of it all week.'

'No chance,' Annabelle said. 'You look lovely, Felicity, by the way, I've haven't had a moment to tell you until now. Are you enjoying yourself?'

'I am.' She joined them at the table, glancing at her watch as she sat down. 'Not long to go.'

Caroline appeared at their table. 'It's eleven-forty, do you think we should start rounding people up?'

'Good idea,' Felicity said, standing up. 'I'll get the DJ to make an announcement at a quarter to.'

'Hopefully everyone will have come to their senses,' Rosemary, Alex's mother, said, pulling up a chair.

'Let it drop, will you, Mum?' Caroline said. 'It's what Alex wants. Can't you let him do this one thing instead of complaining? It's his wedding day. Yes, we all know it's a mad thing to do but he isn't going to change his mind now so why not get behind him.'

Felicity put her hand on Rosemary's shoulder. 'It's natural to worry. My mum's the same. But try not to. Alex knows what he is doing, he's a strong swimmer. Mentally, it's going to help him let go. I'll keep an eye on him.'

Rosemary sighed, patting Felicity's hand. 'Thank you.'

Felicity spoke to the DJ, who waited until the track ended before fading the music out. The babble of voices stopped, and people looked around wondering what was going on.

'OK, everybody, it's ten minutes to midnight and I've been reliably informed by the blushing bride that some of you are going for a midnight dip. Sounds crazy to me and I for one won't be joining you. So if those of you who are taking part would like to get ready, please would you fetch your cossies and your budgie smugglers and make your way down to the marquee on the beach, where you can get stripped off for the midnight swim. And please be sensible, no swimming if you've had too much to drink, so strong swimmers only. For those of you sensible people who are staying on dry ground, here's a little tune to wish them on their way.'

'Good Vibrations' by the Beach Boys blasted out from the speakers and while a few people carried on dancing, others quit the dance floor and made their way outside.

'Let's stay for this one, then go,' Felicity heard Tania say to Miranda. 'Oh no.' She poked Miranda in the ribs. 'Look to your left,' she said, 'Alex's aunt.' She said something Felicity couldn't hear and then the two women were laughing hysterically. Caroline spoke to them before shouting out to rustle up any more swimmers.

'Five minutes to go,' she said. Most people who'd got changed were shivering under their towels, waiting until the last minute to expose their skin to the night air. Felicity went to find Alex.

'It's midnight,' she said. 'Time to get changed. Are you sure you want to go ahead? Everyone would understand if you don't.' She stared out at the black mass in front of them, hearing the sound of the waves she was unable to see. She shivered.

TWO

'Of course I'm sure,' Alex said. 'I thought you wanted to.' He cupped her face. 'Promise you won't worry about me.'

'I'm your wife now, it's my job.' She kissed him.

'Thanks, wife.' They both laughed.

'We don't want all our training to go to waste. And look at everyone.'

The scene on the beach was akin to a farce; all around them, people of all ages were stripping off their finery and wriggling into swimming costumes. Others were taking off their shoes, raising their hems for a paddle. A flash of white skin caught her attention.

'Oh no.' She averted her eyes. 'Your cousin is obviously totally fine with being nude. Honestly. Some people have no shame. Good job it's dark.'

'Trying to upstage me, Phil?' Alex called, laughing. 'I hadn't expected so many people to take part. It's going to be fun.' He followed her across to where they had left their kit, ready for this moment, the climax of their wedding day.

He pulled the towelling robe over his head and took off his shoes and socks, folding them neatly and putting them into the bag. He moved quickly, eager to get into the water and get on with the challenge. He took out the cashmere sweater and jeans, and placed them on a large flat rock, ready to change into after the swim. His body relaxed as he lost the suit he'd been buttoned into all day and slipped into his swimming trunks. Tania and Miranda from the regular swimming group joined them, giggling and tripping on their towels as they lost their balance in the dark.

'Are you sure this is a good idea?' Caroline asked. The sight of her white bathing cap with pink flowers on it set them off laughing again.

'Honestly, you two.'

Tania peeled her dress over her head and dropped it into her bag, to reveal a black and silver tankini.

'I don't know why everyone is making such a fuss, most people are wearing shift dresses and already have bare shoulders.'

'Which is completely different out here, and after getting in the water,' Caroline said, pulling on a pair of rubber shoes.

'You've got goose pimples already,' Felicity said. 'Here, this will set you up.' She handed Alex his red flask and he welcomed the warmth of the tea inside him. These rituals were important to him, to be prepared.

'Where's your flask?' Alex asked.

Felicity wrinkled her nose. 'In the bag. I don't fancy tea right now.'

Tania lowered her voice, not realising Felicity could hear every word. 'I can't believe Felicity has brought that bloody flask,' she said to Miranda. 'Do you think she's brought sandwiches too? She's going to make such a good housewife.'

Let them think what they like. She turned her back on them and focused her attention on Alex.

'More people are taking part than I expected,' he said. 'This is great. Ready?'

Two elderly gentlemen were in the water already, paddling. A bald head glowed under the moonlight.

Alex drained the flask, took Felicity's hand and flashed a grin at them. He raised his hand, leading the way across the short expanse of sand down to the sea, as everyone moved towards the water, splashing and yelling, while those who weren't participating cheered and clapped. It was surprising how much colder it felt as they neared the water.

Most people who were swimming were either in the water now, or dipping toes in and squealing; one man in blue speedos was running back and forth to warm up. A man in a suit, beer in hand, watched on with a look of bemusement.

Somebody called Alex's name as he took Felicity's hand and ran the last few metres, wading out into the water. He waved without turning.

'Catch me.' He raised his hands to the sky, palms together as if in prayer, and dived into the approaching wave. He sliced through the sea. Felicity followed him into the water. A cheer went up from the crowd and the swimmers joined them at varying paces. Miranda raced towards the sea, stumbling as she reached the water, landing on her knees.

'Are you OK?' Tania asked. 'Sure you're not drunk?'

'No, just tripped on some seaweed.'

Tania helped her to her feet. Up ahead, Alex and Felicity had disappeared into the black void that was the sea. A woman shrieked as she ducked her shoulders under. More swimmers struck out into the water, laughing and calling to one another. Miranda lowered herself back under the water and swam a slow breaststroke, shivering at the shock of the cold.

The moment the water slid over Alex's feet, the babble of noise from the party and the chatter of the swimmers following behind him had faded into insignificance. He'd let go of Felicity's hand and focused, mentally checking out from the music and laughter and dancing behind them, and devoting his attention to the vast expanse of water in front of him. The sea required his full concentration, especially at night after a day of celebratory feasting and drinking, dancing and laughing. He'd been restrained, knowing the challenge awaiting him at the end of the night.

Not just any night either, but his wedding night.

He closed his eyes and prepared himself for the initial shock of the cold as the water covered his ankles, his calves, his thighs. His skin prickled and stung, and he controlled his breathing, striding now, anxious to be fully immersed in the water. The warm glow inside from the warming tea he'd drunk to prepare himself was a mere memory, as the freezing water, both delicious and terrifying, reached his waist. He cast a look behind him before plunging underwater, gasping with a mix of surprise and delight as he struck out and ploughed forward, towards the infinite darkness of sea and sky, the latter lit only by a pattern of stars and the half moon, a glimmering slice of opal.

As his body grew accustomed to the temperature, sounds from the others behind filtered back in, shrieks and gasps at the shock of the cold, arms thrashing and splashing, and the midnight swim was underway. It wasn't the coldest water he'd swum in by any means, but he knew the risks. He'd trained his body to expect the unexpected, to respect mother nature and to always be prepared for surprises.

The tingling on his skin was almost painful now, a burning sensation on his thighs and across his shoulders. He switched to front crawl, hoping the speed and friction would warm him up. Night swimming wasn't a new experience, but it was a rarely experienced pleasure. He trained his eyes ahead as advised, the pale light of the moon picking out a path, hopefully keeping him on course. One lap adjacent to the shore, where the lights from the wedding party guided him, then back again.

It was when he turned to go back after the first lap, when all that lay in front of him was an expanse of nothing that the unwanted thoughts burst into his mind and he experienced a surge of terror at the danger that lurked out there. He pictured her face and was swamped by a sense of desolation.

His arms were tiring and his chest felt tight. He tried to whip his head around, but his reactions had slowed. He appeared to have drifted, as the lights from the wedding party, *his* wedding party, were further away than he remembered. His stomach was churning and a spurt of nausea made him gag. Salty water filled his mouth and burned his throat and he was coughing and spluttering, desperately trying not to swallow more water. His mind wouldn't work properly, his legs had lost their power, his fatigued arms battling the sea, which was rougher now, and oh so cold. He slid under the water, then forced himself back up, gasping as his head emerged, then was knocked back under by a wave. Where were the others? It was eerily quiet. When he resurfaced, he tried to call out; he needed help, he couldn't do this alone. He wouldn't let this be the end. His lungs burned, and he focused on his breathing, dragging air into his lungs, battling against the waning strength as his limbs got heavier and his thought processes duller. The strength he'd always prided himself on was letting him down. All those hours in the gym, in the pool, running along the sea front and... A wave smashed against his chest and he was screaming inside, his terror as cold as the water as he dropped down, down, the fight gone as his mind became a blur of shapes and colours. It was eerily quiet.

THREE

'Alex.' Calling him was futile; he was off in the zone. After years of training, his strong arms powered through the water. Felicity, with her school swimming lessons and slim build, couldn't possibly keep the same pace. She felt a flutter of anxiety, willing him to turn back, but already she'd lost sight of him.

She slowed down and swam back towards the shore. Every muscle was alive in the cold temperatures. Most people were sticking close to the shore, a young couple only getting as far as paddling before running back to the makeshift tent. The two old men were still standing ankle deep in water, talking and gesticulating at each other. A small boy was stamping his feet, his face red and furious at not being allowed into the sea. Felicity looked back, hoping to see Alex returning but all she could see was the dark water glinting where a wave caught the moonlight. Caroline swam breaststroke towards her, chin held up out of the water.

'Gosh, it's cold,' she said, treading water when she reached Felicity. She frowned. 'Where's Alex?'

'He went ahead. I can't keep up with him.'

'I can't even see him. If it was anyone else I'd be worried. Shall we head back in?'

'Yes.' Felicity was shivering since she'd stopped moving. A man slid past them swimming front crawl, but the glimpse of a bald head revealed it wasn't Alex. Most people had stuck close to the shore and those who had gone further out were making their way back in now. They must have been in for at least ten minutes.

Felicity and Caroline swam back, reaching Tania and Miranda. They were looking past them out to sea.

'Where's Alex?' Miranda asked. 'We thought he was with you.'

'He was, but not for long,' Felicity said.

'Why has he gone so far out?'

'Typical macho guy behaviour,' Tania said. 'Couldn't resist showing off.' She looked at her watch. 'I'm getting out. Fifteen minutes is plenty of time. What do we think the temperature is?'

'I reckon it's about seventeen, it was eighteen yesterday morning, but it's been warmer today.'

'Felicity.' Her mother, Sheila, was waving to her, holding her towelling robe. 'Come in, you'll catch your death.' They walked the last few metres to the shore, feet heavy in the sand. Felicity welcomed the warmth as she slipped into the outstretched robe. 'You're shaking,' Sheila said, rubbing Felicity's arms.

'It was exhilarating.'

Sheila tutted.

'Where's my stuff?'

Sheila went to help Tania. Excited chatter buzzed in the tent as people struggled to get their clothes back on. Felicity pulled on the sweater and warm joggers she'd brought with her; it was too cold to put her wedding dress back on. Her fingers shook as she pulled warm socks and trainers over her feet. The trainers glowed white in the dark. Getting dressed quickly after a cold swim was crucial to avoid hypothermia no matter how good you might be feeling. She hoped everyone had read the information pack about cold water swimming she'd sent out when inviting people to join the swim. She pulled her warm robe back over her clothes and walked back to the shore. Her skin was tingling. Alex should be coming in soon. A nugget of worry tightened her throat. She joined Caroline and her parents – her in-laws, as Felicity should now think of them.

'Enjoy it?' Rosemary asked.

'Yes.'

'Did Alex say how long he was swimming for?'

'No, but he knows what he's doing so he won't overdo it.'

Uncle Brian wandered over to them. 'Alex isn't back yet. I knew this was a stupid idea.'

'You know he's a good swimmer,' Caroline said, putting her arm around him. Felicity felt a chill; going so far out was foolhardy as it was impossible to be seen from the shore. As other guests joined them, Felicity wandered closer to the water, craning her neck, peering into the infinity of the ocean, waiting to see Alex materialise in front of her.

'He almost made the Olympics, you know,' Alex's father was telling anyone who'd listen.

'How was it?'

Hamish appeared at her side. He and his wife, Sarah, had been amongst the first members of the swimming group, joining shortly after Annabelle.

'It was great,' Felicity said. 'Did you see Alex in the water?'

'No, I couldn't see anything much and I was keeping an eye on Sarah. She hasn't swum at night before. Here, I got you some hot chocolate.'

Felicity warmed her hands on the cup. Sarah joined them, her large swimming robe dwarfing her. Her cheeks were glowing.

'That was glorious, I love the delicious after-chill when I'm all wrapped up and cosy. It's a beautiful wedding, Felicity. When are you off on your honeymoon?'

'Two days' time. I can't wait, a whole week in Cornwall.'

'Lovely. More swimming then.'

'Of course. It's not a holiday otherwise.' She scanned the sea. Most of the swimmers were back now; even the two elderly men had their shoes back on and were clutching beer bottles while they continued their conversation. One of them turned and saw Felicity. 'Alex not back yet?' he asked.

'No,' she said. More people emerged from the changing area, wandering down to join them. Cold breath hung in the air.

A sense of unrest was rising in the crowd. Alex's parents were talking in low voices. His father, Derek, came over to them.

'Does anyone know how long he's been out there?'

'We came out after fifteen minutes,' Miranda said, looking at her phone. 'That was at least ten minutes ago.'

'It takes longer than you think to get dressed again,' Tania said.

'How long is too long for you swimmers?' Derek sounded impatient. 'At what point should you stop?'

'People swim the Channel, Dad,' Caroline said.

'Don't be flippant.'

Around them people were holding their phones up as torches, the lights small pinpricks against the mass of the sea. 'How long has he been in now, Felicity?'

'At least twenty-five minutes.' She strained her eyes to see if she could see anyone out there, but all was still save for the gentle lapping of the sea. 'We said we wouldn't stay out longer than fifteen minutes.' She bit into her lip. 'He's usually very precise.'

'Exactly,' Derek said. He looked around him. People were

forming a huddle around him, asking what was happening, where Alex was.

'Should we be worried?' a voice from those gathered asked.

'Yes, maybe we should do something,' another voice added.

'We could wait a bit more.'

'I can't see anything but it's so hard to tell,' Tania said. 'At least the sea isn't rough.' She shivered, and looked back towards the water, saying what everyone was thinking. 'He really should be back by now.'

'It's been thirty minutes,' Felicity said. 'I agree, I'm worried, seriously worried.'

Derek shook his head. 'We need more than a torch. My son could be in trouble. I'm calling for help.'

'You ring 999,' Felicity said. 'I'll call the coastguard, give me a phone.' Someone handed her their mobile, the illuminated torch blinding her eyes. She raced over to the sign at the end of the beach, her heart pounding, seeing a yellow flash in front of her eyes. This couldn't be happening. She'd run through this day countless times, anticipating what could go wrong. A lost ring, a sick caterer, certainly not this. Her feet sank into the sand, slowing her down. She dialled the number, reassured by the confirmation on the sign that they were open twenty-four hours. Should she use the orange lifebuoy ring, suspended on the board? What use could that possibly be in the pitch black out to sea?

'A swimmer's gone missing.' She gasped the words out, answering the questions put to her, listening to instructions. Each second that went by, Alex was out there, alone. A tremor ran through her body. She untied the lifebuoy ring with shaking hands, before running back to the group gathered on the cold beach, some shivering in their wedding finery, others wrapped up after swimming. A trio of Alex's friends had waded back into the water; others were up to their ankles, spreading out to scan the length of the shore. The mood had changed from vague concern to outright panic, the atmosphere electric with tension. Miranda was running up and down the shore calling Alex's name and Annabelle was physically preventing Uncle Brian from wading out to sea.

Felicity found Caroline barking orders out.

'Spread out, everyone, go as far as you can. This is hopeless.' She lowered her voice on seeing Felicity. 'How can this be happening? To Alex of all people. How long did they say it would be?' The hotel manager had appeared, talking into a walkie talkie.

'Five minutes.' Felicity chewed on her lip, staring out to sea, willing Alex to appear. She twisted her wedding ring around her finger with her thumb, this symbolic link to her new husband suddenly more important than ever; the lifebuoy ring she hoped she wouldn't have to use was in her other hand. She paced up and down as the minutes stretched, wishing there was more she could do. All around her people were going over the swim, what they'd seen, their voices an incessant buzzing of wasps in the air. A couple more people were back in the water, thigh deep, calling for Alex, the words getting lost in the wind.

'They're here,' someone shouted, and all of a sudden the place was awash with screeching sirens and flashing lights. Men and women from the emergency services were running towards them and a boat was being wheeled out onto the beach.

'Over here,' Caroline said to the police officers who'd appeared, pulling Felicity to join her parents. Rosemary was crying, foundation smeared on her cheek. Derek gave them an account of what had happened and a policewoman took charge of the situation.

Felicity stood staring out to sea, recognising words being spoken by the confident young policewoman but not taking them in: statements, witnesses, procedures, doing everything we can. She hugged her arms around herself, shaking violently despite her warm robe. Then her mother was next to her, and she was sobbing into her chest, like a little girl again, broken and desperate.

'Oh, love,' her mother was saying, 'they'll find him, I know they will.'

'It's our wedding day, Alex can't be gone, not like this. He's such a good swimmer, Mum. He was so determined to go ahead with this. I checked he was sure about it, but should I have tried harder to stop him?'

Her mother put her hands on Felicity's shoulders, looking into her eyes. 'Listen to me. This is not your fault. None of it is your fault. We don't know for sure what's happened, so let's just pray for Alex's safety.'

'But after Beth...' Tears blocked her throat and she couldn't speak.

'I know, love, you mustn't think about that.' Sheila let go of her shoulder, gesturing towards the coastguards who were pulling a boat out to sea. 'The right people are here and they're doing everything they can.'

A wail rose into the air, a chilling sound, and Felicity ran towards it, stopping dead when she saw Rosemary on her knees in the sand, sobbing uncontrollably. She ran to Derek, grabbing his arm.

'What is it? What's happened?'

A paramedic crossed the beach and helped Rosemary to her feet.

'Come on, love, let me look after you. You're in shock.'

'She's scared, we all are,' said Derek, stony faced.

A car door slammed next to the lifeboat station and a burly policeman marched across the beach with a determined tread. A police constable stood up straighter when he saw him and after a short conversation he pointed towards Felicity.

'Detective Sergeant Williams,' he said. 'I'll be overseeing the search so any questions, please address them to me. No news yet, Mrs Maitland.' It took her a second to realise this was her name now. 'Initial searches are being carried out and we're doing everything we can. Please be aware visibility is very poor, but we'll continue for as long as we can. It may be that we have to wait until tomorrow to do a more effective search. Alex is a strong swimmer, I understand?'

Felicity opened her mouth to answer but Derek butted in.

'My son is the best swimmer I know. I don't believe he would have drowned. Look at the sea, it's calm.'

'It may look calm but it would be unwise to underestimate the strength of the current, sir,' DS Williams said.

'Did anyone see him out there? What if someone wanted to do him harm?'

'Is there something we need to know about?' DS Williams asked, his tone sharpening.

'Stop it, Dad,' Caroline said. 'No, there isn't.'

His words had given rise to a stirring amongst the gathering. The seed of doubt travelled through the gathering, whispered from one worried mind to the next.

'We'll do our best to find him,' the detective stressed. 'I'd like to take initial statements from all those who witnessed Alex in the sea at any point, starting with those who went in with him.'

'I went in with him,' Felicity said. Her voice cracked as she said the words. The detective took her over to the police vehicle for privacy. Felicity gazed out at the black body of water. Was she a wife, or a widow?

FOUR

ANONYMOUS

He's disappeared under the sea, fitting really. What if he's dead? It won't be a dog walker this time who finds the body, like the opening scene of a television drama, or a novel. Unless he washes up on the shore – no doubt there will be some poor police officer who has to stand out all night in the dark keeping vigil over the sea. Not that you can see anything.

What must it be like, out there in the pitch black? Knowing that deep down underneath the sea is where you're going to end up, being looked at and nibbled at by all sorts of creatures. Does he know he is going to die? That he'll end up fat and bloated like a whale, no longer the handsome man he prides himself on being.

Handsome, but not a nice man. Oh, he pretends to be, he has everyone fooled; it takes a while for his true nature to reveal itself. He lured me in so easily. I'm ashamed that I was so easily had. He used his charm and played with me. And I'm not the only one, which should make it better, but makes it worse. How many more women are there, that he's done this to?

No, when his body washes up on shore – because it will – I

won't be one of those grieving. I'll be celebrating on behalf of all the women he's done this to, on behalf of all the women who've been gaslighted – and more – by a man. He deserves to die. If only it had happened sooner.

We might have all been saved.

FIVE

PRESENT

Hotel staff were busy clearing the back room of the hotel, which only an hour ago had housed a vibrant celebration. Pale, concerned faces contrasted with dark uniforms as the staff worked, taking direction from a police constable. Although prepared for any eventuality given the nature of their job, a person disappearing in the sea had to be a shock. Outside on the beach, bewildered wedding guests stood in clumps, shivering and staring desolately towards the sea. DS Williams gathered the immediate family around him. He watched them all with piercing blue eyes.

'If you'd like to come with me into the hotel I'll run through exactly what is happening.'

They went in and sat around a table in the room that had so recently hosted a wedding reception. The table had been hastily cleared but remnants of silver heart-shaped confetti were sprinkled all over it. A lump lodged in Felicity's throat. DS Williams remained standing while they settled. Derek's leg jiggled under the table, causing it to wobble back and forth. The hotel manager, a tall woman in a burgundy suit, joined them.

'I want to reassure you that we are doing everything we can

to find Alex. We've been working with the local coastguard and a thorough shoreline search by volunteers is currently underway. The search and rescue helicopter has also been deployed. Night vision equipment with infrared light is being used. The staff are experienced and if Alex is out there we will find him.

'The hotel staff are working with us and are providing a hot drink and sandwich station, which will run for as long as needed throughout the night. Police officers have been taking preliminary statements from the guests, and once they have done those they are free to go. As most of the guests are staying in the hotel we've asked them to report to us in the morning. Those who live locally are leaving their details with us before they leave. I advise getting some rest if this goes on for much longer. However, as I said, you are welcome to stay down here while you wait. It is cold outside, hotel staff are also making blankets available.'

'My team will be on shift for as long as needed,' the hotel manager added. 'Anything you want, we'll do our best to assist you.'

'Has this ever happened before?' Felicity asked.

'We've had people get into difficulty in the water at night-time, mostly drunken larks after a night out. Organised events have their own security systems in place.' Were they being criticised? 'Every case is different.'

'Alex isn't a *case*,' Rosemary said, leaning hard on the table as she stood up. 'You should be out there, looking for him.' Her eyes rolled and she crumpled in front of them.

'Over here,' DS Williams called to a paramedic stationed in the room.

'She's in shock,' Derek said, as everyone moved to give the medic some space. Rosemary was treated and taken upstairs by the paramedic, accompanied by Derek and Caroline.

'She's been given a sedative,' Caroline said, when she

rejoined them. 'It's better for her to get some rest. I'm going back outside.'

'Is there anything I can do to help?' Felicity asked the sergeant. 'I feel so useless.'

'My constable is speaking to the hotel staff and we'll be interviewing everyone. If you don't mind answering a few initial questions, that would be helpful. Obviously I'm hoping Alex will be found, but anything you can tell us now could save time should the outcome be any different.'

'Yes,' Felicity said, shivering at the thought. 'Anything you want.'

'I appreciate it, under the circumstances.' He got out his notebook. 'How are you doing?'

The unexpected kindness in his voice made her want to cry. 'I'm bearing up.' She twisted her wedding ring around her finger. It was a solid band and represented so much. She looked up and met his gaze. 'I feel as if I'm in a dream. I can't take it in.'

He nodded. 'Could you take me through the swim itself? From the last hour or so beforehand. I want to be clear about the sequence of events while it's fresh in your mind.'

'Sure.'

'Great, let me sort out somewhere more private to sit.' They crossed the room. 'This table will do.'

Felicity sat opposite him, over the table strewn with empty wine bottles and glasses. A waitress rushed over to clear the table, giving her a much-needed moment to compose herself. She closed her eyes, placing herself back at the scene.

'I've no idea of the timing but we cut the wedding cake halfway through the evening and I was dancing after that for about half an hour, then I got tired and for the rest of the time until the swim I was moving about, chatting with some of my swimming friends; Annabelle and our parents were there too.' That had been the most relaxed she'd felt; physically tired from the dancing and the frenetic activity of the day, she'd been on a high that it was finally happening after so long in the planning. 'It was warm outside and we were enjoying ourselves.' She swallowed back tears. How quickly things could change.

'Were you drinking alcohol?'

Felicity screwed up her face to think. 'Not after the dancing and I hadn't had that much before then. People kept calling me over to talk and I lost my glass so many times. I'm not a big drinker anyway, but once we went outside I made a conscious decision not to drink anymore because I knew we'd be swimming at midnight.

'I was talking to my mum, and Caroline came and said it would soon be time to swim so I asked the DJ to make an announcement, which he did. He reminded everyone about keeping safe.' Her voice faltered.

The detective made a note. 'Take your time.'

'I'd rather get it over with, it might be important.' She rubbed her eyes. 'We went over to the marquee area to get changed. My mum and a few others were looking after our stuff, and waited to help when we all came back after the swim – it's not easy getting dressed when you're cold, even when you're experienced.' She was shivering now, but not from cold.

He nodded again.

'Anyone who was swimming joined us and when we were ready, Alex and I went in the water first, apart from a couple of male guests who were already in the water. Somebody, probably Caroline – she tends to take charge – shouted to everyone to let Alex go first and we went into the water. He was holding my hand...' Here she stopped, her throat tightening. 'Can I have some water?'

DS Williams fetched her a glass of water and waited until she was ready to continue.

'Better?'

'Thanks. As soon as we went into the water he let go of my hand and swam ahead, I followed him but I didn't try and keep up. There was no point, he's much faster than me. He's such a good swimmer.'

'So I'm told,' the detective said.

'He disappeared from my sight so I swam across the bay and back. It was cold and I only planned to stay in for about ten minutes. I know my limits. I looked back for him a couple of times, but it was too dark to see anything. I swam in towards my friends, Tania and Miranda – they're in my swimming group. A few of us swim most mornings. We got out pretty much straight away and got dressed, it must have been about fifteen minutes later that I went back out and not long after, we realised something was up.'

'Going back to when you were preparing to swim, how was Alex's mood?'

'It was good, the day had gone really well. It was such a lovely wedding and he was looking forward to the swim. Everything was fine up until we went into the water.'

'Did he have any reservations about swimming at night?'

'No, he saw it as a challenge. It was his idea. We sent out safety information with the invitations and the DJ reminded everyone about that when he announced the swim. Safety was our priority.'

'Did you have any concerns?'

'When he first mentioned it, I thought he was mad, but when I saw how much it meant to him I got behind it.'

'You thought he was mad?'

'Because it would be dark, dangerous. But that excited him. Before we got changed, I double checked he was still keen to go ahead and he was. Alex loves a challenge and that's what this was to him.'

'OK. How long have you known Alex?'

'Five years in total. We both work at the local university as lecturers in the English department. Alex is my head of department.'

'OK. One final question. Prior to the wedding day, how was Alex? Did he have any worries at all?'

'No, I wouldn't say so. He was excited about the wedding, that's been our main focus for the past year.'

'And work, any problems there?'

Felicity shook her head. 'He loves his job. He's good at it.'

'Any enemies? Any financial problems?'

'No, I've told you already. Nothing like that was bothering him.' She frowned. 'You're making this sound sinister. He just went in for a swim.'

'I'm sorry I have to ask you these questions but the more we know about him the better it is. Can I get you a hot drink? You look exhausted. Why don't you get some rest? One of my officers can run you home.'

'No. I'm staying here until Alex is found. He's my husband.'

SIX

PAST

Felicity was swimming when she first noticed the young couple, climbing down the cliff path, stopping to look around every now and then like tourists. She swam slowly. It was late August and the sun was high in the sky. The tide was out and it had taken a few minutes to cross the wet sand and reach the wall of rocks where she'd left her bag covered by a towel. She savoured the last week of the long summer holiday before she was due back at work. She towelled herself dry, watching the couple, who were looking back to the top of the cliff and pointing. Then they were kissing and she dropped her gaze, finished drying herself and sat down on her towel. She shifted around on the pebbles to get comfortable, leaning back against the rock. From this vantage point she could see the row of beach huts with brightly painted doors stretching along the length of the beach. She reapplied sun cream and by the time she'd finished, her costume was already dry. She tilted her face towards the sun and closed her eyes, savouring the moment, the warm sun on her face, the gentle breeze preventing her from getting too hot, the sound of waves lapping in the distance, the odd shout and the rhythmic beat of a ball being batted back and forth by a pair of teenagers close by. Thoughts of work and the planning she needed to do crept into her mind, the imminent beginning of the university term a reality. In hindsight it was a relief not to have got the head of department post; she'd been in two minds when she'd applied, and she was content doing what she knew she was good at. Let someone else take the extra strain of bureaucracy and the responsibility that went with being the one making all the decisions.

The sound of footsteps crunching on pebbles close by and a woman laughing made her open her eyes. The couple she'd seen up on the cliff were crossing the beach in her direction. They were slightly older than she'd assumed, in their thirties or thereabouts. A handsome-looking couple, he was tall with dark hair flopping over his face, contrasting with the blonde and petite, athletic-looking woman. Both were tanned as if they enjoyed the outdoors or had recently been on holiday.

She sat up straight and smoothed down her hair.

'Hi,' the woman said, 'I hope we didn't wake you.'

'I wasn't asleep, just making the most of the sun.'

'Were you swimming?' she asked. She had freckles across her nose and a fresh face. Felicity warmed to her immediately. The man was harder to work out, his eyes hidden behind large sunglasses.

She nodded. 'It was glorious.'

'It looks it. I wish I had my stuff with me.'

'Are you visiting?'

'Kind of, we're moving here next week. One of the houses just up there.' She pointed along the sea front. 'We just thought we'd check out the beach.'

'We're both keen swimmers,' the man said. 'We hope to swim all year round when we're living here.'

'That's great,' said Felicity. 'I'm a swimmer too. There's quite a little community of us in the area.' She smiled.

'Alex,' said the man, 'and my fiancée, Beth.' Beth smiled at him, her face lighting up. A recent engagement, Felicity thought – something about the way he said the word, like he was proud and trying it out for size.

'Once you're settled in, you'll have to come along to one of our swims.'

'We'd love to, wouldn't we, Alex?'

Alex had a quizzical expression on his face. 'I'm sure I know you,' he said. 'Do you work at the university by any chance?'

'I do, I'm a lecturer. English.'

A broad smile crossed his face.

'Of course, I remember now. I'm Alex Maitland. You were in the office when we were shown around on the interview day. How could I have forgotten such stylish glasses? Some people make wearing glasses look cool.'

Felicity laughed, pushing her glasses up her nose. 'It's not often that word is associated with me.'

Alex Maitland, the name she'd been unable to put a face to despite wondering about what he'd be like to work with. She hadn't anticipated being dressed in nothing but a swimming costume when she met her new head of department. So much for making a good impression. She scrambled to her feet and offered him her hand, laughing. 'Not quite how I expected to meet you. I'm Felicity.'

'Oh,' he said. 'That Felicity.'

She laughed. 'Yes, that one. But no hard feelings. I wasn't sure I wanted the job when I applied for it, so it was a bit of a relief not to get it.'

'Are you my second in charge?'

'I am.'

'How lovely,' Beth said. 'We can't wait to move in. We're coming from London.'

'Have you got a new job too?'

'Not yet. I'm a primary school teacher. I'm moving to be

with Alex so I handed in my notice at my job. I can't believe I'm saying that. Being here still feels like we're on holiday.'

The sun had moved behind a cloud and Felicity reached for her jumper, pulling it over her head.

'I can imagine. When are you actually moving in?'

'Next week.'

'You'll love it here. It's wonderful living by the sea and people are really friendly.'

'We should be getting back,' Alex said. 'I need to rescue the car from the car park before I get a ticket. Good to meet you, Felicity.'

'You too. Good luck with the move.'

She sat back down and watched them make their way back towards the cliff. She remembered Alex now from the small group of candidates that had gathered in the doorway of their office. The tall one, standing at the back. He had the sort of voice that made you pay attention. He should fit in well with their small, friendly team. It was time they had a bit of fresh blood in the department. He was certainly a refreshing change from Professor Dinwoody, who was set in his ways after thirty years in the job. She'd invite them for dinner once they'd settled in, she decided. She closed her eyes and dozed.

SEVEN

PRESENT

Felicity woke with a start, and looked around the room. She was in her bedroom, not in the bridal suite at the hotel as planned, anticipating the imminent honeymoon. She turned to look at Alex's side of the bed and her stomach lurched. The events of last night surged through her mind and she leaned out of bed and gagged.

Her heart drumming, she pulled herself up in bed and drank from the water glass she kept by her bedside. Yesterday had been her wedding day, yet here she was alone in her bed. She reached for her phone. It wasn't yet seven. Only four hours ago they were still all on the beach. She rubbed her thumb over the diamond ring on the third finger of her left hand, proof that she was a married woman now. Or was she? That depended on Alex's fate. She felt sick.

Her phone screen was covered with messages she didn't want to read. The detective from last night had said he'd call her after nine with an update. He'd driven her home, insisting she 'get some sleep'. She'd thought sleep was out of the question but she'd managed a couple of hours. She ran her hand over the cold sheet on his side of the bed. Where was Alex?

She threw back the duvet and paced up and down the room. Nervous energy propelled her back and forth. She scrolled through the messages, checking she hadn't missed any updates, but they were all outpourings of sympathy, the same meaning expressed in different ways:

Keep strong, it's so awful, I don't know what to say, OMG...

Crass, that last one. From Tania, obviously.

She paced some more, not knowing what to do with herself. No way was she waiting two hours for a phone call. She had to get back to the beach. On automatic pilot she did what she always did, what *they* always did first thing every morning without fail.

Her swimming bag was on the floor where she'd dropped it last night. Inside, her costume was rolled up in a bag, still slightly damp and smelling of the sea. She grabbed a fresh towel from the downstairs bathroom, but the damp costume would have to do. The house made her feel claustrophobic and she had to get out into the fresh air. Now she'd decided what to do she wanted to get to the beach as soon as possible, back down to where it happened, where she might be able to find out more. She pulled her swimming robe off the peg, pulling it on as she left the house, zipping it right up to her neck, seeking comfort in the warm lining.

She scurried down to the beach as she'd done hundreds of times before, a twelve-minute walk to the cove they regularly swam in. As she got closer, she saw the blue and white police tape flickering in the wind. It stretched around the perimeter of the hotel and a uniformed policeman was leaning against the wall, reading something on his phone. If they'd found anything there would be much more activity going on, people in white suits and little signs with numbers on where evidence had been found. Her heart beat faster. She stopped, not wanting the policeman to see her. If he recognised her, there would be questions and he couldn't possibly understand her need to be back in the water after what had happened last night. She wouldn't be able to convey to him her need to submerge herself in cold water to clear her mind, to rid herself of this terrible angst. How it was only going to get worse the longer Alex was missing. How she wasn't afraid of the water, despite what had happened. If anything, she would be physically closer to Alex. The thought made her feel cold; if Alex was still in the water he would no longer be alive.

The pebbles crunched under her feet as she crossed the beach, welcoming the discomfort to her soles, needing the pain to distract from the heaviness in her chest as she batted away a constant barrage of memories from the previous day. If she allowed her mind to go there she wouldn't be able to keep herself together. She placed her bag on the large flat rock as she did every morning, only she usually had company. Aside from Alex, on any given day there would be up to eight of them, shivering and chattering as they got dressed. Today she changed in silence, struggling to pull on the damp costume, which felt clammy on her skin, before whipping off her dry robe and spreading it over her belongings. She did this out of habit as today the sky was clear of clouds, and it didn't look like rain. She removed her glasses, then hesitated, putting them back on. She might be able to find Alex if she left them on.

She waded straight in, stopping only to splash her arms and chest with water. It was June and although the water was cold, she'd swum in zero degrees in January and was fully acclimatised. The bite of the water crept up her legs, the sensation slightly different from any other swim as it always was, her arms burning as she struck out, swimming as fast as she could, focusing on her breaststroke technique and keeping her breathing steady.

As she got into her stride, she allowed her mind to wander

back to yesterday, knowing she would have to process what had happened.

A flash of movement from the beach caught her eye. Two figures were walking down to the sea, and she recognised the royal blue robe and the purply red hair of Miranda, the smaller figure of Tania just behind her, her blonde hair covered in the orange woolly hat she always wore for a swim. So she wasn't the only one who couldn't resist the pull of the water. They probably needed it too after the horror of yesterday. Miranda had been distraught, and was one of several people being treated for shock last night. A waiter from the hotel had wrapped her in a blanket and made her some sweet tea to pacify her, Tania calming her down. Felicity wasn't one for theatrical gestures; she was used to keeping a level head in a crisis. The police interview had made the situation real for her, striking her dumb. This wasn't something she'd be able to sort with a list and a plan. She checked her watch; another five minutes and she'd better get out. The waves were strong this morning, making her bob up and down. She focused her attention on the physical, embracing the cold water, her shoulders feeling the temperature the most. Tania waved but she hadn't the energy to respond. Miranda sat down on the rocks as Tania slipped out of her robe and waded towards her.

'Felicity. How are you? I can't believe what happened.' She started swimming as soon as the water reached her waist. 'I wondered if you'd be here,' she said, reaching her and treading water. 'Aargh it's so unbearable, have you heard any more?'

'Nothing,' Felicity said, wiping drops from her glasses before checking her watch again. 'The police will be updating me at nine. I didn't know what else to do,' she said, treading water too, her eyes stinging from the splash of a wave. She gesticulated towards the sea around them. 'It might seem strange to some people but...'

'You don't have to explain it to me,' Tania said, her eyes

going to where Miranda sat staring out to sea. 'She's not coming in, but she didn't want to be alone. It's such a shock.'

Felicity turned to face out to sea, her eyes filling with tears as she gazed at the endless stretch of water, so beautiful yet so lethal. An icy chill made her gasp. Was Alex still out there somewhere? A mental image of a shark, fin sliding dangerously through the water towards her, jolted her into action.

'I have to get out,' she said, swimming away from Tania, more salty water landing on her lips, making her gag. Water, she needed fresh water. The presence of the other women should be a comfort but danger surrounded her, with the inevitable drama of the day about to unfold, and there was nothing she could do to stop it. She thrust her arms through the water, frantic now, her toes numb with cold and her breathing less strong. More droplets landed on her glasses, smearing the view. With relief, she plunged her feet into wet sand. She hurried towards Miranda, whose pinched face was staring at her. She reached for her robe and pulled it over her head, pulling the hood tight, wiping her glasses dry and burying her face into the material as her body trembled and she finally allowed the tears to fall. Miranda looked away, out to sea.

The police constable was standing to attention now, talking into his radio. He was looking towards the hotel, where two police cars and a van were parked. More police officers were moving like a swarm of ants down on the beach but it was too far away to see what they were doing. He ended the call when he saw the women approaching him.

'Bit parky out there isn't it?' he said, grinning at them before his expression went from confusion to seriousness when he noticed Felicity.

'Ah, Mrs Maitland. I didn't recognise you from a distance.'

He was looking at her, but once again Felicity took a moment to register the name. She was Mrs Maitland now.

'Are you alright, ma'am?' He glanced back to his colleagues.

Tania followed his gaze. The policemen were bending over something on the sand.

'What's going on down there?' Tania narrowed her eyes, black mascara smeared under her eye from the sea. 'Have they found something?'

'I'm not sure,' he said, looking back towards the water. 'If you wait here, I'll go and find out.'

'You look so pale,' Tania said, noticing Felicity's colouring. 'Maybe we were stupid to swim. Sit down on the wall, I've got some tea in my flask.'

'It's OK,' Felicity said, 'I've got a bottle of water in my bag.' Alex would have brought the flasks, had he been here. She rubbed her eyes.

The three of them sat in silence, staring at the shore. Felicity had pulled on warm clothes, but her fingers were only just starting to thaw. Their policeman had reached the others and was pointing in their direction. A woman was walking briskly towards them. As she got closer, Felicity recognised Alex's sister, Caroline. Only yesterday she'd been their brides-maid. She was still wearing the pastel-blue trouser suit she'd worn to the wedding, her skin grey with fatigue. The two women embraced without speaking.

'Any news?' Caroline asked in her clipped tones.

Felicity shook her head. 'How are your parents?'

'Dad's gone into overdrive, demanding answers. He agrees with me that this is so unexpected. Mum is in pieces. She wanted to come with me but Dad insisted she get some break-fast. As if that's going to bring Alex back.' She surveyed the police activity. 'Why are there so many people in one place? I hope they know what they are doing.'

'They haven't found him yet,' Miranda said. 'Don't give up hope.' Caroline looked over towards the cordon.

Tania was still standing, narrowing her eyes to try and see what was going on.

'I think they've found something,' she said, her normally loud voice quieter. 'Someone's coming over.'

At that moment another police car pulled up outside the hotel and a man jumped out of the passenger seat and hurried towards them. Felicity recognised him as the detective who'd taken charge last night.

'Mrs Maitland,' he said, his expression grim.

She took her hood down, wanting to stand but not sure her legs would support her.

'What is it?'

'Could I speak to you in private?'

'You can say it in front of my friends, whatever it is.'

But she knew what he was going to say from the pained expression on his face.

'We've found a body,' he said. 'As yet we haven't formally identified him, but it is a male fitting the description of your husband.'

Caroline cried out. Felicity put her hood back up. Tania moved to put her arm around her.

'Don't,' she said. 'I want to be alone.'

She walked away from the others, up past the dunes, her gaze sweeping across the bay, coming to rest on the police tape that was flapping in the wind, the officers pulling on white suits and masks. Then she was running towards them, needing to check for herself that her husband of less than a day was deceased.

EIGHT

DS Williams led Felicity over to the table where Mr Maitland was seated, staring at a cup of coffee with wrinkled skin on top. He stood up when they approached.

'Well?' His face was sunken, the answer inevitable.

Felicity nodded, her throat too swollen to speak.

'I'm afraid it's him,' DS Williams said. 'I'm sorry for your loss, sir. How's your wife?'

'How do you think? We've lost our only son.' He ran his hands over his face. 'I can't take this in. Alex, our boy, leaving us like this. Rosemary is asleep, Caroline is with her. I shouldn't have made you identify the body, Felicity, I'm sorry.'

She nodded again. DS Williams pulled out a chair for Felicity and she collapsed into it.

'Do you know what happened?' Derek asked.

'Not yet but we will. This morning we're going to be interviewing everyone who was at the wedding and the hotel last night. The hotel has given us this room to work in and the lounge areas for people to wait in until they've been interviewed. The most likely outcome is a tragic accident but for now we're treating it as an unexplained death until we're able to find evidence of what happened. Please rest assured that we are doing everything we can.'

A young police officer appeared at the table. She smiled warmly at Felicity. She wore her hair in a ponytail and had an energetic air about her. 'Do you want me to start the interviews, boss?'

'Please. Why don't you go over Mrs Maitland's statement from last night and I'll start with Mr Maitland here. If you're both ready that is?'

Derek gave a curt nod.

'Yes,' Felicity said.

'Would you like to come over here?' the police constable said to Felicity. 'I'm PC Chloe Button.' She helped Felicity out of her chair.

DS Williams turned his attention to Mr Maitland.

'Is it alright if I call you Derek?'

He nodded. 'It's my name. I want to show you something.' He reached under the table and pulled out an A4-size leather pouch. He unzipped the case and took out a pile of documents. He jabbed his finger at the one on the top.

'Look at this. Gold medallist.' He moved to the next one. 'Gold again, silver, best in age group, silver in the Europeans... He has hundreds of these going back to when he was a small boy. And here, he was swimming for the county at ten.' He leaned back in his seat, wiping sweat from his brow.

'Derek,' DS Williams said. 'I understand how competent a swimmer Alex was. This is an outstanding achievement. You must be very proud. But you must understand that against an overpowering wave, a rip tide or a fast current, he wouldn't stand a chance. Channel swimmers have a whole team right behind them as the sea is dangerous. Nature is so unpredictable and accidents occur far too regularly. We will find out what happened to Alex and I hope that will help lessen the pain a little.'

Derek visibly wilted in his chair, like a tyre deflating.

'I can't accept he's gone. My boy, my only boy.' He swallowed hard, shifting into a more upright position. 'What do you want to know, officer?'

'How was Alex at the wedding?'

Derek sighed. Alex had looked so much like him on his own wedding day, he'd thought his pride might burst out of the waistcoat that fitted somewhat snugly over his mound of a stomach. They'd sat at one of the barrel tables in a quiet corner outside before the ceremony and had a glass of champagne, just the two of them.

'Thanks, Dad,' Alex had said, 'for doing all this. You didn't have to. I could have financed this myself.'

'I wanted to,' Derek had replied. 'It means the world to us that you've found someone to share your life with. Felicity will make an excellent wife.'

'She was a good match for him,' Derek said to DS Williams. 'I wasn't sure at first, she wasn't the usual type he goes for, but she shared his passion for teaching. He deserved some happiness after his first fiancée died. We were talking before the wedding and he was full of his plans for the house. He wanted to completely rebuild it into one of those modern glass boxes. Stupid idea, but he was excited, making plans.'

'Did he mention the swim?'

'Yes. He was looking forward to it. I should have tried to stop him but he's headstrong, my son, gets it from me. I should have listened to Brian, my brother. Rosemary, my wife, wasn't thrilled with the idea but I understood why Alex wanted to do it. He's been challenging himself since he was a kid and swimming at night wasn't something he'd done often. Having his friends and family with him made it special. He confided in me once that he'd always felt he'd let us down when he didn't make it to the Olympics. Crazy thoughts, he'd been injured. He didn't need that medal; he was already a winner in our eyes.'

'Did you see him in the water at all?'

'He led the swimmers out, him and Felicity. I watched him swim off. I was proud, you know.'

His voice cracked.

Caroline was next, and she was doing well under the circumstances. DS Williams had seen the father's vulnerability; she was the one holding this broken family together and he would need her now.

'You were the witness for their wedding, I understand.'

'That's right.'

'Tell me about your relationship with your brother.'

'It was good. We were always close. He's two years older than me and I wasn't the kind of kid that needed looking after, but I always knew he was there for me if I needed him.'

He nodded. 'And how did you feel about him getting married?'

'It was what he wanted so I was happy for him. Felicity is a good match. They were colleagues and friends first – the best way to start a lasting relationship, in my opinion. They've both got swimming in common too. Alex is very passionate in his hobbies.'

'What was Alex's mood like yesterday?'

She snorted. 'Good, obviously. The wedding ran like a dream. I'm an experienced events manager and made sure everything ran smoothly. Even the weather worked in our favour. He pulled me to one side after the signing and thanked me for making the day special.'

'Did anything out of the ordinary happen at the reception?'

'I was busy keeping an eye on my elderly aunt a lot of the time but no, not that I noticed. I'm afraid we aren't the sort of family to have huge bust-ups in public.'

'And outside of the wedding itself, did Alex have anything he was worried about, at work, or financially?'

'No. He loved his job and as I've already told you he was happy with Felicity.'

'OK. Back to the wedding, could you run through what happened prior to the swim.'

'Of course. I was with Felicity. We asked the DJ to make an announcement ten minutes before so that those people who were swimming could get ready. People went to the tent and I rounded people up so I was one of the last to get changed. I was concerned that a couple of the women had overdone the alcohol as they were a bit hysterical beforehand but they are both competent swimmers.'

'What are their names?'

'Tania and Miranda. Not sure of their surnames.'

'No problem, I've got a list of all the guests. How was Alex? Had he been drinking?'

'My brother was a very controlled person. He wouldn't have got drunk and then got into the sea, he just wouldn't. He folded his clothes up neatly as he always does. He was talking to Felicity right before they went in – they went first and everyone cheered them. I was distracted by the women giggling and was more concerned they were going to be OK, plus I had my uncle Brian telling me it was a bad idea.'

She looked directly at DS Williams.

'He was right though, wasn't he? It was a bad idea.' A look of pain crossed her eyes, the first sign he'd had of her losing her composure.

'Did you see him swim?'

'I saw him walk into the sea holding Felicity's hand.' She screwed up her forehead, trying to remember. 'No, I didn't see him actually swimming though, because we were all getting in then and the cold water was a shock and my attention was focused on that. When I next looked up Felicity was swimming a bit further out, but I didn't see Alex.'

She clenched her hands together, swallowing hard.

'Would you like a drink?' he asked.

'Like that's going to change anything. But yes, I would please, tea, no bloody sugar.'

He signalled to a police constable, who rushed to the tea table and came back in record time with a cup of tea and a digestive biscuit. Caroline pushed the plate away from her, before sipping her drink.

'Tell me about the swim.'

'Not much to tell. I swam around in circles for a bit, chatting with people. I took part because Alex wanted me to, not because I'm a huge fan of swimming itself. I stayed in for about ten minutes, maybe fifteen, it's hard to tell. I didn't see Alex, and when I joined Felicity in the water she said she hadn't swum with him at all. I even mentioned not needing to worry about him as he's a good swimmer. I know Dad's told you all about that.' She shook her head at the last sentence. 'He's a bit much, my father, but he means well.'

'No need to explain. It's understandable.' Didn't she realise how like her father she was?

'After that I got changed quickly and we all chatted on the beach, waiting for everyone to come in. Uncle Brian was concerned, but we didn't take it seriously at first as he'd been going on all afternoon to anyone who would listen about what a stupid idea it was. Then Dad got concerned, and Felicity called you, I think. I was focused on Mum as she gets so anxious.'

She drank her tea.

'What do you think happened to him?'

She sighed, putting her mug down. 'He must have got into difficulty. Yes, he was the strongest swimmer I know but...' She made a gesture with her hands. 'You can't fight nature.'

'One last question. Do you know of anyone who would wish your brother harm?'

'No. Goodness, I think I've got more enemies than him. He's been through a lot, and we all supported him, especially after Beth.'

'Ah yes, Beth.'

NINE

PAST

A cool breeze through the open sunroof tickled Beth's neck as Alex steered the car deftly around another bend and countryside sped past in a blur of green. Alex was tapping his fingers on the steering wheel in time to the dance track playing through the speakers. The playlist of summer tunes summed up the mood perfectly. He turned to grin at his fiancée.

'Not far now. Are you excited?'

'Yes,' she said, 'now the horrendous packing and loading the van is over, I can't wait to get into the cottage. I hope it's as charming as I remember.'

Excited didn't really cover the array of emotions she had experienced since they set off on the journey from London, leaving their rented two-bedroom flat for the very last time. Four weeks ago she'd been at the traditional end-of-term leaving barbecue out on the school roof terrace, the panoramic view of the London skyline a backdrop, a vista she never grew tired of. Not only was it end of term, but she was also leaving her cherished job of the past five years and saying goodbye to several friends and respected colleagues. They were a tight-knit team and leaving them was a wrench at her heart. As for the pupils, seeing their little faces covering the whole mael-strom of emotions for the last time had made her cry big fat tears.

As she'd stood at the railings framing the roof that formed a barrier keeping them safe from the sheer drop onto the concrete piazza below, she marvelled at the brilliant blue sky, a sky she'd seen go through a whole spectrum of colours and movement, from dark moody rainclouds of early morning, to the radiant red glow of the early evening sun. She'd never forget the morning she'd come to work and watched in horror as a plume of thick grey smoke trailed under the line of clouds, as the catastrophic fire at Grenfell Tower they'd watched with horror the night before continued to burn.

Likewise, she doubted she'd forget her last day at Angel Primary School where she'd been so happy. Butterflies had lined her stomach. Even though she'd planned her speech and talking to a large group was something she was comfortable with, it was a big moment for her to stand up in front of everyone and say her goodbyes. It would mean she'd really done it, she'd quit the job and the city she loved for the man she adored; she was plunging into the unknown, no new job yet arranged to go to and moving into their own home for the first time. As she looked down at the unforgiving concrete below, a cloud had drifted across her mood.

Was she doing the right thing?

'Look, you can see our cottage.' Alex broke through her reverie. She craned her neck to follow the direction he was pointing in. They were travelling downhill and as well as the sea spread before them, the red chimney of their destination was just visible on the outskirts of the village.

'I'll unpack the kettle when we arrive,' Beth said. The kettle and tea things were safely stowed in the boot.

Alex laughed. 'No need to tell me, I wouldn't expect any less.' He reached out and touched her leg, giving it a squeeze.

'I'm so happy we're finally going to be living in our own home together. I love being with you.'

She shifted angle so she was facing him. She enjoyed watching him drive. He was such a confident man, so good-looking with his thick hair and his striking cheekbones, and a smile that made people instantly warm to him. He had a trust-worthy face and he charmed people wherever he went, as he'd charmed and impressed the panel when he interviewed for his new job, the job they were leaving London for. At the age of only thirty-five he'd achieved his ambition of heading up a university department in a prestigious university on the south coast of England.

'First thing I'm going to do,' he said, flashing a grin at her, 'is to carry you over the threshold. Good job you're such a light-weight slip of a thing.'

She laughed.

'Second thing I'm going to do is ravish you on the new sofa.' His eyes glinted.

'You're not,' she said. 'I'm dusty and tired and I want that memory to be special.'

'Spoilsport.'

She shifted position to look out of her side window, hope blossoming in her chest. At moments like these it was hard to imagine the doubts she'd been having, the finger of fear that crept up her spine at times, flicking at each of her ribs. Alex wanting to be with her all the time was what she wanted too; it was part of being in love and this gorgeous man was in love with her. He told her so often enough, though his behaviour some-times made her wonder. She'd also feel more secure if she had a job lined up; she'd wanted to wait until she found another posi-tion before joining him, but Alex had insisted they move in together ready for when he took up his post in September. It was now mid-August and they had two weeks left to get settled in the cottage. Alex had it all planned; by the time they arrived the removal company would have deposited all the boxes in the appropriate rooms, then she would focus on unpacking and arranging their stuff how she wanted it, while he was going to sort out his books and prepare his work for the university and make sure he was ready for the beginning of term. Although the students weren't arriving until later in September, he was contracted to start at the beginning of the month. Even if he wasn't, Alex would have been in there weeks early preparing; everything he did had to be carried out to perfection. He had something in mind for her too, he'd said, but refused to elaborate.

'You're frowning,' Alex said, and she snapped out of her daydream.

'Was I?' His constant awareness of what she was doing made her shift in her seat, trying to get comfortable. She hoped they'd run into the woman from the beach again, Felicity. Making friends would take away the sting of leaving her job.

They were sailing down a hill into the village now, and as she took in the red brick roofs and thatched cottages in front of the backdrop of glorious blue and green sea that she couldn't wait to swim in, she banished her doubts and channelled her mind back into the heady euphoria she'd been feeling earlier.

'I don't know why because I'm so excited I could burst. I've got a feeling we're going to be really happy here.'

'I love you,' Alex said as he pulled up at a red traffic light, leaning across to kiss her.

'I love you too,' she said.

The roads were getting a little more familiar as Alex drove at a slow speed through the village, past the two pubs, post office and the line of shops and cafés which made up the town centre. The school she'd worked at in London had been between a mainline train station and a Tube station, on the edge of a thriving market in the middle of several estates and high rises, surrounded by grid locked roads, traffic fumes and the sound of emergency sirens, with everything from takeaway chicken shops, dingy old men's pubs, to gastropubs and restaurants on their doorstep. Having a limited choice of shops and amenities was going to take some getting used to. They were now on the outskirts of the village, a field of sheep on the left and a signpost for the university campus on the right. The campus was a thriving hub, and the nearest town was only a twenty-minute drive away. Plenty of life for her there. As they neared their destination, they also got closer to the sea, and she leaned out of the window to inhale the salty air. She'd spent her early childhood in bustling Brighton and despite some reservations about village life, the sea had always felt like a magnet, drawing her back where she belonged.

Alex turned into their street, past the woods on the left and a handful of houses, and pulled up in front of their cottage. The large removal van was parked outside and the driver was sitting on the cottage wall drinking from a flask.

'That was well timed,' he said. 'We finished ten minutes ago. Good journey?'

'It was great,' Alex said. 'Not as long as I expected. Can I get you guys a beer? We've got some handy in the boot.'

'No, you're alright, mate. I'll be driving back.'

'Take them with you then.' Alex reached for the cool bag on the back seat. While he chatted with the removal men, Beth walked down the front path, their laughter making her smile. Alex had such an easy way with people, but it took her a while to relax and be herself with others. Inside the small hall, the same smell as last time struck her, a mixture of paint and wood. The cottage had recently been decorated by the owners in order to enhance their chances of a quick sale, but Beth would have taken it whatever the condition. She loved the layout downstairs, the large front room with the reading nook by the window and the quirky kitchen with its low ceiling and the view out over the back garden. Alex had big plans to renovate, but there was no hurry. It was perfect as it was. Upstairs, she looked out from the main bedroom over the small back garden and out to the sea. Her phone buzzed with a text and she took it out to look. As happened every time she got a text, a tiny part of her clung to the hope that it might be Olivia, but it was her aunt, wishing her good luck. She tapped out a quick reply, along with a photo of the view spread before her.

Bet you can't wait to have a swim, Aunt Celia replied.

Beth smiled, despite the pang of sadness thinking about her aunt gave her. She was always so upbeat despite her illness.

'Beth, where are you?' Alex's voice drifted up from the hall, and she ran downstairs to join him. 'Come back outside,' he said. 'I'm supposed to be carrying you in. I hope you haven't put a jinx on the house.'

She hopped over the doorstep and threw her arms around him.

'Sorry, I forgot. I couldn't wait to get into the house. Don't joke about jinxes like that.'

Alex stroked her hair and looked down into her eyes. He was a good foot taller than her. He lifted her up into his arms. She squealed with delight and he laughed at her pleasure.

'You're right,' he said.

'About what?'

He made a point of taking a big stride to lift her over the doorstep.

'We are going to be happy in this house.'

TEN

PRESENT

'Ah yes, Beth. I understand he was engaged, but lost his fiancée three years ago.'

Caroline sighed. 'Yes. It was tragic. But he wasn't feeling guilty and why should he? Beth would have wanted him to move on as did we all. He made a very good speech, he referred to her in it, and how we should all celebrate her memory and take a moment to think about her before we toasted the wedding. He got the tone just right. It was part of the reason they kept it small. The people there were all good friends and family. He was happy again and that's what we were celebrating.'

'Could you tell me about his relationship with Beth?'

'Of course. She was a primary school teacher.' She wrinkled her nose. 'A bit children's television presenter if you know what I mean. Bright clothes and bubbly. Very different to Felicity. She was small and pretty, Alex's usual type. They met when they were both working in London and after a while she moved in with him. She came from a seaside town originally and when Alex got a job near the coast she jumped at the idea. He was happy, they were good for each other, although I saw more of them when they were living in London – as I'm in Surrey and I commute to London for work.'

'Would you have classed her as a friend?'

'Not independent of Alex, no. Felicity is more on my wavelength.'

'How was Alex in the period after Beth died?'

'He's not one to show his emotions and he threw himself into his work and exercise. He kept himself busy. But he's a positive person and he has always had plans for his life. The big house by the sea, the wife and family.' She shook her head.

DS Williams nodded, checking through his notepad.

'That's all I need to know for now, thank you.'

'What happens now?'

'Once we've taken all the statements, I'll speak to you and your parents with an update.'

'OK. I'll be up in their room if you need me. I can't settle until I know what happened to my brother.'

Gavin Williams needed to stretch his legs. He made himself a coffee, going over the last interview in his mind. The picture of Alex's life was still sketchy but hopefully by the end of the interviews he'd have built up a better picture of the man. Until the post-mortem findings were in, he was keeping all options open. Once he'd made his coffee, he located Annabelle Victor.

'Ms Victor, would you like to come over here please?'

Annabelle looked to be in her sixties. She managed a charity shop in the local town and was a friend of the couple through the swimming group. She was wearing a green trouser suit over a black T-shirt, a silk scarf at her neck.

'This is a terrible business,' she said as they crossed back to the table.

'Indeed. How did you know Alex Maitland?'

'He swims with our group. A few of us meet in the mornings for a swim, usually between around eight and ten o'clock. People drop in, but I'd say there are about eight regulars.'

He passed a handwritten list of names to her.

'Have we missed anyone?'

She pulled a pair of green-rimmed glasses from her pocket and took her time scanning the list.

'No, I can't think of anyone else, but I only manage a couple of times a week.'

'When did you first meet Alex?'

She sat back in her chair, thinking.

'It must be about five years now.'

'So you knew his former fiancée?'

A look of sadness crossed her face.

'Beth, yes. In fact, I knew Beth better than I know Alex. She gravitated towards me to chat, whereas he was more focused on his swimming. I was part of the group before they moved here. Felicity and I were there in the beginning. Alex and Beth bumped into Felicity one day and ended up joining.'

'How were they together as a couple?'

Her face lit up. 'Delightful. They were engaged and so happy. It was quite sweet really, they were always together. Sometimes we go swimming later in the day or in the evening, but they always liked to swim as a couple. They were both excited about moving here. Beth, in particular, loved the coast. She came into the charity shop and talked about her plans. She was hoping to return to work as a primary school teacher. She'd have made a lovely teacher, the little ones would have adored her. She was so warm and friendly, enthusiastic. I'd hoped she might come and volunteer in the shop while she was between jobs but she didn't take me up on it. I was surprised. I thought she would. As far as I recall she didn't go back to teaching.'

'Did you ever meet socially, other than in the shop?'

'No, never.'

'What about Alex?'

She laughed. 'Oh no, that wouldn't have happened. We chatted about swimming but he was more distant. He was popular and he could be charming, but we weren't friends, more acquaintances. Occasionally, members would do something social together, for example Tania held a barbecue once, but they didn't show up, although they'd said they were coming. When I asked Beth she said they'd been away for a surprise romantic weekend.' She stared at the table, before looking up at the police sergeant. She had tears in her eyes. 'Talking about her brings it all back. It was a terrible thing to happen to such a lovely couple. He's done well, it can't have been easy for him carrying on without her. I liked to think we were all supportive. And now he's gone too.'

'Tell me about what happened to her.'

Annabelle sighed, her face falling. 'It was terrible. She drowned, after a swim. It was daytime, the sea wasn't too rough. Alex was devastated; we all were.'

Gavin allowed her to sit for a moment with her grief, before letting her go. The fiancée's drowning needed looking into. Time for a catch-up with Chloe, to see what kind of picture they were able to put together.

PC Chloe Button had only been on the team six months and was one of his best officers, always bright and energetic no matter the occasion. He'd asked her once how she managed to remain so cheerful.

'Boxing, boss. Give me a punch bag to thump and I turn it into whoever I want it to be. That and rock-climbing. The adrenalin buzz.' No doubt she'd understand the fanatical swimmers. The thought of willingly getting into cold water turned his stomach.

'I've got some sandwiches for us,' Chloe said. 'I know you won't stop otherwise. What are you thinking at the moment?'

'Obviously the body changes everything. An accidental drowning, most likely, but I'm keeping an open mind. It doesn't matter how much his father protests that he was a champion swimmer, the sea cannot be toyed with. Ask me again in a couple of hours and my answer may well be different. We'll investigate as if it's suspicious as we don't want to lose valuable time.' He sighed, rubbing the stubble that had appeared overnight on his chin. 'Has anything interesting come from your interviews?' he asked, once they were settled in some comfy chairs with their lunch and more tea. He'd lost count of how many cups he'd had.

'I've been through a few of the initial accounts of what happened around the swim kickoff that we took at the time and they all pretty much match up. He went in with his wife, holding hands, then he swam off ahead leaving them all in his wake. It was too dark to see him and Felicity was the last one to speak to him. They all reported him being in a positive mood, the day had gone well and he was excited to swim. I've also been asking about his previous fiancée.'

'Snap. Go on.'

Chloe consulted her notes.

'By all accounts, they were very much in love, moving here was a bit of a dream and they hoped to start a family. They were engaged and she was planning her wedding, she was also looking for a new job but doing a bit of teaching. She was liked by everyone, and Felicity was quite friendly with her, which is interesting. I couldn't find anyone saying anything negative about her. I haven't checked through the investigation report yet.'

'Hmm. A bit too good to be true, do we think?'

She nodded. 'Definitely. We might need to widen our questioning to people who knew them but weren't at the wedding. Alex got together with Felicity fairly soon after and that raises a few questions. We need to clarify for sure.'

'Any news on the post-mortem?'

'Not yet. I'll give them a call after this. Have you finished your interviews?'

'I've got one more on my list for today. Tania Beckford. Plus Miranda Deacon is calling into the station in the morning. Both swam regularly with Alex.'

'We'll speak again once you've finished before I speak to the parents. His mother would be better off at home, she's been hit very hard.'

'Suspicious?'

'Highly unlikely,' he said. 'OK. Good work, I'll catch you later.'

Chloe found Tania with Hamish and Sarah from the swimming group.

'Is it my turn?' she asked, sounding oddly eager.

'Yes.'

Chloe led her back to her table.

'I presume you know all about Beth drowning?' Tania said as she sat down. 'His fiancée. It was terrible. She drowned too.'

Chloe nodded. 'We'll be looking into that but for now I'd like to focus on the wedding night.' She ran through Tania's statement from the previous night.

'I'd like to go through this again to make sure you haven't forgotten anything.'

'No problem,' Tania said. She took her through the day, reaching the point where they were getting ready to swim. 'It sounds terrible now, but me and Miranda were messing about, we got the giggles and couldn't stop laughing. Caroline was annoyed with us and that made it worse because she was wearing this ridiculous hat.' Her mouth twitched and she bit her lip. 'The thing is, we'd said we wouldn't drink too much but I got carried away and I was having such a good time that I kind of forgot. Because of the swim, I mean. Felicity made it clear we had to be sensible. She's like that, a bit of a mother hen.'

'Was Alex there with you?' Chloe wanted to keep Tania on track.

'Yes, him and Felicity, and she was fussing after him then. I made a comment about her flask.'

Chloe straightened slightly. 'Flask? You didn't mention that before?'

'Didn't I? I was probably still a bit tipsy then. Yeah, it was a thing they did but I couldn't believe they were drinking tea at their wedding. I mean who does that? I said to Miranda something about bringing him lunch too.'

'Tell me exactly what happened.'

'She took the red flask out of the bag and offered it to him. She said something about it being good for him. He drank some tea.'

'Did she drink any?'

'I don't remember. She usually had her own, I think.'

'Did anyone else drink from the red flask after that?'

'Not that I saw. Alex was doing everything quickly, like he wanted to get in the water. Maybe he was cold, too, that's normal not to want to stand around. I think he dumped the flask on the floor after and went off to swim.'

Chloe made some notes. 'Can you describe the flask?'

'It's red, plastic, a normal flask, he's had it for ages.'

'You've seen it before?'

'Oh yes, that's what I said, Alex drank tea before and after every swim. It was a ritual of his. He was like that, big on his routines. He was the same with Beth. He had the flask back then too.'

'Did you see the flask after the swim?'

Tania looked at her with bemusement. 'No. I was straight out of the sea and into my clothes. It was freezing. I didn't notice anything. Why do you want to know?'

'We like to build up a complete picture. Thank you, you've been very helpful.'

Chloe flicked through her notepad once Tania had gone. She was sure nobody else had mentioned a flask. She highlighted the words 'red flask' in her notepad and doodled lines around it. If the death proved not to be accidental then it could be significant. She sent Gavin a text to say she'd finished. Maybe the post-mortem results would be in. They'd been careful to preserve the scene but she needed to double check there had been no flask.

Her nerves fizzed with anticipation. DS Williams was always telling her about a police officer's gut instinct. Was this it?

ELEVEN

PAST

It only took them about ten minutes to walk down to the beach. Alex held Beth's hand as they made their way down the rocky slope.

'Look,' he said, tugging her gently to turn her around and show her what he was looking at. 'You can see our cottage from here.'

She stood on tiptoe. 'Just about. Isn't it wonderful? I've always wanted to live back by the sea, and now it's really happening. And with you.' She kissed him lightly on the lips. 'It's a dream come true.'

He grinned. 'You deserve it. After all the worry over your aunt it's about time you were able to have some fun. Come on.'

They rounded the corner and there was the sea. The tide was out and their feet crunched over the pebbly beach. A row of beach huts with brightly painted doors in different colours ran along the length of the beach.

'Imagine if we could own one of those. It would be ideal for all our swimming gear instead of lugging it out with us every morning.'

'Maybe one day,' Alex said, 'but they so rarely come onto

the market and there's always a high demand. I heard last time one became available people queued through the night.'

'I'd queue,' Beth said, gazing out to sea. Her grandfather used to rent a beach hut every year for their family holiday in Cornwall, and she'd loved playing in the little house by the sea. 'I wonder what temperature the water is today.' The sun could be seen behind a cluster of clouds. 'Oh look, there are some swimmers. I wonder if Felicity is with them.' A group of people were getting changed over by the rocky wall that separated this section of beach from the next. Beth watched as they discarded swimming robes and donned brightly coloured hats before wading into the sea. They looked to be around the same age as them. One woman charged in, shrieking as she ducked under the cold water. She waved across at them and Beth waved back.

'Come on,' Alex said, 'I'm getting cold. Let's get in the water here, we can chat to them afterwards.'

They had been looking forward to their first swim in the sea together. In their previous home they'd swum in the local pool every morning; today was the first of many outdoor swims to come. Swimming in the sea was the activity she'd missed most when she moved to London to study for her teaching qualification. Finding a job in a local primary school shortly after meant she'd never returned home. She was so excited to have finally made the move back to the sea.

After the swim, Alex spread a towel out over the rocks and poured them some tea from the flask he'd prepared. The sun was out now and it promised to be a beautiful day.

'That was heavenly,' Beth said, sipping her tea and gazing out to sea. 'So much nicer than the pool.'

'I've got used to counting my lengths,' Alex said. 'It will take some getting used to for me. I'll just have to go by time instead. Time to upgrade my watch, I think.'

Sometimes Beth wished he'd be a bit more chilled about everything. He wrote down his daily exercises in a notebook and set himself goals. For her it was more about the way the water made her feel, and the challenge of a cold-water swim. Mentally it helped, giving her a space where she could switch off from her problems.

Once they'd finished their tea, they gathered up their stuff and slowly walked across the beach. The group of swimmers were out of the water, drinking from flasks and chatting.

'Hi,' one of the women called on seeing them.

Beth wandered over to them. As she got closer, she realised the tall woman with short dark hair, wearing a vintage floral fifties-style dress, was Felicity.

'Hello again,' Beth said. 'It is you. Alex, it's Felicity.'

'Hi,' he said. 'Every time we come to the beach you're here.'

'I didn't recognise you without my glasses. It's my happy place here. How was your swim?'

'It was fabulous,' Beth said. 'Do you come every day?'

'Most days.'

'She only lives ten minutes away so there's no excuse. I try and get here several times a week. Depends how hard I've been partying the night before,' another of the women said, grinning. 'I'm Miranda. I haven't seen you two here before. I'd have noticed such a striking couple, I'm sure.' Beth turned to smile at Alex. Miranda was just being polite; Alex was the good-looking one in their relationship and she'd often felt she was punching above her weight when they first started dating. His good looks attracted women like bees to honey but she was confident in her own skin. Her sunny disposition attracted friends to her; it was juggling friends and the demands of a relationship she found to be a challenge. Her life here was a chance for a fresh start for her in all areas of her life.

'We've only just moved here,' Beth said, addressing Miranda. 'Alex is going to be working with Felicity at the university.'

'Small world,' said Miranda. 'This is Tania.' She indicated the tall blonde in a long-sleeved costume and bright pink boots.

'I'm Beth, and this is Alex.'

'Hello,' Alex said. He shook hands with all three of them, a smile across his face, making eye contact with each of them. He had the knack of making each person he met feel special.

'It's great to see some new faces in the area,' Miranda said. 'Where were you living before?'

'In London. Alex is a lecturer and he's got a new post here at the university. I'm a primary school teacher but I haven't found a new job yet so I'm doing some online teaching helping sixth formers retaking their GCSEs.'

'Alex is our new head of department in the English faculty,' Felicity said to the others.

'Now you know where we meet, you can join us,' Tania said. 'There are a few more of us, including another couple. If you come on a Saturday that's when we get our biggest turnout. From eight-thirty onwards.'

'Sounds good,' Alex said, looking at Beth, who agreed.

'Great,' Felicity said. 'And don't forget, Beth, if you need anyone to show you round the area or just meet for a coffee, I'd be happy to do that. I know what it's like when you first move here and don't know anyone. Especially if you're not working yet. That's the natural place to meet people.'

'I might do some volunteering while I'm between jobs. It would be lovely to meet you for a coffee.' Beth took her phone out of her pocket. 'Let's exchange numbers. What's yours?'

'I'll get it for you when I'm at work,' Alex said. 'We should be getting back.'

'I might as well do it now,' Beth said.

'No,' Alex said. 'I'm expecting a call. I'll get it from you, Felicity.'

'Sure. I won't let you forget. You're starting in two weeks, right?'

'Yes, on the Tuesday. Guess I'll see you then. Good to meet you all.' He flashed the women another smile, before taking Beth's hand and leading her back over the beach.

'They were nice,' she said. 'I'd love to join them. It would be fun to be part of a swimming group, and it would help us make friends around here.'

He put his arm around her. 'I'd like that. Let's join them on Saturday. Not that I don't like it just being me and you,' he said, 'but we can do both.'

On Saturday morning Beth and Alex strolled hand in hand across the beach.

'We're a bit early,' Beth said. 'I hope we don't miss them.'

'Hello there.' They both turned at the sound, which came from behind them. A woman wearing a bright green hat with a huge pom pom on top was walking towards them, the pom pom jiggling as she negotiated the pebbles.

'You must be Beth and Alex,' she said, removing her hat to fluff out her hair. 'I'm Annabelle.' Her silver hair was cropped and when she smiled it transformed her angular face. 'Felicity told me to look out for you as I'm usually here early on Saturdays. It's great that you've decided to join us. I can only come on Saturdays, I run the charity shop in town and I have an assistant who opens up for me today.'

'You'll have to tell me where it is,' Beth said. 'I love a good rummage.'

'Not more junk,' Alex said. 'We got rid of loads of stuff when we packed, we can't undo all the good work already.'

'Ah, here's our other male swimmer,' Annabelle said. 'Hi, Hamish, hi, Sarah.'

They turned to see a couple approaching. The man had a beard, wore square black glasses, a burgundy hoody and jeans. Sarah wore a long flowery sun dress, her pale blonde hair twisted up into a knot. She smiled at them both with striking blue eyes and Beth was struck by how pretty she was.

'Hello,' Hamish said, dropping his bag onto the floor. 'Anyone know what the temperature is today?'

'Warm, I hope,' said Annabelle.

'Nice to see new faces! Where are you from?' Sarah asked.

'London,' Alex said. 'I take it you're local?'

'Yes, I was born here, but Hamish is from Manchester originally.'

'That's where I went to university,' Alex said, taking his flask from his bag. 'Anyone want some tea? I've got a spare cup.'

'No thanks, I'll wait until after I've had a swim,' Hamish said. 'Some of us go to the café after, if you're interested. I heard you're at the university. I teach art at the local secondary school.'

'I'm a primary teacher,' Beth said, folding her robe and putting it on top of her bag and looking over at the sea. 'I'm getting straight in. It looks glorious.'

'I'll wait for Felicity,' Annabelle said. 'She's just coming.'

Hamish joined Beth, chatting about his job as they wandered down to the sea, Alex and Sarah following them. Beth ran into the water, preferring to immerse herself immediately rather than easing herself in as Sarah was doing, while Alex talked to her. *He's such a gentleman*, Beth thought. Usually Alex dived straight in, darting off before she could catch him. Lifting her feet from the bottom, she turned around in the water to see Annabelle embracing Felicity. She smiled, striking her arms out to swim breaststroke, feeling gloriously alive and at one with nature; it looked like they were making friends already and the last week of the summer stretched in front of them like a welcoming smile.

TWELVE

PRESENT

Gavin sat in his car and looked at the house. It was a detached cottage at the end of a lane. Beth had lived here with Alex, and now Felicity. Only one of them was still alive.

Felicity had been welcoming when he'd phoned. 'Drop in any time,' she'd said. 'I want to help.' He wasn't used to people inviting him into their houses. Mistrust of the police was getting worse. With good reason in some areas of the country. If you couldn't trust the police, then who could you? Shaking his head, he got out of the car. Solve cases and get results for people, that's how he would prove himself. Young Chloe was shaping up to be a good copper. He hoped she'd stick around and not get disillusioned like her predecessor.

Chloe had arrived at work before him this morning.

'I've got something, boss,' she'd said. 'Alex drank tea from a flask before he went into the water. Tania remembered it in her second interview. I made a couple of phone calls and jogged some memories. Caroline saw it too, and so did Felicity's mother, who was minding their bags. It might be significant if the death turns out not to be accidental.'

'Interesting,' he said. 'We might need to locate it. I assume it will have gone back in the Maitlands' beach bag. If it was left on the beach we'll never find it. You can take your bucket and spade along, see if you can dig it up if you want.'

She looked taken aback at his attempt at a joke, and then grinned.

'I might just do that.'

He accepted a cup of tea and sat opposite Felicity at the kitchen table. The kitchen was light and airy and smelled of coffee. He liked to see people in their home environment; it helped get an insight into who they were and how they operated. The phone call he'd taken just before he'd rung the doorbell changed everything. The post-mortem results revealed Alex had a significant amount of sleeping tablets in his system. Checks with his general practitioner revealed he had never been prescribed any sleeping medication. He got out his notebook.

'How are you doing?'

'I'm bearing up.' A mug of black coffee sat in front of her. She twisted her wedding ring around her finger. She looked up and met his gaze. 'I didn't expect to be a widow the day after my wedding.'

'I want to go over a few points with you.'

She nodded.

'I understand how hard this must be for you, but any small detail may help.'

She nodded again.

'We're following up a particular line of enquiry at the moment and I have a few questions for you. First, I'd like you to tell me what you remember from the half hour prior to you all going into the sea.'

'I've already given my statement several times.'

'Yes, I've seen those but I'd like you to go over what you remember again for me. It shouldn't take long.'

Felicity went through the events of the wedding. She spoke in a monotone, her emotions still dulled by shock. If she hadn't seen Alex's body, she'd have refused to believe he'd drowned. He always appeared invincible to her.

'Taking you back to the swim itself. You said Alex was...' He read from the statement. '"In a good mood".'

'Yes.'

'How did other people feel about it?'

'Some people felt uncomfortable.'

'Uncomfortable why?'

'Because they aren't swimmers, and they wouldn't understand what was driving us to do it. We'd talked about it a bit before the wedding, me and my friends when Alex wasn't there, and I know a couple of them thought it was in poor taste. I'd told Alex but he was adamant.'

'Did you share their reservations?'

'It was complicated. Beth was a close friend, and I could understand their reaction.'

'Yet you went ahead with it. Were you angry?'

'No, of course not. It was my wedding day. This all happened a while before and it was important to Alex, so I agreed.'

'Why was it so important to Alex?'

'I'm not exactly sure. It was a barrier he had to get over, prove to himself he could swim at night I think.'

Gavin studied the woman in front of him. He'd get Chloe to do some background digging, find out more about her. She was keeping her composure, despite the terrible situation she found herself in.

'Beth was a good friend of yours, I believe?'

'Yes.' Felicity inhaled a deep breath. 'To lose her was horrendous but now this...' Her shoulders slumped. 'I can't take it all in.'

He understood her reaction; a terrible tragedy was playing

out here. For Alex to find happiness again and then to die in a similar way, she must be feeling terrible guilt about the swim. Was she guilty of anything else, that's what he had to determine. Everyone was a potential suspect now.

'Whose idea was the swim originally?'

'Alex's.'

'You said a moment ago you weren't sure why it was so important to him. Are you saying you didn't know your husband very well?'

'No, not at all.' Felicity fidgeted in her seat. 'It was complicated.'

He made a note in his book. 'Carry on with your account of the evening.'

'We went over to the area near the water where we'd stored our swimming kits. He stripped off straight away, he doesn't feel the cold – didn't, I mean.' She faltered then carried on. 'I was a bit slower. Tania and Miranda joined us and they were giggling, and I was worried they might have been a bit drunk, but they insisted they were OK. I was concerned about my dress but Caroline took it over to my mother to look after.'

'Wasn't Caroline swimming with you?'

'Yes, she came straight back.'

'So you got changed, did the others change then too? It's a bit public, isn't it?'

'We had our swimming robes, they're made so you can get dressed under them. I certainly wouldn't have got changed without it. You have to understand it's totally normal for us, it's what we do every morning. Well, it was...' She shook herself, and continued. 'Tania and Miranda were messing about and they took longer to get changed. I was feeling cold and I started shivering. Alex had the flask...'

'The flask? You didn't bring that up last time.'

'Yes, it had hot tea in it. It was so typical of him to be that organised. That's the kind of person he was. He always had a hot drink before we swam. I did too, but I didn't fancy tea at the wedding.'

'Who did the flask belong to?'

'It was Alex's. I don't know how long he'd had it.'

'Can you describe it to me?'

'It's red, plastic, medium kind of size. It's a flask.'

'Every detail is important. Go on.'

'I had a blue flask in the bag but I wasn't in the mood for tea, I'd had enough liquid over the evening.'

'What were you drinking?'

'Water for the last couple of hours. After the cake, like I said. Before that I was drinking white wine mostly. A glass of champagne at the beginning.'

He looked at her expectantly. 'The tea?' he reminded her.

'Yes, Alex drank it. He was very into his routine, he had to do things in a certain way. He always had a hot drink before and after his swim. He insisted on preparing it himself.' Her voice faltered and she looked down at her lap. 'He didn't get to drink after his swim that night.'

'I know this is hard for you.'

'It's OK. Once he'd had his drink he said "Come on," and he went first and I followed. The others were behind us because when I reached the water, I turned round to check they were still there. Which they were. By the time I turned back Alex was already swimming out to sea. I swam after him but he's faster than me. I mean, he was.'

She paused, taking a deep breath. 'It was dark out and I didn't go out very far because I was a bit scared. I swam parallel to the shore so I could be guided by the lights from the wedding reception. I didn't see Alex after that.'

'Did you hear anything?'

'Only Tania whooping when she got into the water. Giggling, shouting, she was making a lot of noise.'

'You said you didn't see Alex again. Were you worried about him?'

'Not specifically. He's... he was such a good swimmer. I had a certain level of anxiety about the whole thing. I didn't swim for too long, maybe ten minutes and then I got out. Tania and Miranda came back at the same time as me and we got changed straight away and it was shortly after that we got worried.'

'OK. Back to the flask – did you see anyone else apart from Alex drink from the flask?'

'No. I was the only person he would share it with but I didn't that night.'

'You mentioned Alex always...' He consulted his notes. 'He always "insisted he prepare it himself". Did you see him do this?'

'Yes, I was in the kitchen with him but I wasn't studying what he was doing. I was aware of it. I wasn't even supposed to be there.'

'What do you mean?'

'We talked about me staying at my mother's the night before the wedding – superstition, you know. It's meant to be bad luck. "Superstitious nonsense," Alex said.' She looked sad. 'Obviously it wasn't.'

'Do you know what happened to the flask once he'd finished his drink?'

Felicity thought for a moment. 'He would have put it back in our bag, but I don't actually remember. There was a lot going on and I was psyching myself up to swim.'

'Can you describe the bag?'

'It was a large canvas bag, blue and white horizontal stripes. My mother was keeping an eye on the bags, she must have taken it. Is it important?'

'Every detail is important.'

THIRTEEN

ANONYMOUS

The body was found sooner than I expected. Better to get it over with, I suppose, let the investigators pick at the pieces like creatures will have picked at the body, crawling into the eyes and burrowing under flesh. It was covered with a tent, hidden from prying eyes, but it was obvious what lay underneath, the swollen corpse, no longer the handsome man who lived amongst us and swam like a fish in the sea.

I wasn't the only one who hated him. The police will soon find that out. I wonder how long it will take them to wonder about the previous death, to wonder what he was capable of. The similarities will stand out, files will be looked at, the previous investigation picked over. It hasn't been that long, after all, that's part of the problem. Will it be the same team working on it? A new team would want to prove themselves, prove they can do better. Questions will be asked. Too many people could comment, whisper words that raise the suspicions of the police. Not only will they look at the former partner but there is the money, money he'd helped himself to, which not everyone will approve of. I certainly didn't, and neither did she. That's two suspects already.

FOURTEEN

PRESENT

It was Alex, hideously transformed but undoubtedly him. Rosemary hadn't wanted her husband to leave her when they were asked who was going to identify the body. Felicity had wanted to know for sure; maybe that way it might sink in because at present she was in a state of disbelief. The image of Alex wouldn't leave her.

Felicity stopped when she reached the top of the cliff, the wind gently lifting her hair. She inhaled a large lungful of sea air, closing her eyes and willed her mind to stop. To stop spinning round on a loop, going over and over the interview with the detective. A seagull flew in circles above her.

DS Williams had mentioned Beth and it had all come rushing back. It hit her every so often like a ball in the head. The realisation that Beth had gone. She hadn't expected to miss her so much.

It often happened while she was swimming. She'd been floating out towards the horizon where the sea and sky merged into one and the sense of space ahead and below her had overwhelmed her and caught her breath. The thought of Beth swimming out here and what might have happened had filled her with fear. If she were to give in to it, stop kicking her arms and legs and allow her body to sink down and down until she lost consciousness she wouldn't have to go ahead with the promise she'd made. She turned to face the beach where she could just about see the splash of green that was her bag. How long would it be before anyone would notice she'd gone? A huge wave slapped her from behind, catching her unawares, propelling her forward and she was swimming fast, the survival instinct kicking in, desperate to leave the dangerous thoughts behind, powering her arms forward, lungs burning as the life she loved flashed before her. She shook her head to dispel the memory.

She'd been racing Alex that day, leaving Beth to swim in the other direction. She wasn't usually into racing; she preferred to swim slowly and soak up the atmosphere, be present in the moment. But he'd challenged her. They'd gone further than usual and Alex had won. How long had they been out there? They'd never been able to give a precise timing. Alex had timed the race, which took fifteen minutes, but they'd chatted on the return; the weather had been good and neither of them were due in work until later.

They hadn't made it into work. As they'd swum towards the shore, Alex had noticed that Beth wasn't back yet and they'd both sped up. Her clothes were untouched, a forlorn pile on the sand. Alex went back into the sea to look for her and as soon as Felicity saw him on his way back, without her, she'd called the coastguard.

How long had it been before the gossip started? A month? Hamish and Sarah's garden party, that's when it had begun. The group had got closer after Beth's death; the shock of it all had made them look out for one another more, and, as death often does, had made them all more aware of how important life was. Sarah had issued the invitations and Hamish had done the cooking. They hadn't known whether Alex would turn up or not, but he had. He'd brought champagne and told them that he'd inherited all of Beth's aunt's money. It had been a huge headache for him, not knowing whether he'd be able to continue the extension they'd started. He hadn't gone into the details, saying it was far too complicated, but he'd broken down in front of them and cried. It was what Beth would have wanted, he'd assured them.

That night had been a turning point, when he'd come out of the fog of sadness that had surrounded him since then. Felicity had been the one to comfort him, to give him a hug, and they'd talked for ages in the car after on the way home. Some time after that she'd gone swimming with Sarah one afternoon and at the café over mugs of hot chocolate, Sarah had confided in her that Hamish was speculating about Alex's sudden windfall, how convenient it was and that something just didn't add up. Hamish had sworn her to secrecy but it hadn't taken much persuading for Felicity to get out of her that Alex had had an affair during his relationship with Beth. He'd confided to Hamish in the pub one night and although he wouldn't reveal the name, he said it was someone they all knew.

It hadn't stopped Felicity acting on her feelings for Alex.

And now he had drowned too.

FIFTEEN

Chloe ate a bite of her home-made cheese and pickle sandwich before discarding it on her desk. Her phone was still blank. Why hadn't Gavin got back to her? He must still be interviewing the wife. Widow, rather. This case was turning into something very different. Interesting to hear how Alex's fiancée had drowned in similar circumstances. Her gut was telling her this was no straightforward accidental drowning.

When her phone rang ten minutes later, she snatched it up. It was Gavin.

'Have you finished the interview?'

'I've got one more to do.' She pulled her notepad across and flicked through it. 'Miranda Deacon.'

'I'll be back in an hour. Catch you after the interview. I have news.'

Miranda was waiting in the interview room. She'd had to go into work the previous day, so instead of waiting around at the hotel she'd offered to come back. Chloe thought how striking she was with her mass of auburn hair and dark makeup. She was scrolling through her phone when Chloe entered the room. She put it face down on the table when she saw her.

'Thanks for coming back. How are you doing?'

Miranda ran her hands through her hair.

'OK, you know. It's all such a shock. Especially after Beth.' She shook her head. 'You read about this kind of thing happening to tourists who don't know the area or teenagers messing around, jumping from cliffs, but Alex? It's so cruel how history is being repeated. Such a lovely couple too.'

'I've read through your initial statement but I'd like to go over a few points. How long had you known Alex and Felicity?'

'About five years or so. Since they moved down here. I've known Alex as long as Felicity has. I hope she's OK.'

'I'd like to go back to the day Beth drowned.'

'I wasn't there,' Miranda said. 'Alex and Felicity were with her, and we arrived shortly after they'd called for help.'

'We being...?'

'Me, Tania, Sarah and Hamish.'

'Could you describe what happened?'

'Felicity was on the beach waiting for the ambulance. She had her phone out and had zoomed in on the camera to see if she could see anything out at sea. Alex had gone back into the water to search.'

'So you didn't see Beth?'

'No. Felicity was calm but that's how she is. She's the kind of person you want around in a crisis. Alex came back in and he was distraught, I've never seen him lose his composure like that.'

'How well did you know Alex?'

'A casual friend, I'd say. Same as I know the others. Apart from Tania. She's a good mate and we see each other outside of swimming. Occasionally we do social stuff as a group but not often.'

'And Beth?'

'I had less in common with her but she was lovely. They

were a devoted couple, anyone could see that. He was protective of her.'

'Did she need protecting?'

'No, but he was quite full of himself; he had a respected job at the university and she wasn't working as far as I know when she died.'

'How did the group feel about Alex getting together with Felicity?'

'We all thought it was great. I think Annabelle was a bit unsure at first, but she's older than the rest of us and a bit more traditional in her values.'

'That's Annabelle Victor?'

'Yes. From the charity shop.'

'Going back to the wedding evening. Did you notice anyone using a flask before the swim?'

She chewed on her lip, thinking.

'Yes, actually. We thought it was funny. Tania made a joke about how only those two could drink tea as if this was a normal swim on their wedding day. I mean, who does that?' She shrugged. 'It doesn't matter now, does it?'

Chloe remained silent for a few seconds, noting the sadness that shadowed Miranda's face. She noticed Chloe looking and shifted herself up in her chair.

'Is that it?'

'Is there anything else you can remember about the wedding day, particularly around the swim itself?'

'No, everyone was having a great time up until then.' She looked up at Chloe. 'I was being silly right before they went into the water. I can't imagine messing around like that now, this has really stunned me. I feel like I'm in a stupor half the time.'

Chloe watched Miranda thoughtfully as she left the station, before returning to her desk and the initial news report about the fiancée she'd located earlier, to make sure the details were fresh in her mind. It had needed no digging at all to locate this piece of information as she was working through the files on Beth's drowning. Had the police done an adequate job on that case? She sighed. Given the bad press they'd had lately, it wasn't a bad inference to make. It was up to officers like their squad to prove them wrong. Proving herself on her first case here was exactly what she intended to do. She opened the article.

FIANCÉE DIES IN TRAGIC ACCIDENT

Coastguards were called to Eastsea bay yesterday morning to reports of a swimmer failing to return from a swim. A woman went into the water with her fiancé and a friend. Despite not swimming out as far as the others, the woman did not return to the beach. Police and coastguards carried out an extensive search of the area but no sign of the woman was found.

The couple were engaged to be married next spring.

DS Williams was back when Chloe returned to the office and he beckoned her to join him. 'What have you got for me?' he asked as she sat down facing him.

She ran through the interview with Tania Beckford and the details she'd revealed about the flask. 'And I've just conducted my last follow-up interview with Miranda Deacon. She remembered the flask, recalled the joke Tania made about it, said it was typical of the pair of them. I've also checked the inventory of items seized from the scene and there is no red flask present. It's described as an ordinary red plastic thermos flask. I also asked Miranda about his first fiancée. She said the swimming group were largely supportive of the new relationship with Felicity. How did you get on with her?'

He recounted his interview. 'She mentioned the flask voluntarily before I brought it up. Plus a stripy bag they carried it in.'

'We've got a stripy bag,' Chloe said.

'She also saw him make the tea and fill it himself.'

'That's interesting. Maybe it's not important. I'd still like to know where it went though.'

'Finding that flask is going to be crucial.' He swivelled his laptop to show her an open email on the screen. 'The post-mortem results are in,' he said. 'The contents of his stomach reveal a sleeping drug in his digestive system. Alex Maitland was murdered.'

'Murdered,' Chloe said. 'How terrible. I thought it was a coincidence given what happened before. I've got the files here on his former fiancée's drowning.'

'Good. Get stuck into it and see what you can find. I'm beginning to think this is not going to turn out to be a straight-forward investigation. I've already spoken to his employer and uncovered a student who had some problems with him. I've arranged to speak to the student, a Judy Michigan.'

Chloe took a large bite of the sandwich that still languished on her desk. This case was getting more and more interesting.

SIXTEEN

PAST

Felicity headed towards the beach, but instead of stopping by the sea she took the coastal path in the direction of the next town, one of her regular walks.

Alex had only been in post for a few weeks, yet already she had no qualms about leaving him without her support for the day. He'd fitted into the department amazingly well, winning them all over on the first day by producing a much-needed coffee machine for the office, and making a point of remembering their preferred drinks. He'd picked procedures up quickly without needing to rely on her at all. It was such a change from his predecessor, who'd relied on her constantly. A weight had been lifted and her shoulders relaxed as she slowed her pace to take in the view of the sea she never tired of.

Despite the sunshine, the wind was strong and she noticed a woman ahead continually pulling her hair back from her face. At times like these she appreciated having short hair. As she neared the woman, she recognised her as Beth, Alex's fiancée. The couple now swam regularly with the swimming group. They were a welcome addition, both friendly and keen swimmers. Beth, she'd found particularly easy to get along with. She called out her name and the woman turned.

'Hi, Beth, I thought it was you. How are you?'

'Great, thanks. I'm trying to get to know the area.' She waved a guidebook of local walks at her. Felicity recognised the cover.

'That's where I originally found this walk. It's my day off. I only work four days a week. Where are you off to?'

'A walk along the cliff, following a route to Cliffhead and back.' Beth showed her the route in the book.

'I'm heading that way too. Mind if I join you?'

'Oh I'd love you to. I won't have to keep on referring to the map. Aside from the company, of course.' They laughed.

'Alex is settling in well,' Felicity said.

'That's good, he's enjoying it. He's aware of being an outsider coming in and taking over the department, but so far he feels welcome.'

'He won't face any problems on that score, we're just relieved to have a new head. The last one didn't cope with change very well. Anyway it's good to get new blood in with fresh ideas to shake us all up a bit.' She laughed. 'I'm so pleased you've joined our swimming group too. We missed you this morning, Alex said you weren't well.'

'I had a headache,' Beth said, 'I thought a brisk walk in the sea air might clear it away.'

'Is it working?'

'A bit.' Beth looked out to sea.

'Did Alex mention I wanted to invite you both over? I asked him to check with you when I gave him my number for you.'

'He must have forgotten. He didn't give me your number either. But we'd love to, thanks.'

The track narrowed and Felicity slotted in behind Beth. Alex had surprised her this morning. Sarah had got to the beach before Hamish and she'd arrived to find the pair of them engrossed in conversation, Alex openly flirting with her. He'd stopped when he saw her arrive but once the others turned up he gravitated back towards Sarah in the sea and they were splashing each other and laughing. She'd never seen him behave that way with Beth; would he have behaved like that if Beth had been there? Felicity put him out of her mind; she was far more interested in getting to know Beth.

'Tell me more about you,' Felicity said. The rest of the walk was taken up with conversation and the rapport between them was as if they'd known each other for ages. Beth told her about the school she'd worked at and how much she'd loved the children she taught. She wasn't having much luck so far in her hunt for a new teaching post.

'Term has already started so my options are limited. Even if I could line something up for January it will soon come round.'

'What about supply work?'

'Alex doesn't want me to.'

Felicity laughed. 'What do you want?'

'I wouldn't mind. But he's right, the kids can play up more when you're a supply. I'm sure I could handle it, but he doesn't want me to.'

'If you think you can manage it...'

'No,' Beth said. 'It's not a good idea.'

'OK.' Felicity was a little taken aback at her vehemence.

They walked in silence for a while. When they arrived back in town, they stopped to say their goodbyes.

'Sorry I overreacted,' Beth said. 'I don't like to upset Alex, he's been so good to me. We should do this again.' Her cheeks were flushed from the sea air and the vigorous walk.

'I'd love that. Let me give you my number.'

They had just exchanged numbers when a large gust of wind took them by surprise, lifting Beth's hair. Felicity caught a glimpse of a large blue bruise, before Beth pulled her hair back behind her ears. She frowned as she watched Beth walk away.

Felicity looked up from her desk, sighing at yet another interruption. Alex's office was directly opposite hers, and he was proving very popular with the students. Faculty staff were encouraged to leave their office doors open when they weren't giving tutorials or having meetings, but the constant flow of traffic to see him was making it difficult for her to get on with her work, and his voice was rather loud. She'd hoped the novelty of having a good-looking male in the department might have worn off by now, after all he'd been in post for a month, but his students were just as keen as ever. Two young women were currently having a loud conversation right outside her door about when their next deadline was. She looked up and frowned. Judy, one of her tutees, was standing in line again. She was forever coming up to see Alex. She hoped she wasn't getting behind in her coursework. Judy was under Felicity's pastoral care and she made a note to check in on her at their next meeting.

Unable to concentrate, she decided to leave her marking for later and opened up her emails instead. Her attention was caught by an address she didn't recognise but a name she did. She smiled as she read the friendly email with a link she might be interested in attached. That was a coincidence when she was just thinking about her new colleague. It was from Beth, Alex's fiancée. They'd been in contact a few times since the walk and swapped details.

A knock at her door made her look up.

'Alex, hi. You're very popular today, aren't you? I'm surprised you can get any work done.'

'What can I say?' he said, grinning. 'It must be my innate

magnetism. Seriously, I don't mind, I want the students to feel they can approach me. I don't want to be one of those distant heads of departments who leaves all the hands-on work to the rest of the team.'

'That sounds great,' Felicity said. 'Your predecessor had a very different outlook. He avoided the students as far as possible and used to use his office as a hideaway, letting everyone else pick up the work he should have been doing. It's a breath of fresh air having you here, to be honest.'

'Still no hard feelings about not getting the job? Everyone thought you'd get it. It must have been a disappointment.'

'No, honestly, I wasn't completely convinced I wanted the job. It's a lot of extra work that isn't teaching, and teaching is what I love to do.'

'The students speak very highly of you.'

'Good to hear. I noticed Judy Michigan has been to see you a lot. She's my personal tutee. Is everything OK with her?'

'Judy... oh yes of course, Judy with the blonde hair, I've been giving her a bit of help with her latest assignment as she was struggling but I think we've got it sorted.'

'That's good. Did you want something?'

'Yes, do you know where this room is?' He showed her a copy of a timetable on his phone. 'I'm teaching there this afternoon for the first time.'

'It's on the third floor, right at the far end of the corridor.'

'Thanks.'

'By the way did Beth tell you what a nice time we had last week?'

'Beth?'

'Your fiancée, don't tell me you've forgotten her.' She smiled.

'Ah of course, I thought you meant a student.' He looked at his watch. 'Yes, of course she did. Catch you later.'

Felicity watched as he crossed the corridor and closed his office door behind him. She got the distinct impression that he had no idea she'd seen Beth. Why pretend he had?

The following week Felicity was waiting for her last student of the morning. Once a month she had in-depth meetings with each of her personal tutees to see how they were getting on with their course and with student life in general. She checked her list to see who was next. Judy appeared in the doorway.

'Hello, Ms Harrison.'

'Felicity, please. Come in.'

'OK.' Judy folded herself into the chair and crossed her legs. Her blonde hair was tied back into a loose ponytail. She was tall but her posture suggested she was still growing into her coltish limbs.

'Tell me how you've been getting on with your course.'

'Alright, I think, my grades are OK so far. I worried I might be out of my depth before I came as it's a big step up from A levels. But my tutors have been really helpful.' She picked at her fingernail, looking at her hands. 'I had a few problems last year and missed some school time. I'm not sure if you are aware of this.'

Felicity cursed herself for not checking through Judy's notes before she came in.

'Why don't you tell me about it now? I'd like to hear it from you.'

'I had depression. I'm doing better now though. I just get a bit anxious.'

'Was there anything in particular that caused it, or have you struggled with this for a while?'

'A bit of both. I split up with my boyfriend and got behind in my schoolwork.'

'Did you receive any help, counselling or medication?'

'I saw the school therapist for a while.'

'Was it helpful?'

'Yes, it was.'

'Are you still having counselling now?'

'No, it was a lady at school I saw.'

'We have student counsellors on site, you know, although there may be a waiting list. Is that something you'd like to explore?'

Judy studied her hands again. 'I don't think so. I've made a couple of friends who know about it, and Mr Maitland has been very good.'

'Has he?' Felicity checked Judy's timetable. 'You're in his medieval literature seminar group, is that right?'

She nodded, more alert now. 'It's my favourite class and he's really helped with my confidence. I got my first A last week. He really encourages me.'

'Congratulations. I'm so pleased you're doing well and it's normal to be a little anxious at the start of a new course. It sounds to me like you have everything under control for the moment. Don't forget, I am your personal tutor and my door is always open. If there's anything I can help you with, or you find your mood getting low, don't feel you can't come and see me. Talking helps. I wouldn't want you to suffer in silence.'

'Thank you.'

Later that day, she went to make herself a coffee in the faculty office. Two of her colleagues were engrossed in a conversation and she hesitated before going over to sit with them.

'Can I join you?' she asked.

'Of course,' Helen said, and Steve moved his coffee out of the way so Felicity could fit hers on the table.

'You looked like you were having an intense conversation there.'

Helen and Steve exchanged a glance.

'We were,' Helen said, looking over her shoulder. 'How are you finding our new head of department?'

'He seems to be settling in OK, and he's very popular with the students from what I can gather.'

'Hmm,' Helen said. 'The female students.'

Felicity raised an eyebrow. 'What do you mean?'

Steve lowered his voice. 'I've noticed he's very tactile with the female students.'

'You have to be careful here, Steve,' Felicity said. Alarm bells were ringing immediately. They all knew how important boundaries with students were, and any allegation against a head of department would be a difficult scenario, heading down a very dark track. 'What are you saying exactly?'

'On two occasions I've seen him with different first-year students standing very close to them. With one young woman he was stroking her arm while he was speaking to her. We all have to respect boundaries, but especially as a man, I'm hyper aware of this and how careful you have to be. I wouldn't behave as he would, let's put it that way. Students can be very impressionable, especially first years when they're away from home for the first time and feeling their way as adults.'

Felicity frowned. 'He has a lot of students come to see him when he's off timetable, and now you mention it, I've noticed they are mostly female. What about you, Helen?'

'He's not great about respecting personal space, I'm always having to step back. But maybe he's like that with everyone.'

'I'm glad you've brought it to my attention. I'm his deputy, so you've done the right thing. I'll keep an eye on the situation.'

'I'm not making a complaint or anything,' Steve said, scratching his leg. 'If he were on the same level as me I might suggest going for a pint one day and having a friendly chat. But he's my line manager so I'm not going there.'

'I know.' Felicity thought about her meeting with Judy

earlier and how lit up she'd been when she mentioned Alex. Surely he wouldn't take advantage of her? He'd been extremely professional so far in all her dealings with him. Felicity recalled Sarah, and the way he'd been behaving with her in the sea. Beth was so genuine; Felicity hoped her fiancé was too.

SEVENTEEN

PRESENT

DS Williams surveyed the room. He'd called the briefing as soon as he'd got in early this morning. He had four staff working this case, which wasn't enough but he knew better than to waste time trying to find more resources. His team were well up to the job.

'Now this is officially a murder case we need to make up for lost time.' He pointed to the photo of Alex Maitland stuck to the whiteboard behind him. 'Alex Maitland died from poisoning at his own wedding. The post-mortem revealed traces of sleeping tablets in his system. We were fortunate to have all the guests readily confined in one space and we were able to gather interviews from everyone present at the wedding. Chloe.'

Chloe got to her feet. She stuck a photo on the board. A woman with shoulder-length blonde hair gazed out from the photo. The shot was of her head and shoulders and the sea was behind her. She was smiling, a wisp of hair across her cheek.

'This is Elizabeth Curran, Alex Maitland's former fiancée. She drowned three years ago after swimming out from the same beach. Beth, as she was known, was due to inherit a tidy sum from an aunt, Celia Davies, who was ill with terminal cancer at the time of her disappearing. The aunt bequeathed everything to Alex after Beth's death and she died two months later.

'A body washed up to sea a few weeks later; it was too badly decomposed to be identified, but was presumed to be Beth's. It could be worth looking into.'

'Thanks, Chloe, good work,' said DS Williams. 'I want us to focus on the family and close friends, in particular the people they swam with. Who was Alex and did he have any worries, any enemies? We need to dig deeper and see what we can find out. Murray, I'd like you to help Chloe go through the investigation into Beth's drowning and see what you can find out. Who was around on both occasions? Tim, I want you to come with me and we're going to go to Surrey to re-interview Alex's family, this time focusing on his relationship with Beth. I've already informed them and Felicity Maitland of these developments. Chloe, I'd like you to speak to the swimmers again, see what you can find out there. Right, let's do this.'

Chloe was logging on to her laptop when the phone rang.

'PC Button.'

The caller was Annabelle Victor, one of the wedding guests who'd joined in the swim.

'I'd like to speak to you please.'

Chloe picked up concern in her voice. Once she had established that Annabelle was working at the charity shop on the nearby high street she arranged to call in on her there.

'I'll be there in half an hour.'

Chloe hadn't done the initial interview with Annabelle Victor so before she went, she had a quick look at the file.

The charity shop was on the main shopping street. The window display showed a colourful display of autumn wear and a gorgeous pair of brown chunky lace-up boots caught her eye. The doorbell jangled as she went inside. She recognised the tall woman with stylish grey hair at the counter, who nodded towards her as she went in.

The interior was small, with racks of clothes arranged by colour at the front and shelving full of books and trinkets at the far end. She was the only person in the shop. Annabelle came out from behind the desk and locked the front door, turning the sign round.

'I'm due a break now anyway. Come into the office and I'll make you some tea.'

The small office at the back was stuffed full of bags of donations which were piled high in boxes. Chloe stepped over a large bag of books which had fallen over and were spilling onto the floor. She sat on a wooden chair in front of a shelf of battered-looking jigsaws.

'Sorry about the mess,' Annabelle said, crossing to a small sink area and switching the kettle on. 'It was good of you to come at such short notice.'

'It's my job,' Chloe said. 'I had you on my list for re-interview anyway.'

'Oh?' Annabelle brought two cups of tea over and handed one to Chloe.

'I'm afraid we've uncovered evidence that Alex Maitland was murdered.'

'Oh no, how awful.' Annabelle looked shocked as she made some space on a table so she could put her cup on it. 'I can't believe that.'

'Was there anyone who Alex didn't get on with in the swimming club?'

Annabelle frowned. 'No, I wouldn't put it as strongly as that.' She twisted her hands in her lap.

'Anything you can tell us at all might help us find the killer, no matter how trivial it seems.'

'You're right.' She sighed. 'Alex was a terrible flirt, that's all, and he was very friendly with Sarah. Her husband,

Hamish, was part of the group too so it was a bit awkward at times.'

'Did Hamish say anything or confront him?'

'Not that I saw. But I got a sense that something happened. Apparently they'd had words at a party round at Hamish's but I wasn't there and don't like gossip so I ignored it. The atmosphere changed. I don't swim very often, only on days when I'm not working alone, you see, and I don't like to gossip. What was it you wanted to talk to me about?'

'Beth, Alex's first fiancée. You must know about her?'

Annabelle nodded.

'I liked Beth. She was a lovely girl and it was so sad. I might be wrong about this but I had some concerns. I've given it a lot of thought since Alex's death and I didn't tell you everything at my previous interview as I was in shock.'

'Why don't you tell me now?'

Annabelle thought back to the first morning Beth had come into her shop. She hadn't recognised the petite woman who entered, assuming she was a tourist. The doorbell jangled announcing her arrival. As she was browsing through the books Annabelle recognised her as one of the newcomers at the swimming group.

'Hello, Beth, isn't it?'

'Yes, I'm sorry I've forgotten your name.'

'Annabelle.'

'Of course. So many new names to remember. I love that orange jumper in the window. Could you tell me what size it is?'

'Lovely isn't it. It's a twelve. Is it for you?'

'Yes, but that's too big. Never mind. I don't really need it. I can't justify it anyway as I'm not working at the moment.'

'Remind me, what do you do? You're not the only one who doesn't remember everything.'

Beth laughed. 'I'm a primary school teacher.'

'How lovely. You must have a lot of patience.'

'I'm pretty easygoing. I love it though, it's such a rewarding job.'

'Do you have children yourself?'

'No, we want to get married first. We're engaged,' she said, showing Annabelle her ring.

'That's beautiful.'

'Isn't it? Maybe we'll think about children in a couple of years after the wedding once we're more settled. This is a lovely shop.'

'It is, but it's in danger of having to close down. We're really short of volunteers.'

'That's a shame. I was just thinking how I'd like to sort the books out over there.' Her hand flew to her mouth. 'I didn't mean to be rude.'

Annabelle had laughed.

'None taken. They're a mess. That task is high on my to-do list. Maybe you might like to volunteer. We have a couple of people who come in at the weekend, but weekdays are a struggle. The shop is very popular but we're in danger of losing it if we don't recruit more helpers.'

'I'd love to.'

'Oh how wonderful. We could do with some young people around the place. All the other helpers are my age, I'm afraid.'

'I am looking for a new teaching job though, so I'm not sure how long I'll be available for. I'm currently doing some teaching online but that's only a few hours per week. Right now I could fit in a couple of afternoons.'

'That would be such a help. Shall I take down some details and I'll be in touch once I've worked out the timesheet for the next couple of weeks?'

Chloe cleared her throat, bringing Annabelle back to the present. She told Chloe how Beth had originally expressed an interest in volunteering in the shop.

'You mentioned you had some concerns.'

'Yes. When she showed me her engagement ring her sleeve fell back and I noticed bruising on her arm, bad bruising, like someone had twisted her wrist.'

'Did you mention it to her?'

'No. I didn't know her well enough.'

'And did she come and work at the shop?'

'No. The next time I saw her was at the swimming group the following weekend. Her fiancé was there too, and after that they were usually together when I swam. That first time stuck in my mind though, because when I asked her about working in the shop, she denied offering to volunteer saying she wouldn't possibly be able to as she wanted to devote her time to finding a job. I didn't press her on the matter as it would have been awkward but I knew she was lying. A bit later, when I was in the sea and her fiancé had swum further out she joined me and told me she didn't want him to know as he wouldn't like her to work in a charity shop. It struck me as odd, and combined with the bruising I was slightly concerned for her. But they seemed happy together.'

'Did you notice any more bruising? She wouldn't be able to hide much in her swimming costume.'

'She always wore a wetsuit, not a full-body one but with long sleeves and short legs so she was pretty well covered.'

Chloe made another note. 'Is that unusual?'

'Not necessarily. In the summer more so, but she may not have wanted to burn her skin as she was quite fair.'

'How well did you get on with Alex?'

'Like I said I didn't know him that well, but I liked what I saw of him. He was very interesting to talk to as he was an English professor and we occasionally discussed books. I mentioned a reading group we run from the charity shop as we get a lot of books donated, but he laughed and said he wouldn't have time. But the next time I saw him he brought a load of books for the shop and drove me home so I didn't have to carry them. He was thoughtful like that, and always making sure we were all comfortable in the water.

'It was odd though, when I said I hoped Beth would volunteer in the shop he said she wouldn't have time as they were very busy in the evenings. Yet I got the impression she didn't do a great deal. He was a member of the sailing club and spent a lot of time there, because Beth joked one time about not being able to drink in the evening as she often had to go and collect him. They seemed close, but I got the impression it was all about him, and she was a bit subservient.'

Chloe went to a café once she'd wrapped up the interview and over a sandwich and a glass of water she mulled over Annabelle's words. Were Alex and Beth as happy as everyone made out? Her gut instinct was telling her no.

EIGHTEEN

PAST

Felicity had swum out much further than the others. Tania and Miranda had finished swimming and were chatting as they swam back and forth across the bay. Every few minutes they'd stop and tread water. Usually she swam along beside them but today she needed time alone to organise her thoughts.

The pastoral meeting she'd held the previous day was still troubling her. She'd woken up during the night and once she'd remembered, she'd been unable to get the unwanted thoughts out of her head. She'd tried replacing them with jumping sheep, which normally worked for her, but not last night. She'd ended up making a chamomile tea and watching the sun come up, willing the morning to arrive so she could shed her worries in the water.

The sun was fully risen now and she welcomed the warmth on her shoulders. Unlike Beth, who always wore long sleeves, she preferred to swim in her costume, with hat, gloves and boots to keep her extremities warmer during the winter season. It was getting into winter now, and she had worn her gloves today for the first time this season, aware that she hadn't slept well and ever mindful of the hazards and unpredictable nature of the sea.

The water was just about warm enough for them still to be able to get in a decent swim. Two figures emerged, making their way down the rocky steps onto the beach. Her stomach sank. It was Alex and Beth; she'd hoped not to cross paths this morning after the events of yesterday afternoon. She wasn't very good at hiding her emotions, and she wasn't clear whether she needed to take action or not. She ducked her head under the water and pushed forward. She was overthinking everything; they wouldn't be speaking about work with the others around.

She shook water from her hair as she emerged from the water, turning round and swimming back towards the bay where they'd left their stuff. Tania and Miranda were wading through the sand, deep in conversation, followed by Sarah. Hamish hadn't been able to make it today. She must do something about encouraging new members; she could do with someone she had more in common with to swim with. Tania and Miranda were close; they didn't mean to exclude Felicity but she wasn't quite on their wavelength. Her life was so busy, despite only working four days. She spent so much time marking and on her research project, she really didn't have time to spend on membership of the group. Under normal circumstances she'd be happy to see Beth as she'd connected with her instantly, but unfortunately she was the partner of Felicity's head of department and given what had happened yesterday she could foresee problems if they pursued the friendship.

Judy Michigan had come to see her yesterday afternoon, knocking hesitantly on the door even though it was wide open.

'Have you got a minute, Ms Harrison?'

'Sure, come in.' She'd given up telling her to call her by her first name, although she'd heard her calling Alex by his without any problems. Judy stood awkwardly and she beckoned her over.

'Sit down, Judy, how are you today?'

'I'm OK,' said Judy, shuffling into the seat opposite Felicity, who was sitting by her desk.

'What can I do for you? Is it the homework I set? Do you need the title clarifying? I've already had two students in about that earlier today.'

'No, er, it's not that. It's a bit awkward.'

'Let me shut the door, give us a bit of privacy,' Felicity said. The girl was fiddling with her hands and wouldn't look her in the eye. She hadn't seen her this anxious before.

'Is something worrying you, Judy?'

'A bit.'

'Is it to do with your anxiety that you told me about last time?'

'Hmm, not really. It's to do with Mr Maitland.'

Interesting that he wasn't being called Alex today, thought Felicity. Aloud, she said, 'You're in a safe space here, let me know what the problem is and I'll see if I can help you.'

Judy stared into her lap.

'You've come this far so you might as well tell me. Would it help if he was here too?'

Judy whipped her head up. 'No, definitely not. The thing is, we've been getting on really well like I told you and he's been really encouraging me with my coursework. He asked me to come and see him after my last lecture the other day and when I went into his office he had a bottle of wine out and he offered me a glass. I don't drink much but I didn't want to offend him.' She breathed in and let the breath out slowly.

'Go on.' Alarm bells were ringing again for Felicity.

'The thing is, miss, I don't want to get him into trouble, so this has got to be confidential. Otherwise I won't tell you.'

'If Mr Maitland has behaved inappropriately I have a duty to report him.'

'No, he hasn't. I was just a bit alarmed and I'm not making a complaint, I just wanted to ask what you thought.'

'Go on.'

'He gave me a large glass of wine and sat down next to me on the sofa. You know he has that couch in his room and usually he always sits behind his desk or in the armchair. It was evening and dark outside and there was a different atmosphere. He sat really close and put his arm along the back of my chair, and his hand landed on my shoulder. I jumped up and ran out. I panicked. I think he might have got the wrong message from me but I feel silly now. I behaved like a stupid little girl.'

'No,' Felicity said. 'It doesn't sound entirely appropriate to me and you have definitely not done anything wrong.'

'I really like him and I have been coming up to see him a lot. I talked to him about splitting up with my boyfriend too and he's been so nice. I'm worried I've messed everything up.'

'You haven't, but it might be better given that you were feeling uncomfortable if next time you're feeling anxious you come and talk to me instead. If you feel comfortable doing so, that is.'

Judy nodded. 'I feel so stupid. He's in a relationship anyway. He's got a picture of his girlfriend on his phone and she's really pretty.' She sighed. 'I know I've been naive but I didn't think he'd be like that.'

'I'm hoping you've misunderstood his intentions, but I will have to speak to him. I promise you won't have anything to worry about.'

'OK.'

'Is there anything else you want to add?'

Judy shook her head.

'Let me check my diary.' Felicity flicked through the pages. 'You're due to see me early next week, so come back then. I'll have spoken to Mr Maitland and we can take it from there. Try and have a nice weekend, do something fun. Have you made friends here?'

'Yes, there are two girls on my corridor in halls I get on well with.'

'Good. Maybe you can do something fun with them, take your mind off your course for a bit.'

'Yes.'

'I'll see you, Judy.'

The cold snapped Felicity back to the present, as she swam towards the shore. She was interrupted in her thoughts by Miranda's voice. She was waving her bright yellow float high, crossing the beach to join Alex and Beth, who were arranging their stuff on the rocks, Beth pulling on her bathing cap. Felicity walked across the warm sand to join them. Sarah was towelling her shoulders dry. She took out her sun cream, squeezing a blob onto her shoulder.

'I'll do that,' Alex said, taking the bottle from her and spreading the cream across her back. Sarah held her hair out of the way and giggled.

'Hey, that tickles.'

'Ooh, me next,' Miranda said. 'I can't remember the last time a good-looking man smeared cream on me.'

'Come on, Alex,' Beth said, ready for her swim.

'You go ahead,' he said.

Watching Beth walk off to the sea alone made Felicity uncomfortable.

'Thank you so much,' Sarah said.

Miranda picked up her sun cream.

'I'll do you,' Felicity said. 'Beth is waiting for you in the sea,' she said pointedly to Alex. After the scene she'd witnessed the other day, this added to her suspicions about Alex and Sarah.

Miranda scowled. 'I'll do it myself, thanks.' She turned her back to Felicity. Felicity pulled the towel vigorously across her back, so hard the friction caused her skin to burn. If she were Beth, she'd be furious. She watched Beth swimming out on her own, while Alex and Sarah chatted in the shallow area.

She'd speak to Alex today about Judy. She wouldn't let her professional relationship with Alex interfere with her friendship with Beth. She'd get in touch with her, invite her round for a coffee.

She stepped onto the beach, the wind bringing goose bumps to her skin. Alex had his back to her, and he held Sarah's arm as they headed towards the sea. She shivered as she watched them go.

Felicity went to see Alex the next day. He was eating pasta from a plastic lunch box and had a drop of what looked like tomato sauce on his chin.

'You might want to wipe there,' she said, pointing to her own chin. 'I know you won't thank me if I let you go to teach like that.' This conversation would be awkward enough without having him look ridiculous. She wanted him to take her seriously and vice versa. She was determined to keep her friendship with Beth intact.

'Cheers.' He wiped his chin with a serviette from the table. 'Almost done,' he said. 'If I don't eat this now I won't get a chance for the rest of the day.'

'Shall I make us some coffee?'

'White, no sugar please.'

She made them both a coffee from the Nespresso machine.

'What can I do for you?'

'It's a bit delicate.' She sipped at her coffee, wincing as it was hotter than she expected. 'Judy Michigan came to see me. She was concerned after a meeting she had with you earlier this week.'

Alex groaned. 'I know exactly what you're going to say. It was all down to bad timing, so unfortunate. It was the end of a brutal day – no time for lunch, incessant appointments and not a moment to stop, so when I finally did I couldn't wait to pour myself a large glass of chianti. Judy turned up at that moment and I offered her one. I shouldn't have. It was a simple mistake but it's not as if we're secondary school students, she's an adult, but... she's very young for her age and I think she misinterpreted my intentions. Is that what she said?'

'She said you put your arm along the sofa.'

'I quite often do.'

'She thought you were going to put your arm around her. That's why she left.'

Alex looked horrified. 'Honestly, I would never...'

'Obviously I only have your two accounts to go on but that does correspond with what she said. I suggested she bring her problems to me in future, I am her personal tutor after all. Are there any concerns about her work? She mentioned you'd been giving her extra help.'

'She just lacks confidence, that's all. I didn't ask her to come and see me. As far as I'm concerned she's coping fine with the work. Her grades are good. I got the impression she wanted attention.'

'I agree she's young for her age. Without going into detail, I don't think she's had it easy.'

'Would you like me to speak to her with you present? I really would like to clear this up. Doing well here is very important for me.'

'I don't think that's necessary. Just be careful, that's all. As I said, I've suggested she bring her problems to me in future. We all have to protect ourselves these days – we're under such scrutiny because of the responsibility we have to young people, but that's how it should be. You seem to be fitting in well here. How are you finding it?'

'Great, it's full on but I thrive on that.'

'Excellent. And are you settling into the area OK?'

'I am. The swimming group is fun and I've joined the sailing club too, which is something I've always wanted to do.'

'Beth mentioned that you'd joined.'

He frowned. 'Did she?'

NINETEEN

Once Felicity had cleared the air with Alex, she'd called Beth and invited her over for a drink. Alex was out at his sailing club, Beth had told her, so the timing was perfect. Felicity had decided not to bring up Alex's flirting with Sarah; she had no proof there was anything going on, after all. She just had a tendency to be protective of her friends.

Beth looked tearful when she arrived that evening. She'd had some bad news about her aunt. Beth had told Felicity how she'd gone to live with her aunt Celia at the age of ten after her parents died, when her whole world had changed. Her parents had lived in an average-sized house in the city, whereas her aunt Celia had married for a second time into a wealthy family and owned a huge house on the coast in Sussex. When her husband died she inherited the house. Beth and her parents used to jokingly call it the mansion when they went to stay there every summer. Celia had a lovely disposition, her kind eyes crinkled whenever she smiled and she was devoted to her brother and his family, as she and her husband had been unable to have children. Beth spent idyllic summers roaming around the grounds in the sunshine and spending days on the beach with her parents and her aunt. After the accident which killed Beth's parents, it had been the obvious solution for Celia to take her only niece back to the mansion where they both grieved their loss.

Celia's diagnosis had happened quickly. A week of nasty stomach pains had sent her to the emergency department where a cancerous tumour had been discovered. After an operation to remove it and a course of chemotherapy, she'd been recovering well.

'I found out this morning her cancer's spread,' Beth said, stifling a sob. 'It's so unfair. She's my only blood family, the one steadfast in my life – apart from Alex, of course. Celia adores him too, as he does her.'

They were sitting on Felicity's back terrace with blankets over their shoulders.

'It was unexpected,' she said, 'and she's only just starting to recover from an infection. I'm worried that her mind isn't as sharp as it was before a fall she had recently, and this will just set her back.'

'Will you go and visit her?' Felicity asked.

'I'll have to see what Alex says,' she said. 'I haven't told him yet. He went straight off to the sailing club.'

'He told me he'd joined. Are you not interested in sailing?'

'No, I don't fancy it. He loves it though, he goes twice a week and there may be some weekend sessions. I don't mind, it meant I could come here.'

Felicity thought that was strange. 'Why does he need to be out for you to do that?'

'You work with him, that's why. He doesn't like mixing work with his private life. He doesn't want me to be friends with you. I won't tell him I'm here tonight.'

'Seriously? That's a bit weird, isn't it?'

'He's always been funny about his work, keeping everything in his life compartmentalised. He has friends he sees without me, because that's the way he's always been. He's not into doing things with other couples.'

'I'd never have guessed. He's very sociable at work. The students love him.'

'I bet they do.'

'There's always a queue outside his door.' Felicity hesitated. 'What is it?'

'Doesn't it bother you?'

'Has something happened?'

'No, of course not.'

'What can I do? Female students are a part of his job. I can't stop him working with half of the population.'

'I hope you don't mind me saying this but it doesn't sound like he lets you do everything you want to.'

'I make it sound worse than it is. The main thing is he doesn't want me to talk to you about his work, and that I can understand.'

'Which is exactly what we're doing. It's inevitable. Look, I've been in my position for a long time and I respect confidentiality. I can't imagine he wouldn't take that as a given. It sounds like this is about you and he's using me being his colleague as an excuse. Has he been like this with any of your friends before you came here?'

Beth hesitated.

'You can trust me,' Felicity said.

Beth went on to tell her how she'd signed up for an evening class in pottery and had immediately hit it off with the woman who showed her how to use the wheel. She hadn't laughed so much in ages. They'd started going to the pub every night after class, until one time Alex was waiting outside in the car for her. He turned up every week after that, insisting he worried about her getting home safely. The friend had tried to arrange other get-togethers, but somehow something always came up with Alex that prevented her from going. Her friend had stopped asking her out and when the course came to an end they were saving up for a move and Alex said their budget couldn't cover enrolling for another term.

'Part of me knew deep down what he was doing wasn't right, but it was early in our relationship and I was flattered that he wanted to spend so much time with me. I wanted to spend all my time with him too.' She laughed.

'That explains his reaction when I mentioned seeing you that first time when we walked along the coast. He made out you'd told him, but you hadn't, had you?'

'No, and he wasn't best pleased.'

'I'd stand my ground if I were you.'

Beth pulled a face. 'I know, but I like an easy life and I don't want there to be an atmosphere at home. If you don't mind keeping our visits to yourself, it would be easier. Do you mind?'

'Of course not.' Felicity didn't mind, exactly, but was it right?

TWENTY

PRESENT

Chloe spoke to Hamish Campbell next. He was of medium height with his wavy hair in a man bun. He wore a loose faded denim shirt and jeans which looked like the rips were from wear rather than a fashion statement. He was softly spoken and sat with one leg crossed over his knee.

'Was Alex murdered?' he asked as he sat down.

'Yes, I'm afraid so. That's why we have to go over the initial statements.'

'Sure, of course. Whatever I can do to help.'

'How well did you know him?'

He shrugged. 'We swam together and we hung out a couple of times as a group.'

'Tell me about your relationship with him.'

'There's not much to tell. I liked him. We met up for a drink quite often after he joined the sailing club. We had a lot in common. He was good at sailing, picked it up really quickly and we talked about going out on the boat one day.'

'You have a boat?'

'Yes.'

'And did you go out on it?'

'No, we didn't get round to it.'

'Where do you keep it moored?' She jotted down the details. They might need to check that out, depending how the investigation developed. 'Going back to you and Alex, I understand there was a garden party at your house when Beth was alive, roughly four years ago. Do you want to tell me about that?'

He shifted in his seat, sitting upright. 'What have you been told?'

'I'd like to hear your version of events.'

'It was years ago. We invited the people we swim with over one afternoon, we cooked some burgers on the barbecue, had a few drinks. Alex and I had words. Look, I liked the guy, but I didn't like the way he acted around my wife. He flirted with her.'

'Was she the only woman he flirted with?'

'No, but it had been going on for a while with Sarah and had started bothering me. I was concerned they would take it further.'

'Had you spoken to Sarah about it?'

'Yes. We had a row about it before the guests arrived. I told her to stay away from him and she said I was being paranoid. I was riled up and after a few beers I couldn't keep my mouth shut. When I saw them huddled in a corner together I went and challenged him. Sarah was furious with me.'

'Were they having an affair?'

'She says not. I spoke to Beth about it and she wouldn't give me a straight answer. It was understandable though, we weren't close friends and she was embarrassed so I let it drop. Although...' He paused.

'Yes? Tell me whatever's on your mind, no matter how trivial.'

'When I was talking to her she kept looking over towards Alex, who was too far away to hear what we were saying, but she looked scared.'

'OK. Going back to your altercation with Alex, what exactly happened?'

'I asked him straight out what was going on with Sarah and he said I'd got the wrong idea. I said I didn't appreciate him flirting and he apologised and said it was second nature with him but didn't mean anything. Sarah took me into the house and had a go at me. When I went back outside Beth and Alex had gone home.'

'How did you get on with him after that?'

'OK, but we stopped going for a drink. We saw each other at swimming and he toned it down with Sarah. If he saw me at the club, he kept his distance. It was a shame as I liked the guy, but his behaviour caused bad feeling between me and Sarah.'

Chloe interviewed Sarah next.

'Tell me about your relationship with Alex Maitland.'

'He was a lovely man. He was friendly and fun to have in the swimming group. He was always entertaining us with anecdotes about his teaching. I liked being around him.'

'I gather Hamish wasn't so enamoured of him.'

She tutted, shaking her head. 'Hamish gets jealous of any man who pays attention to me.'

'Were you having a relationship with him?'

'No.' Her tone was indignant. She sighed. 'To be honest I found him attractive but I would never cheat on Hamish. I love him. It was nice to be made to feel special and I responded. I wasn't the only one. Miranda flirted with him too, and there was gossip about him and one of the students at one point.'

'What about Felicity?' Chloe asked.

'No,' Sarah said, 'I couldn't see it. Their relationship was a real surprise to me. She didn't seem interested in him at all.'

'Tell me about the incident at the garden party.' Sarah gave a similar account of the event to Hamish. 'I was so cross with

Hamish. It was the first time we'd had those people over and he ruined it.'

'Did it cause bad feeling afterwards?'

'Only for a day or so. We're quite volatile as a couple, we blow up at each other but then it's all over. Neither of us bottles things up. Nothing was going on and he believed me. That was ages ago anyway.'

'Had you seen Alex socially since?'

'Only at swimming, with other people. Never on my own. Hang on, am I a suspect? People have been saying Alex was murdered.'

'We're just establishing what was going on in Alex's life. How did you get on with Beth?'

'Poor Beth. Her drowning put me off swimming for a while, I'm not the most confident swimmer. She was sweet, such a friendly person, but I sensed a sadness about her. We had a conversation actually, about what had happened at the barbe- cue. I never told Hamish this. One time we went swimming without Alex and she asked me to go to the café after. She suspected Alex was having an affair because he was out so much, supposedly either working late or at the sailing club. I reassured her it wasn't with me. She wanted to go back to work but Alex didn't want her to and she was struggling with that. I told her to stand up to him. I apologised for flirting with him – she said he was like that with all women and she found it hard. I don't think she was very happy although she made out she was when she was with the group. I keep wondering whether I could have done anything more to support her. She never came out with us, always coming up with some excuse. I got the impression she was quite isolated here.'

Meanwhile, DS Williams was interviewing the last two of the swimmers, Miranda and Tania.

Tania was first on his list.

'I'd like to ask you more about Alex.'

'When his fiancée drowned we all rallied round him as a group to support him. Not that he needed it. He was a confident man, and he was well liked.'

'Did he change after his fiancée's disappearance?'

'Felicity said he threw himself into his work, getting in really early and staying late. That was his way of coping. And then it was natural, I suppose, for him to get closer to Felicity as she was with him at work all day.'

'When did their relationship start?'

'Not for a while after Beth drowned. At least, that's when they told us. Felicity's a pretty straightforward person and she told us all when it started. I don't think she'd lie.'

'Was Alex seeing anyone else?'

'I have no idea. I only saw him at swimming. We're very different people. Miranda's my only close friend in the group.'

Miranda was fifteen minutes late, which enabled him to stretch his legs. Gavin wondered about Alex. Had he been seeing Felicity when he was with Beth? He was about to phone Miranda to check she was coming when she burst into the room wearing a bright red jumpsuit and large hooped earrings.

'I'm so sorry. I couldn't find anywhere to park.'

Once he'd fetched her a drink he ran through her statement taken after the wedding.

'Is there anything you'd like to add?'

'No, it's all there.'

'How did you get on with Alex?'

'I liked him. He was fun, but I didn't know him that well.'

'Were you friends with Beth?'

'Not close friends. She was nice, but quite different to me. Tania's my friend in that group.'

'How did she get on with her fiancé?'

'When we first met them they were so lovey-dovey, but after a while I suspected it was all for show. He got on well with everyone and she wanted him all to herself.'

'What makes you say that?'

'One time he was messing around in the sea with Sarah, she got knocked over by a huge wave and he lifted her out of the way. I saw Beth watching them and she was looking daggers at him. Mind you, Hamish wasn't that pleased about it either. Alex was a flirt and they all took it too seriously.'

'Did he flirt with you?'

'He flirted with all women.'

'I'll take that as a yes. Did you flirt back?'

'Maybe a little, just for fun. He wasn't my type.'

'How about Felicity?'

'I didn't see that one coming. Not being rude but he's good fun and she's dull.'

'When did their relationship start?'

'She told us about it a few months after Beth died. But I had my suspicions that it had been going on longer.'

'Based on what?'

'She was always going round to his house. I saw her car parked outside several times before then, I pass his place on my way home so I couldn't help noticing. I might be wrong.'

DS Williams called Chloe in to go over their findings.

'What do you think about Alex and Beth's relationship?'

'They weren't as happy as everyone made out. He was a flirt, possibly having an affair.'

'Same here. The circumstances of his fiancée drowning are similar so we need to keep looking into that, find out whether he was seeing anyone and if so who? Was it Sarah, or someone else? One of the students? I've interviewed his colleagues and there was at least one incident where he was suspected of being too close to the female students. Or Felicity. She was supposed to be good mates with Beth but when did she start being attracted to Alex? They got together pretty soon after her death and it's worth digging into the dynamics of their relationship. Was he seeing someone else? Somebody knows the truth.'

TWENTY-ONE

PAST

Beth put the hoover away and cast her eyes over the room. She'd worked up a sweat cleaning the cottage and she was looking forward to a lingering shower before Alex got home. He liked everything to be in order and she'd organised her week so that she could spend Friday afternoon getting their home ready for the weekend. Now they'd been here a few weeks the place was starting to feel more like home. Alex hadn't mentioned the renovation plans for a few days and he'd been so against the charity shop she had put the idea on hold for the moment. She'd wait to see if she was able to line up any job interviews before committing himself.

Alex was enjoying his new job and she was thrilled that he'd reached his goal of being a head of department. Hopefully, they wouldn't have to move again for a while. Maybe they could even start to think about having a family.

Beth hummed to herself as hot water cascaded down on her. She sighed with pleasure as she inhaled the new lavender shower gel she'd treated herself to. Yesterday afternoon, she'd been invited round to Felicity's for afternoon tea. She'd baked some fruit scones and taken them with her as a gift.

Felicity lived in a small house not far from the sea front. She lived alone with her cat, Tabitha. She'd originally moved there with her partner Simon, but they'd split up a year earlier and she much preferred living alone. Beth appreciated her frankness about Alex getting the job. This enabled her to work on her garden, a passion of hers, which she proudly showed Beth.

'This is what it looks like in the summer,' she said, showing her a photograph of a sea of wild flowers, every space filled with blues and reds and yellows. It was glorious.

Felicity shared Beth's passion for reading and it was a delight to be able to discuss their favourite authors and exchange recommendations. Felicity's living room wall had a built-in bookcase and every shelf was stacked high.

'I'm running out of space,' she said, and insisted Beth take home two books she hadn't read yet. 'I worried that teaching English would put me off reading, but quite the opposite. The students recommend books to me, and their enthusiasm feeds mine. I don't need to join a book club as most of my time these days is taken up with discussing books.'

Beth was reading one of Felicity's recommendations now, a historical novel set in Cornwall, and she was soaking up the brooding sea atmosphere when she heard Alex arrive home. Felicity had told her just before she left that she'd let slip they'd seen one another to Alex. She hoped he wasn't going to make a fuss about it.

'I'm out the back,' she called. She was sitting in their small garden snuggled up in a cosy fleece with a cup of tea. 'How was your day?'

Alex came into the garden and kissed her.

'Busy,' he said.

'The kettle's just boiled,' she said. 'Do you want a tea?'

'Please.'

She went to make it and he picked up her book.

'What's this you're reading?'

'It's a new author I thought I'd try.'

'Any good?'

'I don't know yet, I've only just started it.'

Alex undid his tie and stretched out in the chair.

'Where did you get it?' he asked. 'It doesn't look new and it isn't from the library.'

She laughed. 'Are you checking up on me? I haven't got round to joining the library yet.' She hesitated. 'I got it from the charity shop.' She gave him a mug of tea. 'Tell me about your day.'

'I'd rather hear about yours.'

'Are you sure?' He'd never shown much interest in her online teaching before. 'I had two lessons. One of my students passed her exam and has recommended me to her friends so that was good. I spent this morning looking for jobs, but there's nothing now the school term has started. No doubt yours was far more interesting.'

He shrugged. 'It was OK. What was interesting, though, was a conversation I had with Felicity.'

'Oh?'

'Yes.' He put his tea down and rubbed his lips together. 'Do you know how embarrassing it was to find out you've been seeing her behind my back? Why on earth didn't you tell me?'

Beth stirred her tea. 'I didn't get a chance, that's all.'

He sighed. 'Look, I know you want to make friends here but why not one of the other women? You know how I feel about keeping my work life separate from yours. And Felicity of all people. She's assistant head of department which means we work very closely together. It's completely inappropriate. Why her?'

'It wasn't planned. I bumped into her when I was out for a walk and she asked to join me. It went on from there. I couldn't exactly say no, could I?'

'I don't see why not.'

'It would have looked incredibly rude, that's why. I don't see why it matters so much. We really hit it off. I haven't met anyone who is so much on my wavelength in a long time. We don't have to talk about the university if that would make you feel better. She's into books and walking and we have loads of other things to talk about.'

'Having a partner who respected my privacy would make me feel a hell of a lot better.'

'Why are you being like this, Alex? I should be able to choose my own friends. I don't mind who you mix with. I wouldn't dream of telling you what to do.'

He picked Beth's novel up and looked at the back cover.

'Did she give you this?'

Beth nodded.

'So you're lying to me now. I knew I was right to be concerned.'

'I'm sorry, it was just easier. I'm fed up because I haven't had any luck with jobs so I might have to see if I can get some supply work. That way I'd meet new people.'

'No, I don't want you to do that. I've got plans for the house and I want you involved with that. I'd thought you could be the project manager. Supply work is too stressful. You've said yourself the kids run riot when they have a supply. You've got enough on with worrying about your aunt. Anyway, I don't like the idea of you mixing with my colleagues. This is meant to be a fresh start for us. You know how much this job means to me. My career is going well and I don't want anything to derail this.'

'The reason I didn't tell you about Felicity – or the book – is because I knew you'd react like this. It's completely inappropriate. It's like Olivia all over again.' Alex had ruined that friendship and she wouldn't let it happen with Felicity.

Alex drummed his fingers on the table. 'I'm not getting into all that. You know I was right. I can't expect you to understand. You've never operated at management level. Think about what

I've said. You're an intelligent woman and I'm sure you'll see I'm right.'

'Don't be so patronising.'

'How dare you?'

Alex slammed his hand on the table and Beth jumped. He had a glint in his eye that she'd never seen before. 'I'm going upstairs,' he said. He paused in the doorway. 'It's been a long day, that's all. I don't want us to argue.'

'Me neither. I'll get dinner ready.'

Beth kicked the table leg hard as soon as he'd gone upstairs. Her instinct when faced with his unreasonable behaviour was to phone a friend. If only she could phone Olivia, but she wouldn't answer.

'Ouch.' The pain helped focus her frustration. Alex's moods were so up and down lately. She never knew where she was with him. He'd just patronised her and praised her in the same sentence. Before they got engaged, he'd never shown any signs of being possessive, yet the trouble started as soon as she met Olivia.

Beth sighed, conjuring up the heart-shaped face and olive skin of her friend. The eyes that were so expressive. Glinting and dancing when they were making plans, having discussions, enjoying life. Dark and mistrusting during the last few months before she and Alex moved away. Not understanding why she couldn't see her anymore, why she was always cancelling at the last minute, why there was always a sudden crisis when they were about to meet. She hadn't understood it herself, at first, until she'd begun to see a pattern. Her husband was placing obstacles in her way, preventing her from seeing Olivia. He'd denied it at first, but it had all come out when she'd challenged him. He wanted her all to himself. They didn't need anyone else; other people were a threat to their relationship. He was being ridiculous, and she told him so. He'd said obviously she could do what she wanted, but in the end it wasn't worth arranging to go out without him as the tension afterwards resulted in a bad atmosphere that lingered for days. And he was right, they were happy when it was just the two of them.

Olivia was no longer her friend, thanks to Alex. She would not let the same thing happen again. Female friendship was essential to her; it helped her be the rounded person she hoped she was. Having some distance now since her friendship with Olivia, she was able to look back and see the pattern, which she hadn't been able to see, or wanted to see at the time. She'd have to be discreet about it, but of one thing she was sure, she was determined to remain an independent person within her relationship. Otherwise, it was doomed to failure.

TWENTY-TWO

ANONYMOUS

She checked her makeup in the driver mirror before she got out, locking the car behind her. She'd been looking forward to this evening so much, but her stomach was churning with anxiety. Seeing Alex only twice a week was getting to her. She wanted more of him, to be more of a permanent fixture in his life. Hopefully he'd come to the same decision too. If he hadn't, well, she didn't know what she'd do.

He told his fiancée he went sailing several times a week when in fact it was only once and the odd weekend. She looked forward to those occasions, after he'd been out on the sea. He was always windswept and full of energy after those longer sessions and their lovemaking was frantic after.

He'd stopped making love with his fiancée shortly after they moved here. Or so he told her; she wasn't naive and she knew what men were like. But she also knew how to get what she wanted and she wanted him. She was in this for the long game. For the first time in her life she had a long-term plan.

Alex was already in the pub. They didn't normally meet here but she'd insisted on it. Usually he came straight round to her flat and into her bed. Yes, he was driven by lust, but she enjoyed the conversations they had afterwards. Alex was like her; he knew what he wanted from life and he went for it. His plans for his new house were so exciting. He had no time for people that got in his way. She had to make him see that his fiancée was doing just that.

He was drinking lager in a booth in a dark corner of the pub. He stood up when he saw her, then kissed her on the cheek, which irritated her; he was always so careful in public. She planted a kiss on his lips and he jumped back.

'Careful,' he said, a look of displeasure she'd never seen before crossing his face, gone so quickly she wondered if she'd imagined it. 'You look good,' he said. 'What are you drinking?'

'Lime and soda please.' He went off to the bar without commenting on her not drinking. She'd wondered if he would notice, but he'd no doubt assume she must be driving. If they were to start a family as she hoped, she had to be as healthy as possible.

'How was your day?' she asked.

'Difficult. I can't get your face out of my mind, do you know how hard that is?'

She smirked.

'I'm going to have a bit of time on my hands this weekend if you're free. Beth has to go and see her aunt as she's not been well and has taken a turn for the worse.'

'Shame for her aunt, good for us. When were you thinking?'

'Saturday evening? You could stay over.'

She grinned. 'That will be a first. I'd definitely be up for that.'

'I've also got an idea for how we can spend more time together.'

'Oh?'

'I'll tell you when I've got something more concrete to tell you. Hopefully on Saturday.'

An image of a diamond ring flashed into her head. Bubbles

fizzed inside her. She'd never wanted to settle down before. 'I'll cook us a special dinner, we'll treat it as a date.'

'Wear that black dress that I like.'

She sparkled inside. The dress had a slit down the front and was the most revealing item she owned. She'd worn it the first time they slept together. 'That was the dress that christened our relationship,' she said. Maybe they'd be christening something else soon. *Stop getting ahead of yourself!* She wanted so much more of him and she'd do anything to get it.

'I have to be sure I can trust you,' Alex said. They were at her flat, curled up together on the sofa. They'd just watched a thriller on Netflix and shared a bottle of wine, although Alex had only had one glass as he was driving. Driving back to his fiancée.

She wriggled up into a sitting position, smoothing her hair back down. She programmed the smooth sound of jazz to play in the background.

'You know you can. I've been discreet about us, haven't I? Not a single one of my friends knows about us. I love you, Alex, I'd do anything for you.'

He nodded, his eyes fixed on hers. His eyes were dark brown and tonight looked full of secrets. She longed to share those secrets exclusively with him.

'Home isn't exactly fun at the moment. I think she suspects.'

'Maybe it's time to tell her.'

'No. I've had a better idea.' He put his trousers and a T-shirt on and sat on her side of the bed. 'Can I trust you?'

'What do you think?'

He stared into her eyes. 'That you would do anything for me.'

She kissed his lips softly. 'True, oh master.'

'I'm being serious.'

She was deadly serious. Alex had no idea how much he was on her mind each day. It had been worse when they first got together, trying to second-guess his movements, never knowing whether he would turn up, how to play it, what to wear. Even her dreams were full of him. Since they got together, she wanted to spend every waking minute with him. If only she could make that step from mistress to partner, only then would she be able to calm her obsession. The one obstacle in her path was Beth. How could she move her out of the way?

He leaned forward and tucked a loose strand of her hair behind her ear. 'I love you for that. I have big plans for us.'

She flung her arms around him.

'I've got to get out of my relationship. I can't stand it anymore, I just want to be with you.'

'That's good, because I don't want to be your bit on the side forever.'

'I know. I've got an idea but I'm not sure you'd be up for it.'

'Of course I would be. I'd do anything for you, if it means we can be together.'

'Anything? Literally?'

She pulled his face towards her and stared into his eyes.

'You can trust me.'

TWENTY-THREE

PAST

Beth walked home at a fast pace, eyes focused on the lights ahead. This path was desolate at night, bushes rustling beside her like whispering voices, and she wished she'd taken Felicity up on her suggestion to get a cab. Next time she would, if there was a next time. Alex had texted to ask how her evening was going and she'd experienced a dart of anxiety. If he knew where she had spent the past few hours he wouldn't be best pleased. And they had discussed him in the context of work, but Felicity was right, it was unavoidable – as was their friendship and she wasn't going to lose it, not even for Alex. Felicity had apologised for letting slip about their meeting – she hadn't realised how important it was to her. Not this time, he'd already lost her two friends. Lights twinkled from far across the sea and she wondered if Alex was still out there as she hastened along, wanting to get home and settled before he came back. She was becoming a fearful person and it wasn't right.

But Alex was far later than she expected and she needn't have worried at all. She was reading in bed when she heard him come in. He came bounding upstairs as if he'd spent the evening drinking Coca-Cola instead of winding down in the pub. She smelled beer as he bent over to kiss her.

'Miss me?'

'Of course. How was it?'

'Fabulous. I'm getting the hang of steering now. It's so great to be out on the open water, so different from academia and it really helps me unwind. How was your evening?'

'Quiet. TV and a good book, pretty chilled. I'm looking forward to our swim in the morning.'

'Me too.'

He was equally animated when he woke her next morning with a cup of Earl Grey. It must be the high of conquering a challenge, as he'd been attempting to master steering alone for the last few weeks.

'I'm going to the club again tonight,' he said. 'No need to pick me up. It's not fair of me to ask that now I'm going so often. I'll take the car.'

Was this another of his obsessions taking over his life? She hoped there wasn't another reason for him wanting to go there so much. She wasn't sure how she felt about it really. At least it would give her some time on her own.

The beach was empty when they arrived, the sea calm, as if waiting for them to disturb it. A couple of women from their group were already getting changed.

'Why don't we join everyone in the café today after our swim?' She might as well capitalise on his good spirits.

'We've brought our flasks,' he said, 'but maybe another time.'

It was a small concession, she supposed. The women were in focus now, and she recognised Tania and Miranda.

'Hi,' Miranda called, 'lovely morning, isn't it?'

'It certainly is,' Alex said, placing his robe over their belongings, flasks and cups to the side, ready for afterwards. If only he would forget it one time, Beth thought. Miranda peeled off her clothes to reveal a bright red bikini, clinging to her figure and accentuating her curves. Tania did the same, revealing a brilliant white costume. Alex was watching them. Beth shivered. She took his arm.

'Hurry up, I'm ready,' she said, and they made their way into the sea. Alex strode forward and plunged into the water the moment it became deep enough, straight into a front crawl, his toned arms slicing through the water. He was a beautiful swimmer and Beth loved to watch him. She ducked her shoulders under the cold water and followed him. She swam after him and he waited for her while he treaded water. As she swam up to him, he threw his legs around her and pulled her in for a deep kiss. The unexpected gesture took her breath away, and her balance, as she dug her toes into the sand and returned the kiss. When she pulled away, his gaze was focused over her shoulder, back towards the shore. She turned her head to see what he was looking at. The women were standing in the shallow water, droplets glistening on their skin.

'I wish you didn't pay so much attention to the other women.' There, she'd said it. In her pockets she clenched her fists. She could do this, stand up for herself.

He indicated right and pulled out onto a busy roundabout, flashing a quick glance at her.

'What did you say?'

'I saw you watching the women getting changed.'

'What? They flaunt themselves in front of us. They're our friends; I don't see them in that way. Are you being serious?'

He looked at her, a hurt expression on his face.

'Maybe I got it wrong,' she said. It was true, they all changed in front of one another, stripping out of their cold things and getting dry more important on a cold morning than modesty.

He gripped the steering wheel. 'I can't believe you said that. You're the only one I want to look at. Obviously, that kiss this morning didn't mean anything. Sometimes I think you don't know me at all.'

Maybe I don't, Beth thought, turning away from him. Perhaps she'd got it wrong, but lately he spent more time away from her. Rain was still hammering down on the windows and she couldn't remember ever feeling so low in her life, apart from when her parents died. There really had been nothing she could do about that and this felt like it didn't need to happen. Alex turned the radio up and the rest of the journey passed without conversation. She couldn't put her finger on why but she didn't believe Alex was being straight with her. She wouldn't be able to see Felicity as much if Alex was using the car to get home from sailing club, now he no longer wanted her to collect him. Had he found out about their friendship? It was almost as if he wanted her all to himself, or was it something else that was bothering him?

TWENTY-FOUR

Felicity paused her marking, recalling the line of students waiting outside Alex's office on her way out of the building earlier, five female and one male and it was past six o'clock. No Judy, and she hadn't seen her up here since their talk. The one time she had seen her she'd been in the library café and had been laughing with two other students. The rumours about Alex in the department had died down. Students sought him out less, and she was satisfied the friendly word of advice had made him reconsider his behaviour. It was a relief that a potentially difficult situation had been avoided, and their even relationship was able to continue. After a bit of light investigation amongst colleagues she'd known for a while and trusted to make sure, she let it go. As long as there were no complaints then she had to assume the gossip was unfounded tittle tattle.

Her mobile was vibrating in her pocket as she let herself into the house. She usually had it on silent when she was at work, since it had gone off in one of her early lectures and she'd been mortified when a burst of the *Star Wars* theme tune had blasted out making her lose her thread along with the attention of the students. She fished it out, hoping it was Beth. It was her cousin. She'd call her later. She switched the volume back on and left it on the table.

She hadn't heard from Beth for a few days, and she'd barely seen her at the beach either, as she and Alex had started swimming earlier than usual. Alex had told her Beth needed to start work earlier so that she could have more time free later in the day. Felicity wondered what she did with her time once she'd finished her online tuition. Beth never talked about going out to restaurants or parties. She stayed home while Alex sailed on the sea and Felicity wondered what else he got up to.

Her phone was ringing. Where was it? Felicity shifted sheets of paper and books from her dining room table, the noise close to hand. An exercise book slid to the floor. The phone was buried under the pile of marking she'd just done.

'Hi, Beth.' She moved to the comfortable chair with a view out towards the garden. It was dark outside. She'd been marking for hours and lost track of time. Her stomach rumbled.

'Beth, are you there?' Beth was on the line but wasn't speaking; she could hear her breath. 'Is everything OK?'

'No, it isn't.'

'What's up? Do you want me to come over?' She'd not been inside their cottage but she'd walked past it several times, ever puzzling over Beth's decision to keep their friendship a secret from her partner. She was concerned for Beth; there had to be some reason she was afraid to let Alex know. It wasn't healthy.

'No, no, you can't come here. I don't know when Alex is coming back.' Her voice was subdued.

Felicity waited, giving her space to say whatever it was she was finding difficult to express.

'We argued. He said some horrible things.'

'What did you argue about?'

'Me getting a job. I don't understand why he doesn't want me to even volunteer at the charity shop.'

'He can't dictate what you do.'

'I know, but... did I tell you about the renovations to the cottage? He's got huge plans and he wants me to be project manager. I don't mind being involved but it doesn't interest me. I'm a teacher, and I want to get back to it as soon as I can.'

This version of Alex didn't equate to the one Felicity knew.

'Why don't you come over here?'

'Best not. He doesn't want me to be friends with you.'

'You have to stand up to him. Don't let him walk all over you.'

'That's what I did earlier but he won't listen to me. We had a huge row and he stormed out. He's always out these days. And my aunt's really ill... sorry but everything got on top of me this evening.'

Felicity sighed. 'And you're talking to me and Alex doesn't know because he won't approve. This is so wrong. Are you afraid of him?'

'I...' Felicity heard a muffled noise from Beth's end. 'It's Alex, I have to go. I'll call you.' The line went dead.

Felicity stared out into the darkness, wondering what it was that Beth was so scared of.

TWENTY-FIVE

PRESENT

The phone ringing took Felicity by surprise. It was DS Williams, asking her to come in for questioning. No, he wasn't asking, he was insisting. When Felicity mentioned a prior engagement, his attitude changed.

'It has to be now,' he said, his voice firm, no nonsense. 'I'm sending a car.'

Thirty minutes later she was waiting in an interview room with PC Chloe Button, anxiety tying her stomach in knots.

'Has something happened?' she asked.

'We're investigating your husband's murder. I would have thought that was enough,' Chloe said. 'Would you like a solicitor present?' Chloe asked. 'It's your right.'

'No,' Felicity said. 'What's going on? Why should I need a solicitor?'

Chloe's face was inscrutable. 'We have a few matters we'd like to ask you about. Would you like some water while we wait for DS Williams?'

Felicity nodded, her throat so dry she wasn't sure she'd be able to speak. They suspected her of being involved in Alex's murder, it was obvious – and she'd been expecting it. The police always looked at the partner first. The door opened with a squeak and DS Williams entered.

'Thank you for coming in,' he said. Felicity didn't respond. She hadn't been given much choice in the matter and now she was here in this characterless room. Aside from the table and four chairs, a jug of water, four glasses and a tape recorder, there was nothing to distract her. She focused on the empty glass. Was she being foolish by not getting a solicitor?

'Felicity? Can I call you Felicity?'

She nodded, tuning back in, and stated her name for the tape recording, her mind racing. She sat on her shaking hands, not wanting the police officers to see they'd rattled her. Did everyone immediately feel guilty in this position?

'How long is this going to take?' she asked.

'We have a few areas we want to explore in more detail,' DS Williams said. 'I'm looking at your statement here and I'd like to go over the timing of your romantic relationship with Alex. You'd been colleagues first, I know. When did it start?'

'Six months after Beth died.'

'Tell us how it came about.'

Felicity summed up the early days of their relationship. 'We bonded through grief.' She'd told them all this before.

'Several other witnesses have mentioned their suspicions that Alex was having an affair while Beth was alive. What do you know about that?'

'Nothing.'

'Was it true?'

'Not that I know of. He was really into Beth.'

'Did you like Beth?'

'Yes.' She couldn't hide her exasperation. 'You know all this. We were close friends.'

'Close friends confide in one another. Did Beth confide in you?'

'Yes, about some things. It was awkward though, because of

our work situation. She kept a lot of things to herself because of Alex and I being colleagues.'

'How do you know that?'

'Because she said so.'

'So if she had suspected Alex of having an affair she wouldn't have told you?'

'She was a very private person.'

'Did Alex confide in you?'

'No, not then, not before our relationship started.'

'Which was when?'

Felicity sighed. 'Six months after Beth's death.'

'You will inherit a large sum of money,' PC Button said, taking Felicity by surprise. 'Your husband was a rich man after his fiancée drowned. We've been looking into your finances.'

'You've what?' She should have got a solicitor. She wasn't prepared for this. 'I have nothing to hide.'

'You have a modest income. Alex earned a lot more than you as head of department. I understand you applied for that job and didn't get it. How did you feel about that?'

'That was years ago. I wasn't even sure I wanted the job. Why are you asking about this?'

'Because Alex was murdered and we have to look into every aspect of his life. You were the closest person to him. You were also present when Beth died.'

Felicity picked up her glass and drank some water, stalling for time. She didn't bother to hide her shaking hands.

'That was an accident. I still haven't got over it.'

'Did marrying her former fiancé help?' Chloe asked.

'What are you getting at?'

DS Williams took over. 'We're merely establishing the facts. I'd like to ask you about the flask now.'

Felicity nodded, feeling numb. They were switching the questions to confuse her. She had to stay calm.

'You mentioned you were present when Alex was preparing the flask on the morning of the wedding.'

'That's correct. But like I said before, I wasn't watching him.'

'Was anyone else staying with you the night before the wedding?'

'No.'

'So we have nobody to corroborate this.'

'No, I guess not. Which doesn't mean I'm lying.'

'I agree, but it's a loose end. You were with him when he drank the tea at the wedding.'

'Yes, I was.'

'Why didn't you drink any tea?'

'I didn't want any. I'd had some water. It seemed...' She hesitated. 'Out of context at a party. It was a wedding. Tea seemed somehow inappropriate.'

'Have you seen the red flask since the wedding?'

'No.'

The police officers exchanged a glance.

'We'd like to carry out a search of your property.'

'What?'

'We can get a warrant to search your property,' Chloe repeated. 'Or you can make it easier and give us your permission.'

'This is madness. Yes, of course you can. I've got nothing to hide. I had nothing to do with Alex's death. We just got married...' Tears spilled from her eyes. 'How can you think I would hurt the man I love?'

'We aren't convinced you did love him.'

Felicity stared at Chloe, wondering what they weren't saying, why they had come to this conclusion. 'Can I go now?' Felicity's throat was tight and she attempted to stand up.

'Please sit down,' Chloe said, not unkindly. 'We're keeping you in for more questioning.'

'Is it compulsory?'

'Yes.'

'For how long?'

'Up to twenty-four hours initially.'

Felicity looked behind them to the closed door. She was trapped.

'I'm not saying any more until I've spoken to a solicitor.'

'What do you think, boss?'

They were taking advantage of the delay in questioning while Felicity waited for the hastily appointed duty solicitor to arrive, and giving Felicity time to get some refreshment.

'Something's not right here but without evidence we're stabbing in the dark. What do you think?'

'She's hiding something, I'm sure of it,' Chloe said. 'Trouble is, at the moment everything is reliant on what she tells us. She wasn't having an affair with Alex behind Beth's back, she saw him fill the flask, but we have no proof. What we need is somebody seeing them together in a romantic situation prior to Beth's disappearance. Miranda mentioned seeing Felicity's car parked outside his house but that doesn't prove anything. They were colleagues, after all.'

'I want you to focus on that once we're done here. She'll be on her guard now and no doubt we'll get a "no comment" interview once the lawyer rocks up, but she's more likely to give something away if she's anxious.'

'She doesn't strike me as a hardened criminal though, boss.'

Gavin laughed. 'She's no mafia moll but it's the quiet ones you have to watch. I'm sure you've learned that by now. Find out where Alex liked to socialise before Beth died, go to those places and see if the staff there remember seeing him with anyone else. Focus on the sailing club to start with. Somebody, somewhere must know something.'

The phone rang and he snatched the receiver, listened then ended the call.

'They've finished the search,' he said. 'No sign of the flask.'

'Damn,' Chloe said.

'That would have been too easy.'

A police constable stuck his head around the door. 'The Maitland lawyer is ready for you now.'

'Right. Let's see if this changes anything. We'll grill her a bit more, then let her go. We don't have enough to arrest her. Yet.'

TWENTY-SIX

PAST

Felicity had a busy timetable that day, which kept her from worrying about Beth. A niggling sense of unease was present all day; it was there throughout her tutorials and distracting her when she was marking. It came to the fore at their faculty meeting after lectures that day.

Unlike their previous head of department, Alex's meetings were efficiently run. He sent out agendas and stuck to the time limit. He organised the room bookings, provided refreshments and they were altogether more useful than under his predecessor. He listened to people's opinions and took suggestions on board. He was charming and relaxed. Felicity watched him in action and thought about what Beth had said. He was so personable, making everyone laugh and managing to keep Steve from rambling on like he always did without appearing rude. Yet she knew he had a whole other side – if Beth was telling the truth. She'd picked up genuine fear in their phone conversation so when Beth had rung to tell her she'd overreacted and to discount everything she'd said, the concern should have gone away but instead it had grown in size all day.

'Who's coming to the pub?' Steve asked as they packed up their desks. 'Alex?'

'I can't, I've got an appointment.'

Felicity made her excuses too and went down to the car park with Alex. Beth had told her he was at the sailing club tonight, contradicting his mention of an appointment, and when he got in his car and drove in the direction of the town, not the coast, which would have meant turning left out of the university car park, she felt sick. Felicity sensed Beth was in trouble and she wanted to know the truth, yet spying on her colleague didn't sit well with her. She had to go with her gut; there was something about this situation that didn't add up.

On the drive home she pondered what to do. She couldn't get Beth's panicked phone call out of her mind. She recalled Beth's insistence that they keep their friendship a secret from her husband. That wasn't normal, no matter what the reason. Alex would know Felicity was a professional and as a person in charge of young people she'd been keeping confidences about safeguarding matters for years. Alex had to have another reason for wanting his fiancée not to fraternise with her. She thought about his efficiency, the fanatical tidiness of his office and how methodical and organised he was. She made a sudden decision and indicated right to go in the opposite direction from her home. Alex was otherwise occupied and she had to see Beth. She was worried about her friend and what was really going on in her relationship. Why wouldn't he want her to do some voluntary work? He even knew Annabelle, the manager of the shop. One thing she was sure about, Beth needed a friend.

Beth opened the door to her dressed in a pale blue jumpsuit and furry slippers, looking like a child ready for bed. Her eyes widened.

'Felicity. You shouldn't have come here.'

'I know Alex is out.'

'He might come back at any point.' Her eyes scanned the street over Felicity's shoulder.

'He's busy, OK? We were at the same meeting not long ago and he told us he was going out.'

'He's gone sailing.'

'Can I come in? I need to talk to you. I won't stay long, I promise.'

'OK.'

Beth checked outside once more, before closing the door behind them. She followed Felicity into the kitchen, past a pile of cardboard boxes stacked in the hall.

'What's going on here?'

'We're preparing for the building work, the extension I told you about.'

'It's definitely going ahead then?'

'Looks like it.'

'Are you project managing?'

'We've not decided yet.'

'You don't have to go ahead with it if it's not what you want.'

'I know but it makes sense to get the work down now.'

'Fair enough.' Felicity was aware she should be careful not to overstep the mark and push Beth too far. Obviously, the couple's affairs were private, as long as Beth wasn't being coerced into doing anything against her will.

'Can I get you anything to drink?' Beth asked.

'Tea would be nice.'

Beth nodded and switched the kettle on. She fiddled with her engagement ring as she waited for the water to boil, twisting it round and round.

'I've been worried about you,' Felicity said. 'You were really upset when you phoned me the other day, and then brushing it off as if nothing had happened didn't make sense to me. I'm concerned, Beth. What's going on with Alex?'

Beth was looking down at her ring the whole time Felicity

was speaking. She poured hot water onto the tea bags and brought the cups over to the table. She couldn't hide the tremor in her hands and a drop of tea spilled onto the table. She sat down and played with the string on the tea bag.

'Look, I know your relationship with Alex is private, especially as I work with him, but I'm worried about you. You strike me as being pretty isolated. You hardly go out, the friends you have are kept a secret. And OK, if Alex was doing the same, just spending all his leisure time here with you, fair enough if that's what you're both into, but that isn't the case. He's out, here, there and everywhere while you're stuck at home.'

'It's only the sailing club he spends time at, he's so passionate about it. He's always like this when he gets a new hobby. He took up cycling last year, joined a cycling club, bought himself a fancy bike and it consumed his free time. If he wasn't out cycling, he was reading about it. You must know what he's like, being his colleague, I'm sure he's the same at work. He's a high achiever and won't accept anything less than perfection. Sailing is his latest in a long line of hobbies.'

'Are you sure that's where he is?'

Beth removed the tea bag and dropped it onto the saucer. She looked at Felicity.

'You mean he might be seeing someone? Yes, it has crossed my mind. He likes women, you've seen how he is.'

'Doesn't it bother you?'

'Of course it does, but I try to be level-headed about it. I can get too jealous. Has something happened?'

Felicity thought of Judy, and her desire for confidentiality. How Alex had settled into the role.

'No. You're my friend and I don't think he treats you properly. Why should you project manage an extension you don't even want? It looks to me as if he controls what you do. It's important you put a stop to it, or get out of the relationship.'

Beth got to her feet and paced around the kitchen.

'You're right. He's always wanted it just to be us two, and I liked that, I didn't need anyone else. I went along with it because I loved him.'

'You're using the past tense.'

She nodded, looked at Felicity, then went back to staring out of the window, as if it were easier to send her words out into a void. Felicity understood she just needed to get it all out.

'Remember I told you about my pottery friend, how Alex sidelined her? That wasn't the only time. Before we moved here, I had a really good friend, Olivia. We met at the swimming pool, she used to go every morning like I did. This was when I was single. We started going for breakfast after our swim at weekends, we got on so well and became friends. We saw each other a lot, going for drinks, cinema, the usual stuff. Then I met Alex and gradually our lives became intertwined. I tried to keep the friendship going with Olivia, but I had to keep cancelling because other stuff came up.'

'Was that other stuff because of Alex?'

'Yes.' She joined Felicity at the table. 'Like he said I'd double booked myself. At first, I thought it was me being forgetful, being so busy I was making mistakes. But after a while I began to suspect Alex was making me think I had, when actually he was deliberately arranging things at the same time I'd arranged to meet Olivia. I couldn't be sure though, and he always denied it. Naturally she got fed up with me constantly cancelling and she stopped asking me to go out. It got to the point where I hardly saw her. Then I bumped into her in town and I suggested going for a coffee. That's when it all came out. She said she didn't think I wanted to be friends because Alex had turned up at the pool one day without me and told her I didn't have the heart to tell her but I found her irritating and didn't want to hang out anymore. He said he was worried about me as I was very stressed and not to bother me. It was all complete nonsense.'

'Did you challenge him?'

'Yes, but he denied it, said she was jealous of him taking me away from her. It was too late for our friendship by then and I knew we were moving so I left it.' Beth joined Felicity at the table. 'That's why when I met you I wanted to keep it from him. I didn't want him to ruin our friendship. When we first met, we instantly clicked and I knew we could be good friends.'

'Same here.' Felicity nodded. 'And maybe it isn't ideal that I work so closely with him but our friendship is important to me. What if he is having an affair?'

Beth was silent for a while. 'Do you know, I'd almost be relieved as it would take the focus off me. It's making me doubt whether I still love him.'

'Oh Beth. Talk to him about it?'

'I accused him of flirting the other day. He said I don't know him. It's true. We're growing apart.'

'You know I'm there for you.' Felicity squeezed Beth's hand and tears formed in Beth's eyes.

'That means so much.' The sound of a text pinged and she jumped, dropping Felicity's hand as if it was hot. She picked up her phone. 'What's the time?' The haunted look had returned to her face. 'You'd better go. He mustn't find you here.'

Felicity had so much she wanted to say to Beth, but the anxiety was catching. If Alex caught her here it would get Beth into trouble.

'Whatever you do, be careful.'

They hugged. Felicity looked back to wave as she got into her car but the front door was already closed.

TWENTY-SEVEN

PRESENT

After a brief catch-up session the lawyer reminded Felicity of her right to no reply. He was a large man in a rumpled suit, smelling of coffee. His voice was gruff, but his eyes were kind.

'I have nothing to hide,' Felicity said.

DS Williams was asking the questions again.

'We'd like to ask you a few questions about your relationship with Elizabeth Curran, Alex's first partner, Beth as she was known.'

'OK.' Felicity nodded. 'We were friends.'

'Tell us about your friendship.'

Felicity told them how she'd first met Beth at the beach, how they had swimming in common, about bumping into her and going for a coastal walk together, the easy friendship that developed.

'My first impression was they were very much in love, engaged to be married and were excited to be in their first home together. Speaking to Alex, you'd think they were happy, one of those couples that did everything together, but the more I got to know Beth, the more I realised that wasn't the case. She didn't want him to know about our friendship for a start. I told her I thought that was weird but she said he liked to compartmentalise his life and he didn't want his home life interfering with work. That was true, although he was outgoing and sociable, he didn't talk about his home life.'

'Did you keep it a secret?'

'I let it slip that I'd seen her once and he wasn't pleased. He was pretty flirtatious back then, he's toned it down a lot since. He got into a bit of a situation with a student.'

'Is that Judy Michigan?'

'Yes.' Felicity was surprised they'd already uncovered that. Were they suspicious of Alex?

'We know all about that. Back to Beth.'

She nodded. 'She thought he was having an affair as he was out so much, supposedly sailing.'

Chloe interrupted her. 'You said in a previous interview that she wouldn't have confided in you about an affair.' She flicked back through her notebook. '"Beth was a very private person". But it sounds like she did tell you?'

'I know, I'm sorry. It felt wrong, betraying her confidence. I didn't think it was important.'

'We'll decide what's important. You have to tell us the truth. We will get there eventually. Carry on.'

'She didn't know who the affair was with – or at least she didn't tell me. She said her feelings had changed towards him so it might be easier if he was. That surprised me, I must admit. She always said she'd share her inheritance with Alex when the time came, she was such a lovely person, that's how she was. He made her feel isolated and wanted her all to himself. She wanted to get a job and he wanted to look after her. They grew apart, I suppose.'

'Did you know about an affair?'

'No.' She sighed. 'I'm not convinced he was having an affair. The Alex she described was totally different to the one I knew. I know it's impossible to know what really goes on in a relationship, but Alex was pretty open about Beth. After we'd been working together for a couple of months he confided in me that Beth had been struggling at work, living in the city was stressful for her and the reason they moved was to be somewhere quiet. Her anxiety was getting worse and they both hoped living by the sea would be therapeutic for her.'

'You think she imagined the affair?'

'It's impossible to say. Alex liked women and was flirty by nature but he loved Beth. Whenever he talked about her you could tell he loved her.'

'Did Beth ever talk about her anxiety?'

'Not about the past, only in relation to the affair. That's why I doubted it. I tried to reassure her.'

'Given how close you were, I'm surprised she didn't confide in you more.'

Felicity shrugged. 'Everyone's different.'

'Talk to me about falling for Alex.'

'We bonded over our grief. He's a genuinely nice man and I never saw that side of him that Beth talked about. Don't think I didn't agonise over the relationship. We kept it secret for a while, but I hated the deception. I told the group all at once. Someone would have found out and I wanted to be upfront.'

'I see.' Chloe made a note.

'Were you having a relationship while Beth was alive?'

'No, I keep telling you. It began six months after that. I would never have done that to her.'

'Is there anything else you can tell me about Beth, anything at all?'

Felicity nodded. 'She had trouble sleeping and she took sleeping tablets occasionally.'

'Sleeping tablets?' Chloe scribbled in her notepad. 'Do you know what kind?'

Felicity shook her head.

'For the tape.'

'No.'

'Go on.'

'She found some of her tablets in Alex's pocket. She was afraid he was going to kill her. I worried about her after that.'

'Because he might kill her?'

'No.' Felicity sounded surprised. 'He wouldn't do that. I was worried about her mental health. She was changing her story a lot and I thought she wasn't well. If I was wrong I'd never forgive myself.'

'One last question – your friend Suzie Hill. Was she at the wedding?'

Felicity held her gaze.

'No, she wasn't.'

Gavin gathered the team together for a briefing. They'd had to let Felicity go. Nothing had been found at her house and the time would be better spent looking for more evidence while keeping an eye on her. Her friend Suzie Hill was worth looking into as according to Felicity's phone records they'd become friends shortly after Beth's death. Before he spoke to them, he went back through interviews with Alex from the time of Beth's death. That investigation had been undertaken by a different team before he moved into the area, and the DS running the case had taken retirement on health grounds after a nervous breakdown. None of his present team had worked on the case. Had a thorough job been done? He wasn't convinced, despite finding nothing in the notes to suggest Alex was suspected of having an affair or having cheated on his fiancée at any time. Beth's aunt Celia had been interviewed, and she had confirmed that she was helping both Beth and her fiancé financially and she was not being coerced in any way to give him money. Unfortunately, she was no longer alive. Alex was popular at work, and colleagues from his former workplace spoke highly of him. An incident with a student early on in the job hadn't led to any disciplinary action. No enemies, or anyone with a grudge had been uncovered. Not finding anything didn't deter the suspicion forming in his gut that Alex Maitland had been a smooth operator. They needed to dig deeper into his life at the time.

'So you think Beth was killed by her fiancé?' Chloe asked. 'Felicity dismissed Beth's concerns, and she was quite close to her.'

'Not as close to her as she might want us to think. If Beth confided in her about her husband's alleged problematic behaviour, why wouldn't she talk about her problems with anxiety?'

'She told Felicity she was taking sleeping tablets so she was aware to a certain extent.'

'I've spoken to her former employer and there was nothing in her references about it,' said a police constable, but lots of people wouldn't shout out about mental health issues. There's still a lot of stigma around about it.'

'See what you can find out from her medical records. Find out the details of the sleeping tablets, what was prescribed and exactly when. And how long they would be effective for, given the time lapse. You'll no doubt come up against patient confidentiality but given the circumstances it's worth looking into.'

'Boss,' the constable said.

'I want to be able to find out as much as we can about this, although given the lack of a body we are limited.' Something about Felicity bothered him. He assigned tasks to the two police constables present to go over the other interviews that had been taken at the time. 'Look especially at those who were around on both occasions. See whose interviews tally with what they said at the time. The current case may have woken up memories that weren't seen as important back then. Was he a harmless flirt or something more sinister?

'Chloe, I want you to look into Alex Maitland. Particularly his love life. There are rumours that he was a womaniser, was possibly having an affair. Felicity says the opposite. Was he just a flirt, or was it more? If he murdered Beth, did he act alone or was someone else in on it?'

'Yes, boss,' said Chloe.

'I'm going to focus on Felicity. I'm convinced she's not telling us everything. Annabelle Victor mentioned bruising, yet nobody else has reported seeing it.

'I know you're all working hard and the hours have been intense over the past few days and I can tell you're all knackered. But let's keep pushing, I'm convinced we're on the edge of cracking this case.' He looked round at them all, saw a police constable suppressing a yawn. 'I appreciate your hard work, and drinks will be on me once this is over.'

He knew from the nods and noises of encouragement that the team were as determined as he was.

TWENTY-EIGHT

PAST

Beth was watching television when Alex came home.

'Is there anything to eat?' he asked.

'There's some leftover pizza in the fridge.'

'Didn't you cook tonight?'

'I thought you'd be eating at the club. You usually do.'

'That sounds like a dig. Why don't you come out and say it?'

'Say what?'

'That you don't want me to go.'

'I didn't mean that, honestly.'

He took out the pizza and slammed the fridge door. 'This will have to do. You need to go shopping, there's hardly anything in this fridge.'

'I would have gone tonight, but you had the car. Maybe we should get a second car.'

'You don't need a car.'

'I might if I find a job.'

'You don't need a job. Talk about ungrateful. You have no idea how hard I work to earn enough for both of us.'

'Of course I do. And you shouldn't have to. I want to

contribute, we should be equal. It feels wrong, not working, relying on you.'

'Most women would love that.'

'I doubt it. What do you mean, "most women"? This is me, Alex, we went into this relationship together and it doesn't feel like that anymore. I've always earned my own living.'

'Felicity was saying today how she'd give up work in a heartbeat if she could.'

'Felicity? Not for a man, she wouldn't.'

'How would you know? You don't talk as friends, do you?'

'True.'

'If you knew her better you'd be surprised at some of the things she comes out with. We talk a lot. I like her, she's got an interesting way of looking at things. I never thought we'd become friends when we first met.'

He took his pizza into the dining room and she stared at the television screen. The quiz contestants were still answering questions but she no longer cared who won. What she did care about was Alex's remarks about Felicity. Obviously they were colleagues but she hadn't got the impression from Felicity that they confided in one another. She felt sick, wishing she could take back some of the things she'd said. Felicity wouldn't tell Alex what she said, would she? It might explain his recent disinterest in her.

Not long ago, Felicity had sat on this very sofa, turning up unannounced, insinuating that her husband was having an affair. What if the affair was with Felicity?

She switched off the television and went into the kitchen. She heard Alex go upstairs. She poured herself a glass of cold water and sipped it slowly, trying to calm herself. She pictured Felicity's face when they'd spoken, the look of concern in her eyes.

No, Felicity was her friend.

Or was she?

TWENTY-NINE

Felicity ducked her head beneath the water and pushed forward, staying under until her lungs burned, focusing on her body instead of the endless chatter in her head. She was right to tell the group about her and Alex, and in an hour from now it would be over.

Less than a year ago Beth would have been one of the people amassing for the swim today. She pictured her as she was those last few weeks, after she'd told Felicity she thought Alex was having an affair. The wary look on her face, the way she'd followed Sarah with her eyes, stepping in to distract Alex when he was with Sarah. Yet Sarah wasn't interested in Alex; she was just being her usual friendly self.

Of course she'd taken Beth's concerns seriously, but she'd been in a difficult position given her professional relationship with Alex. All she could do was observe. Yes, he had standards and liked things done in a certain way, but she witnessed his relationships with colleagues and students, how he was able to make a group feel relaxed with his easy, confident nature. He'd changed his attitude towards the female students, no longer encouraging their devotion, learning from his mistakes, and she respected that. He was interested in people, asking them about their private lives. He'd been very good to a colleague when her partner had suddenly been taken ill, despite the difficulties it had caused for the department. She respected him, and it was hard to square the picture Beth painted as being an accurate one. Yet if her friend was in trouble... She shook her head at the memory of that last day. She wouldn't have done anything differently.

She hadn't expected to feel so comfortable with Alex. They'd always had a good relationship at work, and now she no longer had to fret over what was going on between him and Beth, it was so much easier. Their relationship had surprised her as much as she suspected it was going to surprise the others. Becoming his partner changed everything.

She thought back to that time, when she'd been stuck in the middle of two people she cared about in different ways. When Beth had reached out to her that evening, upset after arguing with Alex, she'd been dreading seeing him the following morning and keeping her anger to herself. But Alex hadn't been himself either.

'Hangover?' She'd attempted a light-hearted reaction to seeing him with dark circles under his eyes and his normally pristine hair in need of a good wash.

'I wish,' he said. 'Can we talk?'

She'd made them some coffee.

'Beth isn't well again,' he said. 'I've been concerned for a while that she's becoming increasingly anxious, like she was before we came here.' He ran his hands through his hair.

'I'm sorry, I hadn't realised.'

He nodded. 'It's so difficult because I'm trying to protect her, but she thinks I'm isolating her. She doesn't understand that getting a job is not right for her at the moment.'

'Why don't you tell her your concerns? If it's happened before she'll know you're right. Would she go to the doctor?'

'It's hard to explain. You're right, but I have to pick the right time. I don't want to send her over the edge when she's home alone a lot of the time.'

'Does she have friends?'

'She's cut them all off.' He sighed. 'I shouldn't have encouraged her but we were so into each other and she only wanted to be with me. It wasn't a problem in London, but here it's a lot worse.'

His version of the situation between the couple was very different to Beth's. If she was on sleeping medication then surely she must have already seen a doctor. Unless she was getting them from the internet, but she couldn't imagine Beth doing that. Once Alex had gone off to his tutorial she'd focused on her work. She couldn't forget the fear in Beth's eyes. Was she ill, rather than frightened?

Incredible to think how far they'd both come, and what had happened to Beth. She could never have predicted everything that had brought her to this day, when she was about to divulge her relationship with Alex.

They were arriving now. She could change her mind; she didn't have to tell them. Yes, she did; hiding what she chose to do with her life was not how she operated. The wind blew her hair into her face and she ducked her head under the water, the cold shock on her face clearing her mind. If she didn't tell them now, it would be worse. There were suspicions in the group already, the knowing looks and the conversations that stopped when either she or Alex walked in. She'd almost bumped into Miranda outside Alex's house the other day; that was what had given her the impetus to tell them.

Tania waved from the beach and she waved back, standing up as she reached the shallower water, pushing her wet hair back from her face. Miranda and Annabelle were getting changed, and Hamish and Sarah were crossing the beach, Sarah a few paces behind Hamish, as if they'd argued before leaving the house. Miranda's red costume stood out like a traffic light against the dull grey sky.

'What's it like out there?' Tania asked.

'It's calm today, cold though. Worth every moment.'

'Hello,' Hamish said, his feet crunching over the pebbles. 'How's everyone today?'

'Good, thanks,' Felicity said. Since Beth's death the group had come together more, each of them aware that it would be so easy to give up, to allow the fear of what had happened to Beth infiltrate them and take over, stop them from doing an activity they all loved. She cleared her throat. 'Will you all come to the café after? I've got some news.'

'Ooh,' Tania said. 'I hope it's good news.'

'I think so,' Felicity said.

'Very mysterious,' Miranda said. 'Is Alex not coming today?'

'No idea,' Tania said. 'He's seemed a lot better lately.'

'He's on a course today,' Felicity said. His absence was the reason she was taking this opportunity to talk to the group. 'I'll get changed and go ahead to get us a table at the café.'

Annabelle was the first to join Felicity.

'It's too cold for me today, I only managed four minutes in the water, and the prospect of the café was too tempting,' she said. 'Plus I wanted to talk to you.'

'Oh, OK. I'll order the coffees now you're here.'

'Has your news got anything to do with Alex?' Annabelle asked. 'You and Alex?'

Felicity hesitated.

'It's OK.' Annabelle put her hand on Felicity's. 'I guessed a while ago. It's understandable in a way, given your work situation, and you knowing Beth.'

'That means a lot,' Felicity said. 'I'm not sure the others will feel the same way.'

'But...'

Footsteps clattered up the stairs, interrupting her, and Hamish joined them, wrapped up in a blue puffer jacket.

'That was a bracing swim. Cheers for the coffee,' he said, looking out of the large windows towards the sea. 'The others are just behind me.'

While Annabelle chatted, Felicity sipped her tea, trying to still the churning in her stomach. The tea had little effect.

'Come on, Felicity,' Miranda said. 'What's your big news?'

Felicity wished she hadn't made such an event of it now but telling them all in one go was easier than having to go through it multiple times. She cleared her throat.

'This isn't easy for me to say. You know what I'm like, I'm more of a private person so I'll just come out with it.' She inhaled deeply, 'Alex and I have got together, as in romantically.' Her cheeks were burning and she gripped her cup, staring into her tea to avoid their eyes. 'It's serious and...' She hesitated.

'Felicity,' Tania said, eyes wide, 'that's not what I expected at all.'

'Congratulations,' Annabelle said.

'Yes, same here,' Hamish said.

'Hang on,' Miranda said. 'You and Alex are dating? You're a dark horse.'

'You don't look very happy about it,' Tania said.

'I wasn't sure what you'd all think.'

'You're scared we're going to judge you,' Tania said. 'It's six months since Beth drowned and Alex deserves another chance at happiness. Go for it, I say. I thought he'd been more cheerful lately.'

'How long have you been seeing each other?' Sarah asked. Hamish shot her a look.

'What does it matter?' he said.

'It's OK,' Felicity said. 'I'd prefer to get it all out in the open. It was because of Beth that we got closer. Alex was grieving and so was I, obviously not to the same extent as Alex, but we already had a good working relationship and were becoming good friends. He needed someone to talk to and help with practicalities. Beth's aunt Celia died shortly afterwards and I largely managed that for him as he was inundated with their affairs to sort out.'

'Being friends first is always a good way to start a relationship,' Hamish said. 'That's how Sarah and I met.' Sarah smiled at him.

Felicity nodded. 'We were colleagues already, so I'd got to know him fairly well.'

'Does Alex know you're telling us?' Miranda asked.

'Yes. He finds it a bit awkward.'

'You wouldn't think so,' Hamish said. 'Alex clearly likes women and I'm sure none of us expected him to live like a monk.'

'Oh, Hamish, let it go,' Sarah said.

'Beth would have wanted him to be happy again,' Annabelle said.

Felicity relaxed. It was going better than she'd imagined. Obviously, they might not say what they really thought to her face but her stomach was no longer churning. Conversation turned to other matters.

'Are you walking back, Felicity?' Annabelle asked.

'Yes, are you?'

They strolled along the cliff path.

'Do you feel better for getting that off your chest?' Annabelle asked.

'I do.'

'Good. It shouldn't matter what other people think as long as you're happy.'

'It's easy to say that,' Felicity said, 'but I feel awkward about it myself. I keep thinking I'm betraying Beth.'

'I understand, but you aren't.'

They walked along in silence for a bit.

'I'm heading off this way,' Annabelle said, coming to a halt. She hesitated.

'What is it?'

Annabelle sighed. 'Don't rush into anything. Alex is still on the rebound. And there's something else. Just now, I overheard Tania and Miranda talking about Alex in the bathroom before we left, when you were paying the bill. They were gossiping.'

'Tell me. I'd rather know.'

'That's what I thought. I'd be the same. They thought Alex was having an affair when he was seeing Beth.'

'With who?'

'They didn't know, although there was that business with Sarah.'

'Nothing happened with Sarah.'

'I also heard them say they thought you were seeing him behind Beth's back.'

Felicity stopped walking and stared at her. 'That's not true.'

Annabelle put her hand on Felicity's arm. 'I believe you, I thought you'd want to know given how important it was for you to get things out into the open. Ignore them. It's none of their business.'

'Tell me the truth, what do you really think? Why say that he's on the rebound?'

Annabelle looked out to sea, as if working out what to say. She sighed.

'I think you should be careful. How well did you know Beth? Were you close?'

'Yes, it was a bit awkward because of me and Alex working together but I'd say we were, or we would have been if... why?'

'I'm not sure she was happy with Alex. Did you sense that?'

Felicity hesitated. 'She adored him initially – a bit too much if anything. She left a job she loved for him. More recently, I know she had concerns. She felt isolated here, she was questioning everything. She had her suspicions about an affair, but

I'm convinced it wasn't true. Look, I don't want to betray confidences, but Beth had mental health issues. I'm not sure she was thinking clearly during those last few weeks. Alex was worried about her too. I had to be objective, but on balance and given what I know I'd be inclined to believe Alex.'

Annabelle frowned. 'I'm only telling you this because I care about you. Maybe I'm being overly cautious, but be careful. I suspect Alex might have hurt her.'

'What? Did she tell you that?'

'She didn't have to.'

THIRTY

PRESENT

'I told Felicity I had my suspicions about Beth the same day she told us she'd got together with Alex,' Annabelle said. 'I thought I should warn her. She took his side, which I suppose she would given she was in love with him.'

'Did anyone else know about this?' Chloe asked. She'd asked Annabelle to come into the station for this interview.

'I don't know. Apart from Felicity I didn't mention it to anyone else.'

'Why didn't you tell the police about this at the time?'

'I wasn't asked. I visited the police station and said I had some information and was told somebody would call round to interview me. They never did.'

'You didn't chase it?'

'It's not my job to do that. I concluded it couldn't be relevant. It was a horrible time. Beth had drowned and we were all devastated. I felt sorry for Alex, who was in a bad way, and I suppose I thought this would cause further problems for him unnecessarily. I had no proof of anything and I'd only ever seen him be kind.'

'Why come forward now then?'

Annabelle sighed. 'I don't believe in coincidences. Alex drowning like this... Before I knew it was a murder, I was already dubious that it could happen again. In theory, obviously it is within the realms of possibility but really...' She spread out her hands in a question. 'I remembered a detail about Beth. It may prove unrelated, but I won't have it on my conscience anymore.'

'Do you have any idea who he might have been seeing?'

'No, I don't.'

Not even the cold sea could still the questions going round in Annabelle's mind resulting from her interview with PC Button yesterday. Had she done enough for Beth? If she was alone with her concerns, then she'd failed. Surely Felicity must have had some idea. She'd planned to ask her, only she wasn't swimming this morning. She was about to ask the others where she was when Tania had appeared, walking so fast she was out of breath as if she couldn't wait to reach them.

'Have you heard the news?' She patted her chest to get her breath back. 'Felicity was taken in for questioning yesterday evening and I couldn't get hold of her this morning. I think they're going to arrest her.'

'You're joking,' Miranda said.

Tania silenced her with a look. 'As if I'd joke about something so serious. I mean, I don't know anything for sure but it's not looking good.'

That decided Annabelle. Maybe it would be good to talk it over with the others.

'Does anyone fancy a coffee?' she asked, as she towel dried her hair.

'Hamish?' Sarah asked. 'We've got time, haven't we?'

He nodded. 'Miranda? Tania? Café?'

'Sure,' Tania said.

'Are you OK?' Sarah asked, as she and Annabelle went on ahead. Tania was still struggling with her costume under her robe, while chatting with Miranda.

Annabelle sighed. 'It's just all this business with Alex. I was questioned again yesterday and it got me thinking about Beth.'

'You're not the only one,' Sarah said. 'They interviewed us too. It looks like they're looking into her death again.'

'I guess they have to rule out foul play.'

'You were quite friendly with her, weren't you?'

They reached the café counter and placed their usual order. 'I'll bring the drinks over,' the waitress said. They sat around their usual long wooden table, which looked out over the sea. The others were coming in now, talking to the waitress.

'Anyone want cake?' Hamish asked.

'No thanks,' Sarah said. Annabelle shook her head.

Annabelle lowered her voice. 'Were you ever worried about her?'

'What do you mean?'

'That Alex was abusive towards her.'

Sarah stared at her. 'No. Did she tell you that?'

'No, but one time I saw she had bruising on her arms, and she seemed anxious to please him.'

Hamish sat down with a piece of apple cake, cutting a huge piece with a fork. 'Who's anxious to please?'

'Hamish,' Sarah said. He ate some cake, frowning.

'It's OK,' Annabelle said. 'We were talking about Beth.' She repeated her concerns.

Hamish and Sarah exchanged a glance.

'Tell her,' Hamish said.

'Beth was worried that Alex was after her aunt's money,' Sarah said. Tania and Miranda joined them and the waitress deposited a tray of drinks on the table, plus two more slices of cake.

'I thought it might help to discuss our thoughts about Beth,' Annabelle said, 'given the investigation is going on and the police are asking a lot of questions about her. I was concerned Alex was hurting her.' She recapped the rest of the conversation. 'I can't help thinking I could have done more. I knew something wasn't right, but she was such a private person.'

'Felicity was her closest friend,' Miranda said. 'Have you asked her?'

'No, I don't like to. She's going through enough as it is.'

'It's all pretty horrendous for her,' said Tania, 'what with his sister making a fuss. Felicity said she was constantly ringing the detective for updates.'

'And so they should,' Miranda said. 'He was murdered.'

The word landed like a stone dropped in water from a great height.

'Are the police thinking Beth was murdered?' Hamish asked.

Annabelle rubbed her eyes. 'Maybe they are. Does anyone else feel they let Beth down?'

'Yes,' Miranda said. 'I got the sense she wasn't happy, but I didn't want to pry.'

'Hindsight is everything,' Tania said. 'But we don't know for sure.'

'I hate to say this,' Sarah said. 'But doesn't anyone wonder about Felicity? What if her relationship with Alex started before Beth died?'

'That crossed my mind too,' Tania said. 'Remember when she first told us about it?'

'Yes,' Annabelle said, 'She wanted to be upfront with us. I don't think she would lie about when it started.'

'It's impossible to know,' Miranda said.

'I can't believe Alex was murdered,' Hamish said. They all looked at one another.

'We shouldn't speculate,' Annabelle said. 'Let the police do their job.' She wasn't the only one whose thoughts turned to Felicity.

The question of who killed Alex hung in the air.

THIRTY-ONE

PAST

Beth couldn't fault the plans. The extension would involve knocking down the existing wall between the small kitchen and the living room, building onto the back of the house to create a huge open-plan kitchen.

'What do you think?' Alex asked, coming up behind and putting his arm around her.

'It looks amazing.'

'Doesn't it? We'll have so much space and light and we'll have a picture window looking out over the sea. It's what you've always wanted.'

Beth sighed. 'It's beautiful, and you've put so much work into the design, but we're losing the character of the cottage. That's what I love about this place.'

'But it's so poky. Wouldn't you like to have an amazing kitchen like this? We can have brand new appliances – even a built-in coffee machine. What's not to like?'

Beth had only ever seen those in interior design makeover programmes on television. It wasn't what she dreamed about. The houses in her dreams were cosy with original features like old fireplaces and patterned floor tiles.

'Of course I'd like that one day, but I'm not in a hurry for it. The one we've got is perfectly adequate. I'm not cut out to be a project manager. I don't know anything about it. I'm still hoping to get a teaching job.'

'You don't need to work, I keep telling you.'

'But I want to. Teaching gives me a sense of purpose, it's who I am. I don't want to waste all my training.'

'The extension is going ahead regardless. Wouldn't you rather have a say in it? You can have free rein with the design. You'll love it, I know you will. Look how you've made this poky old cottage look with a few colourful touches. Think about it, for me?'

'OK.'

'I knew you'd come round to my way of thinking.'

And therein lay the problem. She was having to do a lot of that lately, as if she were losing her sense of self.

He hadn't given her much choice.

Alex was sailing that evening and after she'd eaten a bowl of soup, she logged on to their joint bank account to look through the latest statements. This extension was going to cost a fortune. How could they afford it on one wage? Her wages went into her account and Alex had talked her into sharing an account for household bills, holidays etc. She rarely looked at the joint account as Alex preferred to take care of all the household finances, getting annoyed if she butted in. She typed in the passcode and waited while the broadband clicked in. The connection was so much slower here. She looked through their statements. Alex had made frequent payments to the sailing club. The club had a bar and restaurant as well as running the courses he went on and his club fees. He spent a lot of time in the restaurant. They all went to the bar, she knew, and the local pub. A flicker of unease came over her, recalling the conversation with Felicity. He was spending a hell of a lot of time at the sailing club. Was it just sailing that was attracting him?

. . .

'I met this guy at the club tonight,' Alex announced on his return from sailing. 'He runs a building company. They've got a really good reputation. He's offered to give me a quote and if it's favourable they can start work at the end of the month.'

Beth looked at the calendar. Very little was marked on it. It was a sad indictment of her life she went out so little, and when she did it was carried out in secret. How had her life got so small? It was like being carried along by the sea, the water gathering pace and erupting in a huge wave and spitting her out on the other side.

'That's only three weeks away. I haven't decided yet. I thought we were going to have a chat about it.'

'There's nothing to discuss. If you don't want to be project manager I'll do it myself.'

'You don't have time. You're never here as it is.'

'What's that supposed to mean?'

'You're so busy at work, with sailing. That's an expensive hobby. The renovations are going to cost a fortune too. We should wait until I'm earning.' She pulled a face. 'And I hate saying this, but Aunt Celia doesn't have long left and she's told me she's leaving everything to me. That will more than pay for any improvements we want.'

'When that happens there will be a lot of bureaucracy to get through. Sorting out inheritance tax, clearing and selling a property, all that takes time, years sometimes. Stop being obtuse about this and accept that we're doing this. You really frustrate me. I'm doing the house improvements straight away for you, don't you get that? You're at home all day.'

'Yes, but only until I find a job.'

'You don't need a job.' He slammed his hand on the table, making her jump. 'Talk about ungrateful. You have no idea how much organisation this has taken on top of working full time and having to deal with everything since we made this decision.'

'Since *you* made the decision. Without telling me.'

'What did you say?'

Alex grabbed her chin and shoved his face into hers. His fingers were digging into her skin and she tried to prise his hands off her. He shoved her and she stumbled backwards, lost her balance and struck her hip on the coffee table as she fell onto the floor. The pain was sharp and she shook with shock and fear, staring at this Alex who she no longer recognised. He'd never been this violent before. She tried to pull herself up but pain shot through her hip making her groan. Her neck was sore where he'd dug his fingers into it.

He stepped towards her and she cowered against the floor, unsure whether he was going to help her up or kick her in the ribs. She didn't know this man.

He did neither. He loomed over her.

'This is happening,' he said, poking his finger into her chest. 'Get used to it.'

He looked at her in disgust before leaving the room.

The next morning, she heard the front door slam. Beth waited, listening. Sometimes he came back having forgotten something. Or so he said. It happened too frequently for such an organised person. He had to be checking up on her. But what did he think he'd catch her doing? She sighed.

The car was leaving, the engine noise decreasing and she got out of bed, wincing as a spasm shuddered through her hip. She held on to the wall to steady herself. Pulling on a pair of sweatpants and a T-shirt, she looked at herself in the full-length mirror. Dark patches discoloured her skin where Alex had grabbed her. She wound a scarf around her neck, pulled on a jacket and went downstairs, moving slowly, getting used to walking in a way to minimise the pain.

Alex's swimming bag was in the hall, his trunks slung over the radiator. They were damp to touch. She frowned, wandering into the kitchen to check the time. It was ten o'clock. She'd slept right through and he'd swum without her. Maybe a swim would be good for her aching body.

The beach was busier now; a group of mothers and small children were holding hands, paddling in the sea. Beth parked her stuff by one of the groynes and changed underneath her towelling robe. The cold water made her gasp, instantly taking her mind away from the shooting pain in her hip. She should probably have got it checked but she couldn't face the questions, the false answers she'd have to give. She'd taken some painkillers, that would do, and already the cold was therapeutic. She floated on her back, the events of last night flashing in her head. Alex had shown a side of himself she'd never witnessed before. She closed her eyes and tried to empty her mind, focusing on her body and the sensation of the water lapping over her.

After the swim, she dried herself quickly and dressed, taking her bag over to the sand dunes, her hip protesting as she climbed the sandy verge. She sat behind a dune, sheltered from the wind and out of sight of the people on the beach. The sun warmed her skin and she removed the scarf.

The throbbing in her hip returned, a pulsing reminder of what Alex had done; the hands that had once touched her with care had turned into weapons. She thought of Celia, how fond of Alex she was. What would she think of Beth for allowing this to happen? Once upon a time she'd have been able to confide in her aunt, but she was too sick to burden her with her trivial problems. Only it wasn't trivial. If she didn't act on this, somehow put a stop to it, it would get worse. Her gaze was focused on the sea, the waves gently lapping over one another, the taste of salt still on her lips. The natural beauty took her breath away. She loved it here; she didn't want to leave. She recalled Alex holding her hand and helping her climb the steep descent to the beach for the first time and how the view had filled her with joy and tears poured from her eyes. Then she was sobbing, for Alex, for her aunt, for her lost love.

'Beth?'

She whipped her head round on hearing the unexpected voice, wiping her eyes with the back of her hand, not wanting anyone to see her blotchy face and snivelling self-pity.

'Sarah?' She was blocking the sun, making Beth shiver.

'I heard you crying. I don't want to intrude, but are you OK?' She crouched down next to Beth. Her face crumpled with concern. 'What's happened to your neck?'

Beth instinctively pulled her sweatshirt up to cover it.

'It looks worse than it is. I bashed it in the kitchen.'

Sarah sat down. 'I don't believe you.'

'It's the truth.'

'OK.' She frowned. 'Hamish said you weren't swimming this morning. He said Alex was in a funny mood. Is everything alright with you two?'

Beth pressed her lips together, trying not to cry. 'I don't know. We're going through a bit of a rough patch. We used to be inseparable, but since we moved here, he's out all the time. I can't stop thinking he might be seeing someone else. I've asked him, but he shuts me down, says I'm imagining it. Honestly, if he is seeing someone else I'd rather know.'

'Really? Are you sure?'

Beth looked at her, reading confusion in her eyes.

'You know something. Tell me.'

Sarah sighed. 'It's probably just gossip.' She looked away

from Beth, out to sea. 'Miranda saw him having dinner with another woman.'

'Who? When?'

'I don't know.'

'He has female colleagues. It could have been one of them, a business meeting.'

Sarah nodded. 'Of course. I shouldn't have said anything. You have to talk to him. You can't go round feeling like this. Me and Hamish often have blazing rows but we say what we think and it's much healthier. Lies destroy everything.'

Beth wound her scarf around her neck.

'I know.'

Sometimes a lie is the only way out.

THIRTY-TWO

Sarah gave Beth Miranda's number. She rang her after Sarah left, before she changed her mind.

'Miranda? It's Beth.'

'Beth! This is a surprise. I didn't know you had my number.'

'I need to talk to you.'

'Oh. OK. When?'

'As soon as possible.'

'Really? Gosh. OK, well I'm at the hair salon where I work and I'm due a break in half an hour. Is that soon enough for you?'

'That's perfect, thanks, Miranda. Remind me where your salon is.'

Half an hour later they were drinking flat whites in a café on the high street.

'I must admit I'm intrigued,' Miranda said. She was dressed in the black and white uniform of the salon, stylish cropped trousers and a shirt. She smelled of hair products. 'Is everything OK?'

Beth felt frumpy next to her, despite having rushed into a public cloakroom on the way to wash her face. She twisted her hands in her lap, hoping Miranda wouldn't notice how anxious she was.

'Thanks for agreeing to see me. I won't beat around the bush. One of the swimmers was gossiping about my husband. You saw him out with another woman?'

'Ah.' Miranda picked up a sugar sachet and twisted it. 'Me and my big mouth. Who told you that?'

Beth blushed. 'I'd rather not say.'

'As long as it wasn't Tania?'

'No, it wasn't.'

Miranda narrowed her eyes. 'Intriguing. Look, I'm sorry you had to hear this but maybe it's for the best. I hate men who cheat, it's happened to me more than once and there's nothing worse. I was surprised though, you've always seemed like a great couple to me.'

Beth's face felt even hotter. It was bad enough opening up to a close friend, let alone someone she hardly knew. 'It was probably one of his colleagues.'

'You wouldn't have come all the way to meet me if you believed that.'

'I want to be sure of the facts. What did you see?'

'I saw him at the sailing club in the restaurant, having dinner with a woman.'

'When was this?'

'The first time was about three weeks ago.'

Beth's stomach dropped. 'It was more than once?'

Miranda nodded. 'The second time was last Tuesday. I don't go to the club very often but I've heard him say he goes a lot. It was the same woman in the restaurant with him.'

'It wasn't Felicity?'

Miranda laughed. 'No! I know what she looks like. You don't suspect her, do you? I thought she was your mate.'

'No, I was thinking because she's a colleague.'

'It definitely wasn't Felicity and if it was a colleague then it's no longer just a professional relationship. It was a romantic date, no doubt about that. I would have gone over and spoken to him otherwise, but I didn't because it would have been awkward. Part of me wanted to though, to ask him what he thought he was playing at when he's got a lovely fiancée at home. I'm sorry.' She put her hand on Beth's arm.

'What does this woman look like?'

'Shoulder-length brown hair, thin face. Medium build. Not as pretty as you.'

'And what makes you so sure it was a date?'

'They were kissing,' Miranda said. 'You can't argue with that.'

THIRTY-THREE

PRESENT

After she'd finished questioning Annabelle, Chloe arranged an interview with the manager of the sailing club, warning him she wanted to go through his CCTV footage and speak to his staff. Before leaving the police station, she put in a call to the retired detective who'd led the investigation into the drowning of Beth Curran.

The case had never been closed, he told her. When it had been established that the corpse was too badly decomposed to make a formal identification, he'd visited Alexander Maitland personally to break the news. The pathologist had been able to establish that the corpse was female, aged between twenty and forty, and had never broken any bones. It had been impossible to establish whether the body had any scarring or tattoos, although Beth had neither.

Eighteen months after Beth disappeared he'd informed Alex that most of the officers on the case were being stood down, as they'd exhausted all leads. When pressed by Alex, he admitted he would be inclined to believe the body was Beth's. This had been good enough for Alex.

'He wanted closure,' the detective explained to Chloe. 'It

was understandable. His life had been in limbo and he was moving forward. It didn't mean he would ever forget her, but he believed the washed-up body was Beth's. It was incomprehensible to him otherwise. The case was never officially closed, it remains open today. Are you going to have another crack at it?'

It wasn't how Chloe would have put it, but yes, she was going to be looking into it.

'It forms part of an ongoing investigation.'

'Let me know how you get on. I doubt you'll find anything different; the body was hers, I was always convinced of that.'

Felix Adams, the manager of Eastsea Sailing Club, showed Chloe into his office, situated on the first floor of the club, behind the restaurant. She'd been in the building once before, but that hadn't been for recreational purposes either, unfortunately.

'You can use my office,' he said, 'if you need to go through any of our CCTV files, but we only save them for one week.'

'That's better than a lot of places. This is the man we're looking into.' She showed him a photo of Alex.

'Alex, yes, I thought it might be. Terrible news. Everyone's been talking about it here.'

'He was a regular club user?'

'Oh yes, he had been for years.'

'Was he popular?'

'He was well liked. He was a good sailor – I always knew a boat was in safe hands if Alex was in charge.'

'Who did he come in with?'

'I only ever saw him arrive alone, but there are a couple of guys he sailed with. You might be better off talking to the staff in the lounge area as he often went there after a session. I've only been here a few months.'

The CCTV covered both the main entrance and the back

door of the club, which led out to the sailing area where boats and equipment were kept, the reception desk, gym floor and the bar/café lounge. Chloe focused on the social area, which was only open during the evening. She painstakingly scrolled through the tapes on the dates prior to Alex's death, but he hadn't visited the lounge in that week. She rubbed her eyes, switching off the files. She found Felix in reception.

'Find anything?'

'No. Do you keep any other record of attendance?'

'Members have a card which they swipe in and out with. I'm not sure how far our records go back.'

'Would you have a look for me?'

'Sure.'

'Are there any staff around who were working here five years ago?'

He nodded. 'Josh the bar manager. He's been here for years.'

'Is he in today?'

'He is. He's already in the bar. I'll let him know you're on your way.'

A bearded man with round black glasses was polishing the bar counter.

'PC Button?'

'The uniform's a bit of a giveaway.'

He grinned. 'Can I get you a coffee?'

'Please. A latte, no sugar.'

'Coming up.'

They sat at one of the tables in the bar.

'I understand you've worked here for a long time,' Chloe said.

He nodded. 'Part of the furniture, me. Must be about twelve years now.'

'You must get to know the regulars then.'

'Oh yes. Most people who join come on a regular basis, plus

the restaurant is good, we won best restaurant in the area last year.'

'Impressive. Do you recognise this man?' She opened Alex's photo on her phone but Josh was already nodding.

'It's gutting news about Alex. He's been coming here for years.'

'Who does he come with?'

'He's part of a regular group of four, three other men.' He gave her their names, none of which she recognised.

'What about female company? Did he ever come here with a date?'

'There was someone he came in with for dinner once, but it was a long time ago.'

'Can you describe her?'

'She was wearing a big sun hat, that's why I remember her. I couldn't tell you what colour her hair was.'

'I'm going to show you some photos. Tell me if you've ever seen them with Alex.'

She opened the photos on her phone. The first shot was of Beth.

Josh shook his head. 'She never came here but I know who she is. Her story was all over the news. It's insane how the same thing happened to her husband.'

'What about this woman?' The picture was of Felicity.

'No.'

She went through some more photos of the women around Alex: Caroline, Sarah, Miranda, Tania and Annabelle. Only one photo made him react. He took the phone for a closer look, zooming in.

'It could have been her.'

'When exactly was this?'

He thought for a moment. 'It was before we had the big refurbishment so that would be about four years ago. I know because the table they were at is where the comfy chairs are now. I'm not one hundred per cent sure though.'

The sound of footsteps interrupted the conversation as Felix came through the swing door looking pleased with himself, followed by a young man who went straight off to cover the bar. Felix put a laptop onto the table.

'The swiping in log is never deleted, so you can look back as far as you like. And Chris here has been working in the bar and restaurant recently, if you want to show him those photos once he's finished setting up the tables. The records are on here. You can search either by date or by name.'

Chloe had a beat of excitement. The photo he'd selected had set her mind whirring and she was running through the woman's interview in her head. First, she searched under Alex's name, and a list of dates and times appeared. She spent a while searching through the list of the female witnesses from the wedding, starting with Miranda. She also searched Judy Michigan but nothing came up. Peering at the screen was tiring with none of the names getting results. Until she got a hit. This woman had been at the club a couple of times four years ago after Alex first became a member, and her entry status was 'guest'. She checked back under Alex's name and he had been there at the same time. She came up again one week before Alex's death. Adrenalin shot through her.

'Is this woman a member?' she asked Felix, showing him the name.

'No,' he said, 'it would be stated if she was.'

'Do you know her?' she asked, opening up her photo.

'No,' he said.

'Can I print some of these?' she asked.

'Sure, the wireless printer is automatically set up. Do it now and I'll go and collect it. You can talk to Chris while you wait.'

He called Chris over. Chloe explained about Alex and showed him a photo.

'I know him,' he said. 'Nice guy, always offered me a drink. He used to come in after sailing, plus he ate in the restaurant a couple of times.'

'Was he alone?'

'No, it was a date. They were pretty into each other, I could tell by their body language.'

Chloe opened the photos again, hoping he wouldn't notice her fumbling fingers. His answer was crucial. She showed him Beth, Felicity, Caroline. When she opened the next photo he nodded.

'That's her. They were here just recently.'

Felix appeared with the printouts and handed them to her. Chloe looked for the most recent date that the woman had logged in. Alex had swiped in too. 'Would that have been last Monday?'

'Could have been. Yes, I was working on that Monday night.'

'OK. I'd like you to go through exactly what you remember from that occasion. I'll need to go back through the CCTV footage as I must have missed her.'

'Which woman is it?' Josh asked.

Chloe showed him the photo again.

He nodded. 'Yes, it could have been her wearing the hat.'

THIRTY-FOUR

Felicity thought back to the day after the wedding. How she'd walked up the sand dunes, away from the others and dialled one of the few numbers she knew by heart. Down below, her new husband's body lay lifeless on the sand. A white tent was being erected around him. She wasn't sure she would be able to speak. She managed two words.

'It's over.'

'Oh Felicity, it's you, thank goodness. I thought... when you didn't ring I thought you'd changed your... oh never mind. What's over? The ceremony? You're married?'

'No, yes, I mean yes I'm married but everything is over. *It's* over.'

'What's wrong? You sound terrible.'

'I don't know how to say this so I'll just come out with it.' She gulped down some air. 'Alex is dead.'

'What? He can't be.'

'It's awful. He drowned. I don't know how it happened. We all went for the midnight swim as planned, and...' Felicity made a strangled sound. 'He swam out further than the rest of us and none of us saw what happened to him. It was dark and creepy out there, I didn't venture too far out. Once we realised he hadn't come back some of us went out again but it was impossible to see very far. The police arrived and a rescue party carried out a search but they couldn't find him, until this morning. They found his body, Alex is dead. He drowned.'

Felicity's voice had got quieter. 'I'm scared. That's why I'm using a different phone. The police are going to question us all again this morning. What if they find out? It doesn't look good and I don't know what to tell them.'

'If he drowned that can't be pinned on you.'

'I know, but it's too early to tell. Something's off with the police. They're acting as if they suspect something is strange.'

'I'm sure you're imagining it because of what we've done. Forensic tests will take a while, they can't possible have done a post-mortem yet. What time did they find him?'

'Only this morning, at about eight. We were there when it happened.'

'We?'

'Us swimmers. I couldn't stay at home doing nothing while he was lost out there. I went back down to the beach, I wanted to find him, I had a swim, stupid I know, and some of the other swimmers turned up. They felt the same. It was impossible to stay away. Everyone is in bits.'

'This could ruin everything. What are you going to tell the police?'

'I'll stick to the story. They'll look at my phone, that's why I didn't use it for this call, but they'll see how often we're in touch.'

'That won't tell them anything. We've been careful, right from the start. We're close friends, we ring each other. It's normal. How are his parents? And Caroline? They must be devastated.'

'Everyone is. A lot of the wedding guests are still milling around. The police have asked them all to stay in the area until they've taken statements. I haven't seen his parents yet this morning but Caroline is suspicious. Maybe it's because of her the police aren't assuming anything. She's convinced he couldn't have drowned because he's such a strong swimmer.'

'They believed it about me.'

They were both silent for a while.

'Aside from all that,' Felicity said, 'we did what we planned. This will work in our favour.'

'That's why they must never find out.'

Felicity couldn't move. Once the call had ended, her limbs turned to jelly. The confidence she'd displayed to appease her evaporated.

Alex was dead.

Everything she had done since *that* night had been working towards the events of this weekend. The wedding to Alex. She was now the first Mrs Maitland but she wasn't a wife. She was a widow.

She called Suzie again later that day. She put on some music to make doubly sure she wouldn't be overheard and closed the living room door. They had so much to talk about.

Suzie answered straight away.

'Hello.'

'Alex's death was on the news. What happened exactly?'

Felicity heard footsteps and a door closing.

'Everything went according to plan until the midnight swim. Quite a few of us took part in the end, I was surprised how many of the guests wanted to join in. He swam out far, you know how he likes to show off, only this time he didn't come back. The police have closed off the beach and we've all been questioned. Reporters are buzzing around.' She pulled two slats of the blind apart and peered through. 'Three are outside my house at the moment including that moron from the local paper with the haystack hair. He's all puffed up and acting like he owns the place, showing off to the nationals.'

'There's bound to be interest, but it will die down soon. What happens next?'

'I don't know. The police are still doing their investigations.'

'Into what? He drowned.'

'Yes I know, but there are procedures they have to go through. They're very thorough. Alex's dad is kicking up a fuss, he took all Alex's medals and certificates down to the police station to show them what a proficient swimmer he is... It would be funny if it wasn't so tragic. We have to stay calm.'

'I need to talk to you properly. I'm so isolated here. Can we meet?'

'It's too risky.'

'I have to see you.'

Felicity sighed. 'It won't be immediately. It depends how long the police are around. I can't risk anyone following me. Meeting isn't the best idea.'

'Probably not, but we can make sure nobody sees us. I wouldn't suggest it if it wasn't important.'

'OK.' Felicity wasn't convinced, but keeping Suzie calm was as important. A full-blown anxiety attack was the last thing they needed. Even though she'd rebuilt her confidence over the last few years, her inner fragility was never far away. Who knew what she might do? 'I don't know when yet, but I'll get a message to you. Don't call or text me again. We can meet at Pevensey Lighthouse. That's about midway on the coastal path between us. Nobody will see us there and we can make it look like we bumped into one another if necessary.' She heard the sound of a key in the front door. 'I've got to go. I'll let you know when by email, from that other account.'

THIRTY-FIVE

PAST

Felicity was already in the sea when Beth and Alex arrived at the beach. She hadn't expected to see them. As usual Beth was covered up in her long-sleeved costume. She swam slowly around, watching them drinking tea from a red flask, her hands cramping with cold. She was reluctant to get out of the water and face them. She didn't know who to believe. The water was cold, forcing her out, shivering as she crossed the beach to join them.

'I'm glad I caught you. I wondered if Beth might like to join me and a few friends on Thursday night round at my house for some food and drink. Women only, I'm afraid, Alex, otherwise you'd be invited too.'

Beth opened her mouth to answer but Alex jumped in, squeezing her hand.

'That's such a shame. She'd have loved to, but I've planned a surprise for her that evening.'

'Maybe I could fit both in?' Beth said.

'You won't have time. Come on.' He took her hand and pulled her towards the sea.

Felicity had noticed Beth's reluctance.

Beth phoned her shortly after, insisting they meet.

'It has to be tomorrow.' Beth insisted they meet somewhere far away, a place she had no connection to. Felicity found the forest on a map. It was quite a drive. Was Beth becoming paranoid? Or was she genuinely in danger?

'I have to be careful,' Beth said over the phone. 'I'll explain when you see me.'

The path was narrow, trees bending over and blocking the light, which slipped through every now and then, adding to the unease Felicity felt and the sense that the trees were hemming her in.

She waited until the path was wide enough for them to walk along together before speaking.

'I'm trusting you because once I told you what was going on you haven't told Alex about our friendship, when it would have been so easy for you to do so. I'm going to leave Alex.'

'What?' Felicity stopped walking.

'I'm not happy with him. He's having an affair and his behaviour towards me is threatening. Talking to you has enabled me to see what's going on. I make excuses for him and I'm losing my sense of self. It's so easy to believe a narrative about yourself and I'd fallen under Alex's spell. I can see through him now – I've been so blind. Everything he does is his way and he's moulding me into the person he wanted me to be. He has no idea about this. He apologised and promised to change. I made out it was OK, that his behaviour was understandable. That way he won't suspect I'm planning to get away.'

Felicity was shaking her head.

'I had no idea it was this bad. He's so personable at work, a little arrogant, yes, but charming. Everybody likes him.'

'That's who he is and that's how he was when I first met him. But in our relationship I feel stifled. I can't keep up this pretence any longer and I want to get away. He made me a special breakfast this morning and it was hard not to gag. I know he's seeing someone else and if I leave, he can be with her, whoever she is.'

'Do you really have no idea?'

'I don't. Can I trust you?'

'Of course.'

'Even if it means keeping a secret from Alex when he is desperate to know?'

Felicity nodded. 'I can do that.'

'You'll understand why I'm making such a fuss when I tell you what I want to do.'

'Just tell me.'

'I want to disappear. It's the only way. He won't let me go, I just know it. Will you help me?'

'Why me?'

'Because you've been a good friend to me and you have a car.'

'I don't think you should rush this. You're less likely to pull it off if you rush into it. You'd have to plan carefully.'

Beth shook her head. 'It has to be soon. I found out last night he's been taking my sleeping pills. He's been stashing them away. Why would he do that? Given how threatening he's been lately I'm scared of what he might do. What if he's planning to drug me?' She was shaking.

'Beth, no.'

Despite knowing a different side to Alex, Felicity could understand Beth's fear. She also sensed Beth wasn't telling her everything.

'I'm sorry to spring this on you so suddenly,' Beth said, 'but it's going to have to be this Saturday. After I found the sleeping pills, I couldn't settle. I'm scared, Felicity, scared he wants to kill me.'

Felicity was stunned. 'Surely he wouldn't go that far.'

Beth's face shut down. 'You don't believe me.'

'I do, but if that's true you should go to the police. I'll come with you.'

'I can't take that risk. The police aren't going to take a few threats seriously. They'd have to question Alex and then he would know. I'd be in even more danger. I've thought about nothing else and this is the only way. I'll get away from here, make sure he never finds me again.'

Felicity hugged Beth.

'This weekend is fine by me. We've got to get you out of here before it's too late. I could never forgive myself if anything happened to you.'

'Thank you for believing me,' Beth said, her eyes full of tears.

Beth stayed in the forest long after she'd watched Felicity disappear back down the path to be swallowed up by the dense trees. Leaves rustled above her and she shivered. Was she doing the right thing? Trusting Felicity was huge, but she had to put her trust in someone. She'd considered Annabelle, also Sarah, but her gut was telling her Felicity. After all, it was Alex who'd put the doubt about Felicity in her mind, and Alex liked to play mind games. That wasn't straightforward Felicity's style.

If she was wrong, she'd soon find out.

THIRTY-SIX

ANONYMOUS

She thought back to six months ago. She'd groaned that day when the alarm went off. It was a whole hour earlier than usual but she wanted to get there first, watch them together without them knowing she was present. Although she'd slipped back into a routine with Alex, the illicit thrill she'd so relished in the early days when Beth was alive was becoming stale second time around, tainted by Felicity. The last few times she'd been round to his place, Felicity's toothbrush sat on the shelf next to his. She'd tried to talk to him about it, but he shut her down and refused to discuss it.

'You sound like Beth,' he'd told her more than once. The sight of a rogue toothbrush in the bathroom had brought tears to her eyes. She loved him so much; why wasn't she enough for him? The two of them had also taken to swimming earlier than usual, so that by the time they all rocked up they were often already out of the water and drinking tea from the red flask he'd shared with Beth. If it wasn't for the connection with Alex she'd have ditched the swimming group; she could swim alone and she'd never been particularly close to Felicity. Aside from swimming, Felicity had wildly different interests to her own – she liked to read and go for long walks. Lighten up, she'd wanted to tell her on so many occasions. Obviously she and Alex had shared work interests in common, but personality-wise Felicity was so staid compared to him. She couldn't imagine they had the same kind of postcoital conversations she enjoyed with him. Alex talked to her about how he wanted to make something of his life; his ambition was to build an impressive house with glass windows facing out to the sea, with its own swimming pool and hot tub. She was born to luxuriate in that hot tub, in her designer swimming costume, her lifestyle bankrolled by her husband. He also discussed how he was going to finance it; there was no way he would be sharing that information with Felicity.

The car park was almost empty; only three spaces were occupied, one of them by Alex's car. She parked in the space next to his and went to buy a ticket. Waiting for it to print, she looked down over the part of the beach they swam in. A lone male was in the water; she recognised Alex from the orange flash of his bathing cap. Excitement flickered inside her as it always did at the sight of him, even after all this time. He was the good-looking husband with the traditional film star charisma she'd dreamed of as a teenager. She scanned the beach but couldn't see Felicity. She hurried back to her car where she put the ticket on the dashboard and grabbed her bag. Gravel crunched under her feet as she crossed the car park, moving as fast as she could for the chance of some alone time with Alex in the water.

As she rounded the corner from the car park, a voice carried through the air, and she slowed down. On a bench looking down over the beach was Felicity. She was wearing a padded jacket and talking on her phone. Her back was to her, and she stayed where she was out of sight to listen to the call.

'It's working,' she was saying, and something about her tone of voice told her this was a call Felicity didn't want overheard.

'He's set the date for the wedding. I persuaded him to make it as soon as possible.' She listened to the person at the end of the line. 'Yes, that's exactly what I think. It won't be long now. We're going to pull it off.'

She was rooted to the spot, aghast at what she was hearing. Alex was marrying Felicity? He wouldn't go ahead once she told him about this conversation. It made her feel somewhat vindicated. Her gut had warned her there was something off about Felicity getting together with Alex; now she was proved right.

'I've got to go. He's getting out now, but I'll see you on Wednesday at eleven. Hang in there, it won't be long now.'

She waited five minutes before heading down to join them. Alex was drying himself off and Felicity was pouring him a drink from the flask. She was still wearing her coat.

'Hi, Miranda,' she said.

'Hi.' Miranda focused on Felicity, avoiding looking at Alex, who was rubbing his back with a towel. When she looked at him it was hard not to touch him. 'Not swimming today?'

'No, I've got a cold so I thought it best not to. Do you want some tea?'

'No thanks. I'll go straight in.'

'Hi,' Alex said, pulling on jeans and a jumper. He drained his cup. 'It's glorious out there today.' He sat down on a rock looking out towards the sea, closing his eyes and showing no trace of the awkwardness Miranda was feeling. She undressed quickly, grateful to already be wearing her costume, unusually self-conscious, and ran down to the sea. The water was fairly still and she swam breaststroke away from the beach then turned and headed back, watching Alex and Felicity, mulling over the snatched phone conversation she'd heard. Felicity had to be seeing someone behind Alex's back. He wouldn't like that. He was allowed to have affairs galore but he liked his women's focus to be on him. Miranda had mentioned going on a date once with a guy she'd met at a club and Alex had been insanely jealous. If he knew exactly what Felicity was up to behind his back he'd dump her, she was sure of that. She just needed more proof. When she got into work later she'd book Wednesday off and find out exactly what Felicity was up to.

On Wednesday morning Miranda was parked along the street from Felicity's home from seven in the morning. She was dressed practically for a drive in jeans, trainers and hooded jacket. A pair of heels and a smarter jacket were stashed in the boot so she was prepared for any eventuality. She was eating a chocolate croissant, watching Felicity's front door when she came out of her house just before nine o'clock and got into her car. Miranda dumped the half-eaten croissant on the passenger seat and brushed pastry flakes from her lap, before driving off behind Felicity. She really must get the car cleaned.

She was heading for the motorway going south. Miranda checked the petrol gauge, relieved she'd had the foresight to fill up the previous day. She'd been with Alex last night so knew Felicity had spent the night at home. She'd tried to ask him about his relationship with Felicity but he shut her down, insisting it was nothing more than a fling and changing the subject. An alarm was clanging in her head. Regarding the weekend, he said he was visiting his parents so wouldn't be available. Was he taking Felicity to meet his parents? Combined with the information she'd gleaned from Felicity's phone conversation, all the signs pointed to a marriage proposal. The thought made her feel cold all over. She had to stop this from happening. The last few weeks had solidified her feelings; she didn't want to be with anyone else and she no longer wanted to be the other woman. She wanted to be the first Mrs Maitland, settle down with Alex and have his babies.

Felicity was driving like an old lady, sticking to the slow

lane, rarely venturing above sixty. Going on drives with Alex was exhilarating, speeding round bends in his powerful car, the sunroof open. Miranda stretched out her back with frustration, wanting to put her foot down and get to wherever they were going and find out what Felicity was up to. Her wildest theory was that she wanted to avenge Beth's death and harm Alex, yet she didn't really think Felicity had it in her. More likely was her theory that she was after his money. Felicity wasn't materialistic but maybe she was in debt; that would explain it. How could she find out?

Alex had made no secret to Miranda that part of the reason he stayed with Beth was because she was due to inherit a large sum of money when her aunt died. Her aunt had been very ill shortly before Beth's death, and he'd persuaded the aunt to give him power of attorney while Beth was still alive, and had moved large sums of money to his own account, all with the aunt's blessing. She'd rather the money went to them than get used up on medical bills, and they needed money immediately rather than having to go through the inevitable delay of all the procedures they would need to go through after her death. She'd also given him a lump sum towards the house renovations. She was a sensible woman, and knew that she didn't have long left on earth. Thus, Alex was able to stay in the home he'd bought with Beth, and his financial issues were resolved. He'd hired the architect and the interior designer and his plan was taking shape. If Felicity were to marry Alex she would reap the benefits of everything he owned. Felicity lived a modest life and Miranda didn't imagine she would be earning a fortune as a lecturer. She certainly didn't lavish money on going out or clothes. Yes, debt was certainly looking likely.

A car was overtaking Miranda in the middle lane, sailing past Felicity and onwards. An exit sign appeared for the next town and Felicity indicated and put her brake lights on, as did the two cars between them. They'd been driving for over an hour and it wasn't a town Miranda knew. She kept her distance as they drove round a roundabout and joined a smaller country road. Not long after, Felicity indicated right and turned into a residential cul-de-sac with identical houses on either side. She parked the car and Miranda managed to find a spot slightly further down the road. She waited in the car, watching Felicity take a coat and scarf from the car boot before heading off down a path. She wouldn't be surprised if Felicity were to keep a folding chair in the boot and a pair of wellies. She was exactly that sort of person. Miranda kept the red beret in her sights. A park lay ahead of them and it looked like this was Felicity's destination. Miranda got out of the car. Sure enough, she went into the park and made her way over to a coffee van in the centre of the play area. She came out with two drinks and sat down at a table outside. Miranda was fizzing with anticipation at who Felicity might be meeting. She wandered around looking for the best place to observe her without being seen. Behind the van were some benches. She took a book out of her bag and sat facing Felicity's back. She was too far away to hear a conversation but she could keep her in sight. Felicity waved and Miranda saw a woman entering the area, a little girl holding her hand. She frowned. Had she got this all wrong? She'd anticipated a meeting of lovers. Something was off here. She lowered the book, her pulse picking up as the woman and child got closer, something stirring in her memory. Once they were close enough to see properly, Miranda thought she must be seeing a ghost.

The woman was Beth, who had supposedly drowned in the sea. What the hell was going on? She stared at the woman, her mind whirring. This new development was dynamite.

THIRTY-SEVEN

Seeing Beth alive was like having an electric shock. Miranda's arms were trembling as she hurried across to the small café just outside the park. She bought a pot of tea and took it to one of the tables outside so she could watch Felicity and Beth. The teapot knocked against the cup as she poured tea into it, the china rattling along with the tremor in her hand. Seeing the child had completely thrown her.

Felicity and Beth were walking slowly, deep in conversation. Beth was alive! Adrenalin flowed through Miranda; she was right to be suspicious about Felicity but never would she have imagined something like this. Alex couldn't know about Beth, could he? No, Miranda dismissed the idea. She was sure she was the only person who knew what his intentions to his wife had been.

The adrenalin was really pumping now; this was the ammunition she needed against Felicity. She had to play this right. Had Felicity known from the beginning Beth wasn't dead? Had she played a part in it? She was guilty of withholding evidence from the police if nothing else, and she doubted Beth would have known what Alex was planning.

The women were turning round now, heading back the way they came, walking like tortoises behind the little girl. Miranda lifted her phone and snapped some images, zooming in on the girl and also on Beth. She hurried back to her car and waited for them to reappear. After about ten minutes, Felicity's car pulled out of the car park, and a few minutes later Beth and the little girl emerged from the exit. The girl skipped ahead and went down the path of one of the houses in the cul-de-sac. Once they'd gone into the house Miranda drove slowly past, noting the door number and street name. She drove home in half the time it had taken to get there, enjoying the buzz of the motorway and her newfound knowledge. All she had to do now was decide what to do with it.

She took two days off work and drove over to the area she'd seen Beth in. The little girl, who looked to be about two, went to a preschool nearby, with Beth both taking and fetching her. The second time she saw them they walked past her car and she got a good look at the child in her mirror. Seeing her up close made Miranda feel sick; if only she could find out exactly how old she was.

She waited for hours outside the house that night, but nobody else walked down the front path, no husband returning from work through the neat square of grass and into Beth's arms. When she got home she opened the photos on her laptop and studied the features of the little girl again, the dark hair and deep-set eyes. All too familiar. There was no doubt about it. This little girl was Alex's daughter.

Had Alex known Beth was pregnant before she left him? Would he still have wanted to kill her? Did Beth know Alex had inherited all her aunt's money? Was Felicity plotting against Alex, in league with Beth, or what if Felicity was playing a blinder and dating Alex behind Beth's back? Felicity was an intelligent woman and Miranda would be wrong to underestimate her.

The possibilities were endless and it was impossible to stop going over it all. If only she could share the information, but the risk was too great. After much deliberation she reached a conclusion.

It was time to get Felicity away from Alex.

One month later, Miranda was sitting in the car, parked outside the house she'd identified as the one where Beth was living. Her every instinct was telling her she was right, and if she was, should she tell Alex?

Following Felicity had given her the biggest shock of her life. She'd uncovered a secret so explosive she'd been convinced it couldn't possibly be true. She'd taken it slowly, finding out as much as she could about this woman, needing to be absolutely sure. Alex had told her about the wedding, insisted it wouldn't change anything between them. Wait till he heard this.

A flash of red caught her attention. It was them. The two women and the little girl were walking down the street on the opposite side of the road. As they drew nearer, she leaned over her bag on the passenger seat and stayed there until she was sure they would have passed by. She looked back up in time to see Felicity holding the child's hand and waving from the doorstep as the woman Miranda had identified as going under the name of Suzie Hill, by asking a few questions outside the school gates, got into a car parked outside the house and drove off. So she trusted Felicity enough to leave her precious daughter with her. Miranda wouldn't. Felicity was double-crossing Alex, so why stop there? *Oh Suzie.*

Only she wasn't Suzie Hill. Suzie Hill was no other than Beth Curran, supposedly drowned three years ago, but in reality very much alive and in a town not so far away from East-sea, where she'd left all the people who loved her and made a mockery of them all. Especially of Alex.

The wedding was taking place in a week's time. Seven days to decide how to put a stop to these two women. She dialled a number.

'Alex, I need to see you. You'll never believe what I've found out...'

THIRTY-EIGHT

Miranda paid the taxi driver and checked her phone. Alex was expecting her at eight. He'd invited her for dinner so that she could share her news. Fireworks had been exploding in her head since she'd made up her mind to tell him. A lot depended on what he had to say.

He took the bottle of wine she offered as she hung her short fur jacket in the hall.

'Good choice,' he said. 'I've cooked some fish and roast vegetables. This will complement it nicely. Come into the kitchen.'

She sat at the island. Fish sounded manageable; she couldn't face anything too heavy. Her stomach had been delicate lately and she was nervous about what Alex was going to say. She had to challenge him about his relationship with Felicity and work out where he was at. Alex never drifted into anything; he always had a clear plan about everything in his life.

He opened the wine and poured out two glasses, joining her at the island. He'd knocked through the old living room wall and was building an extension on the back to make one enormous open-plan space. It was going to be stunning when finished. The kitchen island looked out over the sea, where lights were twinkling against the dark background. 'Dinner should be ready in about half an hour. Is everything alright? You look stressed.'

She drank some wine. 'I've found out something which is going to blow your mind.'

He laughed. 'Nothing is ever ordinary with you. That's what I love about you.'

'As much as you love Felicity?'

The smile vanished. 'It's different, you know that. Marrying her changes nothing between us.'

'Marrying her will be a big mistake. She isn't who you think she is.'

'Tell me.'

When she'd finished talking, his face had turned from white to red and back again. Then he stood up and threw his wine glass against the wall. The crack made Miranda flinch, her pulse racing. Red wine streaked the white paint and drops landed on the glass doors. He screamed obscenities at the wall before collapsing onto a chair.

'I knew something wasn't right, but Beth didn't have it in her to pull off something like that. I never for a minute suspected Felicity would do this to me. Why? Why would she?'

'That's what I wondered. She's got to be after the money. Is Felicity in debt?'

'No, but Beth would need money, wouldn't she, and her aunt gave everything to me. How would she manage for money? Or maybe her plan is to get Felicity to marry me and take my money that way. I can't believe I've been so stupid and that she got away with it. I wanted that body to be hers, it gave me closure.'

'There's more,' Miranda said. 'You'll need a drink for this.' She fetched a new glass and the bottle and poured them both a drink. She sat down, and put her hand over his. 'She has a daughter who looks just like you.'

Alex stared at her, his eyes filling with tears.

'You're serious?'

'Of course I am.' Her voice cracked with emotion. She'd debated for hours over whether to tell him, but knowing the extent of Felicity's deception was more important than revealing her desire to be the mother of his first child. She was building up to telling him that, and the time was not yet right. 'You're a father and those women have taken that from you.'

Alex crossed to the window, staring out into the darkness. When he next looked at Miranda, the tears were gone and his eyes were hard.

'What are you going to do?' she asked. 'You can't marry her.'

'Oh yes I can,' he said. 'I'll marry her and then I'll have her under my control. I'll ruin her and Beth and I'll get my daughter back. I should have listened to you all along.'

They clinked glasses and shared a passionate kiss.

'Let's eat,' he said. 'I'm suddenly starving.' He sorted out the food, leaving Miranda feeling overwhelmed. She hadn't expected him go ahead with the wedding. He handed her a plate. She stuck her knife into the fish and pressed down hard. As she cut it into little pieces she thought about Felicity.

THIRTY-NINE

THE WEDDING DAY

Felicity put the finishing touches to her makeup, then spun around to face Sarah.

'Will I do?'

'You look lovely. Let's have a toast.' She handed her a glass of champagne. 'To you and Alex and a wonderful day.'

They touched glasses. The bubbles made Felicity's nose fizz.

'It's so nice of you to come over. My mum offered but she's not entirely convinced I'm doing the right thing. It's happened too quickly for her liking.'

'That's what friends are for. She'll come round once she sees you together. You and Alex make a great couple.'

Felicity felt her cheeks flush. If Sarah knew the truth she'd be horrified. So much was riding on this wedding taking place; it was the only way for Beth to get her money back. Beth would be on tenterhooks right now, wondering what was happening and she doubted she'd get a moment to call her and put her mind at ease.

'Hamish used to worry there was something going on

between me and Alex when we first met him,' Sarah said. 'Did he ever tell you that?'

'No.' Felicity laughed.

'Good. He was with Beth then, but I wanted to make sure you didn't think I had an affair with him.'

'It never crossed my mind. Beth suspected he was seeing someone else but she didn't know who – at least she didn't tell me anyway. That's all in the past. I've made mistakes too, but at our age, we all have a history and dwelling on past relationships makes no sense.'

'Good to know he's been through his midlife crisis.' They both laughed.

An hour later she was hanging on to her mother's arm, sudden nerves making her hold on tight. What if there was a last-minute objection? It wasn't impossible. A cold sensation crept down Felicity's spine. Was she really going to get away with this? Classical music competed with the hum of conversation as she entered the registry office, material rustling and seats squeaking and groaning as heads turned and faces relaxed into smiles. The bride was here, no jilting at the altar or traffic disaster to put a spoke in the proceedings. Felicity smiled with relief as she spotted Hamish, Tania, her old school friend, an uncle, so many people she was fond of... and guilt gripped her chest. Then the tall man in a dark suit standing ahead of her turned around and she noted the small details, the expensive new suit, the hair trimmed shorter than usual showing off his excellent bone structure. His face lit up with a smile and a surge of an emotion it was hard to identify swept over her like a huge wave. Their eyes met and she held his gaze; his belief in her in this moment in time was crucial. No matter what.

The room went quiet and she stepped forward to marry Alex.

· · ·

A car honked outside and Miranda checked she had everything before heading out to the taxi. The registry office was only a fifteen-minute walk away but in these heels five was too much.

'Going to a wedding, love?' The cab driver asked as she got into the back of the car. She gave him a tight smile. Given that her destination was the registry office and she'd spent all morning getting ready, it didn't need a genius to work it out. The cab driver turned his attention to the road and she looked pointedly out of the window.

Tania waved to her as she got out of the cab. She looked radiant in a pale pink dress under a silk jacket. Miranda tipped the driver before crossing the road.

'Gorgeous shoes,' Tania said, 'but how are you going to manage on the beach?'

'I've got a flat pair in my bag.'

'Let's go in and get a good seat. There isn't much room in there. I doubt there will be a big crowd, given the circumstances. It must be a bit strange for him, but I'm so glad he's found someone else.'

'I still don't get what he sees in her. I hope he isn't on the rebound,' Miranda said. 'Felicity deserves better.'

'Opposites attract, I guess, but it makes sense, given they were both grieving for the same person. Beth would want them to be happy.'

If only she could tell Tania, thought Miranda, but it was important they kept the revelation about Beth to themselves. Since finding out about Beth she hadn't stopped mulling over what she and Felicity were up to. Was Beth right to trust Felicity? Alex would be in demand today so it was up to her to keep an eye on Felicity.

They slipped into two free seats at the end of the second row. Alex was already inside, wearing a suit Miranda had helped him choose.

'The colour brings out your eyes,' she'd told him. 'Not that I want you making an effort for her.'

'You know that's not what this is about.'

If only she could be sure.

Looking around, she counted about thirty people. Aside from the swimmers she knew none of them. To think she knew him far better than anyone else here. Alex was scanning the crowd and his eyes lingered on hers for a moment. She looked away. She had to be so careful not to ruin what they had.

A murmur ran through the crowd and she turned along with everyone else to see Felicity in the doorway, a woman in a grey suit holding her arm. She looked like an older version of her daughter, even down to the glasses. Felicity was wearing a blue knee-length dress with three-quarter-length sleeves. Her glasses were gold-rimmed, matching her simple gold necklace and bracelet. Alex preferred Miranda in a dress, preferably one he could peel off easily. Felicity's mother escorted her to the front of the room, one hand on her back. Miranda noticed with satisfaction the dress had many small pearl buttons with those catches that took forever to undo. She wouldn't be slipping out of that in a hurry.

When they were saying their vows, Miranda sat on her hands to stop herself getting up and declaring the whole ceremony a farce. Imagine how the reaction of the crowd would change if they knew why he was marrying this woman – not for love in the traditional sense. While everyone clapped and cheered when they exchanged a kiss, Miranda looked away. It was like one of those ceremonies on *Married at First Sight*, everyone trying to convince themselves it was going to be a success while knowing the chances of it succeeding were slim indeed.

It was a relief to be back out in the fresh air again. A friend of Alex's was taking photos and once that chore was over, they all headed off to the hotel for a meal.

'Felicity scrubs up well,' Tania said as they walked the short distance to the hotel. 'I've rarely seen her out of her swimming gear. I still can't get my head around them planning this swim later.'

'I can. They want to exorcise a ghost. It's understandable. You're still up for it, aren't you?'

'Yes, as long as you are.'

If she was going to tell Tania about Beth, now would be the right time but she swallowed down the words on the tip of her tongue. She couldn't risk anything going wrong.

'We can keep an eye on them, make sure they don't drink too much or go out too far.'

'This is Alex we're talking about. I bet he won't let Felicity out of his sight. He's such a strong swimmer and he's not a big drinker.'

'True, the man treats his body like a temple.'

The rest of the day passed quickly. The meal dragged out over several hours after which everyone moved to the back lounge, which had been hired for the occasion. The large glass doors slid back to reveal tables and chairs on the decking area that led straight down to the beach. It was a different part of the beach from the bay they usually swam in and stepping off the decking would mean sinking straight down into the sand. Miranda changed into her sandals and put her shoes in her bag. The bar was free and she planned to stick to soft drinks from now on. She needed to keep sober to make sure she didn't let anything slip.

Every time she looked for him, he was in a different place, talking to a new group of people. When he was at the bar talking to Felicity's mother, she walked over and stood behind them, touching Alex lightly on the arm. He turned round, giving her a cautious smile.

'Two gin and tonics,' the barman said.

Felicity's mum took the drinks. 'I'll see you later, Alex,' she said, smiling. 'Son-in-law.'

Miranda slipped into her spot at the bar.

'Now you're saddled with a set of in-laws,' she said.

'What are you having?' Alex asked.

'Diet Coke.'

'Not drinking?' He frowned. 'Why ever not?' He glanced quickly around. Most people were outside. 'I thought you would be enjoying yourself.' He lowered his voice. 'Nothing's changed about our little arrangement.'

How could he be so obtuse? No matter what 'little arrangement' they had come to, no matter that she understood his reasons, knowing he was married to another woman gave her a stabbing pain in her chest.

'Alex,' a voice interrupted them from behind. 'Congratulations, mate, I've been trying to catch up with you all night.'

Alex turned and slapped the tall man addressing him on the back.

'What can I say? I'm in demand. How are you? Having fun? I spoke to your better half earlier.'

Miranda slipped away, taking her drink to the edge of the dance floor. It was eleven-thirty. She stood to one side and watched people dancing and chatting. An old disco anthem was playing. Tania poked her in the ribs.

'Look to your left,' she said, 'Alex's aunt.'

A middle-aged woman in a tight red dress was belting out the song at the top of her voice and waving her arms in the air. Alex's uncle was shuffling from one foot to another, a pint of beer held out in front of him. The dress was straining at the seams and Tania mimed it popping, laughing hysterically. Her infectious laugh combined with nerves made Miranda giggle. Tania grabbed her arm and neither of them could stop. Pent-up tension burst out of Miranda as tears filled her eyes.

'Hey!' Caroline was in front of them. 'It's getting on for midnight if you're swimming.' Tania was biting her lip, trying to stop laughing. 'If you're drunk then I don't advise it.'

'No.' Tania wiped her eyes. 'We're just enjoying ourselves. Come on, Miranda.'

'Anyone else swimming,' Caroline shouted. The elderly uncle came over, still clutching his pint.

'This is a stupid idea,' he said. 'I've told Alex this is madness. You've all been drinking, and...'

'Trust me, Uncle Brian.' Caroline patted his arm. 'We know what we're doing. I wouldn't let Aunty Teresa join in though.' She gestured towards the woman in the red dress and Tania started giggling again. Miranda pulled her over towards the beach where Alex was already down to his swimming trunks. Felicity was changing underneath her swimming robe. Miranda looked away.

'Come on,' Tania said, 'I want to get this over with. We must be mad. I can't believe Felicity has brought that bloody flask. Do you think she's brought sandwiches too? She's going to make such a good housewife.' Miranda looked over to see Felicity holding the flask.

They changed quickly under their robes, shivering and stumbling as they pulled their costumes on.

'Are you sure this is a good idea?' Caroline asked. She was wearing a white bathing cap with pink flowers on. Tania snorted when she saw it.

'Honestly, you two. Hey, they're off.'

Miranda looked up to see Alex draining the flask, then dropping it into a bag. 'Alex,' she called, suddenly wanting to stop him, but the wind carried her voice away.

Alex turned and flashed them a grin, taking his bride's hand and running towards the sea.

'Catch me.' He dropped Felicity's hand, raised his hands to

the sky, palms together as if in prayer, and dived into the approaching wave. He sliced through the sea.

Felicity had done it. She'd beaten her to become Alex's wife.

Felicity followed Alex into the water, her hand tingling from the pressure of his palm in hers. She wondered how Beth was feeling – not how she'd told Felicity she was feeling, but how she was *really* feeling. After all, she'd been engaged to Alex not so long ago and she'd never got to marry him. She'd left, knowing she was carrying his child and neither of them would ever see him again. Felicity remembered these thoughts, several hours later, when the wedding guests gathered in clusters on the beach, not because they'd been summoned there by the photographer for a group photoshoot, but because the groom hadn't returned from the sea. Anxious eyes peered in vain out to the horizon, desperately scanning the darkness where spotting Alex was as likely as seeing what sea creatures swam deep in the seabed. A frantic energy hovered in the air, as each person imagined a different scenario for why the strongest swimmer amongst them hadn't swum back to shore, body glistening with sea droplets, an aura of wellbeing after a cold swim visible in his face.

Felicity mulled over these thoughts as Alex's elderly aunt Margaret was the only one to voice what few dared to imagine. Whether in a moment of lucidity plucked from her muddled mind, or whether from confusion.

'Where's Alex? Has he drowned?' Caroline rushed to appease her, to lead her inside and fetch her some water, to stop her asking the question that hours later would be on everyone's lips.

Where is Alex?

FORTY

PRESENT

Felicity had taken the risk of calling Beth and arranging to meet her. The detective bringing up Suzie's name had changed everything, throwing it in at the last moment as if it were insignificant. Did they think she was stupid? Questioning her about Alex and Beth's relationship and whether it was really happy, and why she'd married him. She'd got away with it on this occasion, but it was only a matter of time before they were onto what she had done. She had to convince them she had fallen in love with Alex.

The police would find out. Once they started digging into Beth and what happened to her, the game would be up. She looked into the rear-view mirror, a move she'd done so often during this journey it was almost a twitch. The road behind was empty, as it had been for most of the drive. She wasn't being followed. Yet she wasn't imagining the change in the attitudes of the police during the last interview. Her position had changed from grieving victim to potential suspect. Right at this moment she felt powerless to stop the storm that was heading towards her.

She waited on a wooden bench, facing the direction Beth

would arrive from. She wore the old red beret she'd worn for years. She hadn't changed; it was Beth who had taken measures to change her name and disguise herself. They'd agreed rarely to see one another; it wasn't worth the risk.

A woman got out of her car in the nearby car park and bent down over a small child, pulling a woolly hat onto her head. She took the girl's hand and walked towards her across the sand. Felicity stood up when they were a foot away, recognising Beth, although she still wasn't used to her new hair colour. Felicity crouched down in front of Rosie. Seeing her face again stopped her breath in her throat. She was the image of her father and it was like resurrecting his ghost. She composed herself, so as not to alarm the little girl.

They'd barely spoken these past three and a bit years. It was too risky. The few snatched conversations they'd had were focused on essential matters only. She looked back at Rosie, uncannily like her father to look at.

'We can walk on the sand,' Beth said to Rosie, who was tugging her hand, 'but we're not going in the water, darling.'

Rosie skipped ahead of them on the beach, which was more pebble than sand. The ground crunched as they walked.

'It's so good to see you,' Felicity said, 'and to meet her again. How are you bearing up?'

'I hadn't expected it to affect me so much. I can't believe he's not here anymore.' Beth kept Rosie in her sights as she ran ahead of them, stopping regularly to examine shells.

'That must be a good feeling, right?'

'Good isn't how I'd describe it. It's... complicated. Who would have murdered Alex? Have the police given any idea who their suspects are?'

'Apart from me? They wouldn't tell me.'

'That's normal. You mustn't worry. They want to rule you out. I've watched enough crime shows to know those closest to the victim will automatically be suspects.'

'Hard to think of Alex as a victim.'

'How are his parents?'

'Devastated. His mother collapsed. They'll be leaving soon but Caroline is staying with me.'

'Is that a good idea? She's the one I thought most likely to suss me out.'

Felicity shook her head. 'She doesn't know anything. She's upset and she's angry.'

'She's always been close to Alex.'

'She's grieving, as are we all in our different ways.'

Beth sighed. 'I always thought I'd be euphoric after the wedding, that we'd finally done it after all this time.'

'I know, same here. After so long and such careful planning. We need to hold out for a bit longer. It's natural to worry we won't pull it off.'

'I guess it could be a good thing, as attention is taken away from the actual wedding.'

Felicity stopped walking. Close up, Beth's face looked as strained as she felt. 'I'm worried it's the opposite. Alex's family are kicking up a stink about his death, saying he would never have drowned.'

'I might have guessed. His dad likes to take charge.'

'Must be where Alex got his controlling side from.'

They walked in silence for a moment. 'Even without his dad making a fuss, the police would be investigating, but reading between the lines I think the police are suspicious about how he died. When they questioned me they asked lots of questions about his flask. Who drank from it before the swim.'

'Not that old red flask?'

Felicity nodded. 'Alex always drank tea before his swim. Earl Grey, with a dash of milk. And after.'

'You don't have to tell me.'

Their eyes met and Felicity recognised fear. She touched her arm. 'Don't let it upset you. You're safe from him now.'

Beth looked out to sea. Felicity thought how funny it was to think Alex's life had carried on following the same old routines while everything in Beth's had been completely over-turned. They watched Rosie singing to herself as she drew pictures in the sand with a stick. Beth took Felicity's arm.

'She makes everything worthwhile. I wouldn't change anything we've done. Anyway, I've had it easy compared to you. I wasn't sure you'd be able to pull it off, faking your relationship with Alex to allow me to escape. I can't ever repay you for that. Was it horrendous?'

'No. Any time I wavered I pictured my cousin, what she'd been through.' Her cousin was the reason she'd offered to help Beth by marrying Alex, then divorce him and get back the house and the money – everything that was rightfully Beth's. She'd previously told Beth how her cousin had nearly died at the hands of her abusive husband, and the trauma she and the whole family had gone through trying to help her. At first Felicity had found it difficult to understand why, when her husband hurt her enough to require a hospital visit on numerous occasions, she always went back to him. The turning point had been when the children were threatened with violence; only then had her cousin been able to walk away. Her once vivacious cousin barely left the house, terrified that her former partner would find her again. Felicity had seen the early warning signs with Beth and had determined she would never let that happen to another woman again. By helping Beth she would be saving her before it was too late.

If Alex hadn't been a friend, she couldn't have gone through with it. She liked him, despite everything, which was why she'd been better able to understand Beth's bond with him in a way she hadn't initially with her cousin. He was a personable colleague and she felt comfortable in his presence. Liking him had made it easier but hadn't detracted from her determination to get justice for Beth. Their easy relationship had developed naturally; he was an attractive man and spending time with him was fun. As weeks became months, she'd found it hard to keep up the pretence, but in those moments she thought about Beth, and her broken cousin and the lies Alex had told about Beth that she'd nearly fallen for. Her resolve strengthened. She'd take herself off for long solitary walks to give herself a pep talk and fortify her strength. Having the wedding date set made it easier, as it gave her an end point. Being single suited Felicity, and she had longed to get back to it. Being a murder suspect had not been part of the equation.

Felicity was weak. The truth was, if Alex hadn't died, would she have been capable of going through with their plan? An image of the bloated body on the beach flashed again before her, and she curled her fists in her pockets, willing the pain to go away. How weak Beth would think her for wavering. But Alex was a human being, after all.

'Look!' Rosie was running towards her, her face open, happy and full of childish wonder at the shell she held outstretched. If she'd had a child with Alex, would she have had a little girl or boy who might look just like the one in front of her? She closed the thought down.

Of course she would have gone ahead as planned.

They continued the walk. Rosie ran back a few more times to show them the shells gripped in her muddy hands, insisting Beth keep them in her pocket. The shells rattled gently as they walked, her arm rubbing against Felicity's. Being back with Beth was so natural.

Beth's phone rang and she had a brief conversation.

'Thanks for letting me know, I'll be along as soon as I can. The chemist,' she said to Felicity, looking at her watch. 'That's bad timing. I've got something to collect but I need to feed Rosie before she goes to her swimming class. The chemist is in the opposite direction.'

'I could take Rosie and get her some food and meet you back

at yours. Or I could feed her at your house, whatever you prefer.'

'Would you? That would be a big help. She gets grumpy if she doesn't eat regularly.'

'Of course. You're OK, aren't you? The prescription?'

'Yes. My sleeping tablets. I haven't needed any for ages, but since finding out about Alex the nightmares have started again. I'm hopeless if I don't get a good night's sleep and I need to be on top of my game. In case... you know. Oh Felicity, I'm so scared they're going to find me. Have the police said anything else about what they think?'

'They're asking about his rumoured affair when you guys were together, who it might have been with. Other than that they won't tell me anything. I'm finding sleep difficult too, not helped by Caroline. I'll be relieved when she's gone, she's so full on. I need space to think and it's impossible with her clomping up and down the stairs, ranting about the police not doing their job properly. It's fair enough that she's angry but it's upsetting. I'm finding this harder than expected.'

'You aren't regretting it, are you?'

She could read the fear on Beth's face.

'Of course not. It was the only way. I would never let you down.'

FORTY-ONE

Beth took one last look at Felicity and Rosie, who were waving from the doorstep. Felicity had been mesmerised by Rosie. Her likeness to Alex was striking, but Beth could see beyond the father to the individual she was and had learned to ignore it. As a mother she often watched Rosie in awe, that she could have created this special little person. Felicity had been watching her in the same way. Did Felicity want children? It wasn't a subject they'd ever discussed. Felicity loved her single life, which was why what she'd offered to do for Beth had been so incredible.

She thought back to the moment when Felicity had outlined her plan, that extraordinary suggestion that she was willing to risk everything for Beth. Her cousin had been the victim of an abusive marriage, she'd revealed, and she'd sworn never to sit by and let that happen again. Alex was restricting Beth's life and if she didn't escape now, it might be too late. She was sick of reading headlines about domestic violence and inno-cent women becoming grim statistics.

Beth had been stunned. That Felicity would buy her freedom to help Beth escape was incredible. That she would be willing to pursue Alex herself, with the sole aim of getting

Beth's money back was incredible. Initially the doubts had been there, but she'd seized the opportunity to get away, and Felicity had appeared true to her word. She'd stuck by Beth, aiding her in her transformation into Suzie Hill. It was only later that doubts crept in. Why would Felicity marry a known abuser, given her feelings of revulsion for such men?

She allowed herself to think through the thought she'd shut down several times recently. They'd always known Felicity would have to wait a reasonable amount of time before she could risk divorce proceedings, and that was by no means a dead cert. Alex could have refused; any number of obstacles stood in their way. Getting back what she rightfully deserved was always going to take time.

They'd waited three years already, Felicity taking her time with the relationship until Alex was ready.

What if Felicity had decided to hurry proceedings along by getting rid of him? She gripped the steering wheel. She'd proved to Beth countless times she was single-minded, once decided on a course of action, and that she thought Alex deserved punishing. Alex's death would mean she could get her hands on the money sooner. She'd never before doubted that Felicity would give her what was rightfully hers, but what if she was being naive?

Cold sweat broke out over her back, and she turned the heating up further. One part of her was telling her Felicity was a loyal friend who would risk everything for a woman in trouble, while the other part was screaming at her that a woman who could seduce a man she didn't love no matter how good the reason behind it was a woman who would do anything. What if she had lied about everything? Was Beth being gullible, being played by her friend? What if Felicity had been the one having the affair Beth had known was happening?

'No.' She spoke aloud, taking deep breaths. But she had to stay with this thought. She'd left her daughter with this woman who was capable of incredible deception. Her heart thumped in her chest and she swung the car round, narrowly missing an oncoming motorbike. Her daughter could be in danger. She stepped on the accelerator.

She jumped out of the car, not bothering with the lock and raced down the path. Her keys slid from her fumbling fingers and she swore, gripping them hard to steady her hand enough to open the door.

'Mummy!' Rosie ran into the hall and threw herself at her, followed by Felicity, who was holding a teddy bear.

'That was quick,' Felicity said. 'We've only just started our game, haven't we, Rosie? Did you get what you wanted?'

'The chemist was shut,' Beth said.

'That's a shame. She's adorable, isn't she? Such a bundle of energy. I'm exhausted already. I don't think I could handle being a mother full time.'

Heat rushed to Beth's face. How could she have got it so wrong?

Felicity left shortly after.

'We have to hang on in there,' she said, hugging Beth on the doorstep. 'Seeing you today has made me realise what we've been missing; not seeing you has been hard and I don't know how soon we'll be able to do this again. It depends on the investigation.'

'I feel sick thinking about it. If they find out what we've done I might go to prison. I can't bear to leave Rosie, I won't.'

'I'll do my best,' Felicity said. They hugged. Felicity's phone rang. 'It's the police.'

'Answer it,' Beth said. Felicity spoke briefly.

'OK. When?' She ended the call, her face pale. 'They want to interview me again. As soon as I can get there.'

FORTY-TWO

'Are you comfortable?'

Rosie looked at her with an air of confusion, her eyelids slowly drooping.

'You have a sleep, darling.'

Beth started the car, relieved that within minutes Rosie would be fast asleep, lulled by the rhythm of the car. Breaking her routine wasn't ideal, but she felt compelled to go back to Eastsea, to see where it had happened. A sense of urgency compelled her now that Felicity was being questioned again. How long before they were found out?

If Felicity knew what she was doing, would she try and stop her? She hadn't said a great deal when she'd called her earlier but she'd wanted to keep the call short. No wonder, if she was being questioned by the police. The partner was always the first suspect in a murder case. Murder? Was that what had happened to Alex?

She cranked the heating up in the car; she was still cold and when had she last eaten? Food hadn't been her priority today.

It was rush hour and there was a stream of traffic making

slow progress down the main coastal road. Waiting at a red light, she looked at the other drivers, wishing for a green light and wondered about their lives. Were they normal people, going about their business, or did everyone lead lives as complicated as hers? She knew the answer. For this to happen on the wedding day, the day that had been their goalpost for the past year, was incomprehensible. The woman in the car next to her smiled, and she realised she'd been staring. She gave a robotic smile in return. She had to focus, work out what she was going to say. Was she really going to do this?

She wouldn't use the sat nav. Police could track everything these days. Already, she was thinking like a criminal yet this crime was nothing to do with her. Once she was on the main road she was able to drive on autopilot. Despite having made this journey only once recently the road was all too familiar.

'Suzie Hill?' The ring startled her as she was so focused on the road ahead. She pressed the dashboard to answer the call.

'Yes.'

The caller was male, not a voice she recognised.

'I'm Detective Inspector Gregory. I'd like to ask you a few questions.'

Her stomach lurched. 'What is it to do with?'

'I'd like to talk to you about your relationship with Felicity Maitland. You may know her as Felicity Harrison. She married very recently.'

'Oh yes. What do you want to know?'

'I'd prefer to do this in person. Where are you?'

'I'm in my car. Going home. I live in Chenton.'

'Could you come to Eastsea main station please? Tomorrow morning. I'll expect you at ten.'

. . .

The emergency vehicle that came up behind her, sirens blaring and blue light flashing, caused her to swerve the car, her stomach aflutter. Her pulse raced and she collapsed with relief when an ambulance soared past. If the police were tracking her car they would know she was lying. She shook her head. She was overthinking. It would be a routine call because she was one of Felicity's phone contacts. That was all. Otherwise it would have been more urgent and they'd be coming to get her. She glanced back at Rosie. The sudden noise and lights outside hadn't disturbed her, her lips parting as she breathed out. Everything she had done was worth it for her daughter.

Once she came off the motorway and the sea appeared to her left, she loosened her grip on the steering wheel, wiggling the tension out of her shoulders. She turned off when she saw a sign for a roadside café, a dingy yellow light signalling that it was still open. She bought a cup of tea and a carton of milk, before driving the rest of the distance to her destination.

Rosie opened her eyes when she was wrestling the car seat out, before crossing the shingly beach. The heat from the disposable cup burned through her cold fingers. The beach was empty save for a lone dog walker, and she sat on a wall of rock and looked out at the expanse of water. The tide was in and spray from the waves splashed her. The salty taste on her lips sent her back in time. Living near the coast and swimming every morning, tension easing away as she slid under the water. These days, the closest she got to a swim was taking Rosie to the local baths, which she'd been doing since she was a baby. Beth knew how important it was to learn how to swim. Rosie had taken to it like she'd known she would; it was in her genes after all. Rosie, her water baby. Tears filled her eyes; she loved her daughter so much.

The dog walker had gone without her noticing, and she looked around the deserted beach, then out to the water. She imagined Alex. Who hated him more than she did? Had another woman found out what horrors lay beneath that friendly exterior?

The spare blanket in the car would serve as a towel – it wouldn't be the first time a lack of a towel or a costume hadn't stopped her from taking a swim. She went back to the car and fetched the blanket, found a spot where she could seclude Rosie from the wind and keep her sheltered from the sight of anyone walking along the sea front. A few minutes later she was stripped to her underwear and ducking under the waves, swimming, the cold water exhilarating as she'd known it would be, keeping her eyes fixed on Rosie. Ahead the twinkling lights of the coastline beckoned. She thought again of Alex, imagining his strong arms ploughing through the water, the neat way he swam with barely any splashing, his long legs and arms powering him forward. What had happened to him out there? Did he know he was drowning when it happened? He would have been as surprised as everyone else was. Had he thought he was having a heart attack or some other unexpected health issue, far more likely than a poisoning, or had he known the irony? After all, he'd tried and failed to do the same to her. He was doing something he loved; that would be of some comfort to his family, possibly, when they were able to emerge from the shock and the awful reality had sunk in.

It hadn't sunk in for Beth. She was getting cold. She longed to swim until her arms grew tired, but with Rosie here it would be reckless and out of the question. The current was strong. Alex was such a physically powerful man, and while it was hard to contemplate the reality of death at any time, this had hit her like the slap of a massive wave on her naked skin because of the profound effect he'd had on her life for so long. Once upon a time she used to imagine how she would feel if he were to suddenly disappear; she'd imagined she'd feel free. No matter how hard she'd willed it to happen in reality she couldn't envisage how her life would look without him. Even when he was physically far away his presence lingered. After all, he'd wanted to kill her.

The sea was colder now, her arms tired from swimming back and forth. The white building in the distance was a pub. She could make it out now. It was not dissimilar to the one she'd planned to get married in, and a cold tremor swept through her body. She focused on her breathing and getting back to the shore. She had to go back and face up to what she had done.

Alex was dead yet he'd never felt more alive.

Would she ever be free?

It was early evening. Beth pulled her clothes back on and cuddled Rosie to her, giving her some milk in a plastic cup. The wind had picked up, but the wall of rocks sheltered them from the worst. Rosie drank her milk contentedly, jumping when Beth's phone rang, before going back to it. It was Felicity. She watched her name flashing on the screen. She didn't pick up. She no longer knew who to trust.

She welcomed the darkening sky as it added another barrier to her being spotted. The chances of anyone she knew being around here were slim but taking precautions was second nature to her after all this time. She knew where the body had been washed up – still impossible to accept that it was Alex – so she climbed the steps up to the clifftop where she had a view over the rest of the bay. She paused at the top, bending over to catch her breath and when she straightened up, her eyes landed on her old home, just visible across the rooftops away from the sea. She caught her breath and thought of the woman she used to know. She was long gone. Swallowing hard, she turned away towards the bay, settling on the area popular with swimmers. A flash of white stood out against the muted colours of the bay; something fluttered in the wind. It took a moment for her eyes to adjust, and her brain to comprehend that she was looking at the remnants of the police tape, one end still tied to a post, the other being buffeted by the wind. Here was the spot where Alex had lain.

FORTY-THREE

'You look done in. Come and sit down.'

Caroline ushered Felicity into a chair and fetched a large glass of water, standing over her while she drank it. 'How did you get on?'

'I'm exhausted. The police confirmed Alex had a long-term lover. Did you know?'

'No, and I told them that when they asked.'

'They've found out who it was. Miranda, from swimming.'

'The redhead?' Caroline sat down. 'I had no idea. How do you feel?'

'Numb. Stunned. I need a drink.'

'Coming up.' Caroline fetched a bottle of wine from the fridge. 'Will this do?'

Felicity nodded.

'They must have a reason for telling you.' She frowned. 'Is she a suspect?'

'I don't know, they wouldn't tell me. They were most interested in whether I knew and how I felt about it. They could see I was in shock. I still am. They asked a lot of other questions.'

'What about?'

'Mostly they were asking about the flask he drank from.'

'So it was the murder weapon?'

'It looks that way. It's all so surreal. I still can't believe this is happening.'

'Believe me, it is. They've asked to speak to us before we leave. Being here is making Mum worse so we're going home today. I'm going to stay with them so I can look after her. I appreciate you letting me stay. I'm collecting my stuff now and then I'll be off.'

Felicity stayed in the kitchen while Caroline thudded about upstairs. Having the house to herself again would be a blessing. She had been exhausted after the police grilling, but it had been the revelation about Alex's mistress that had left her feeling stunned.

Beth had suspected Alex was having an affair. Their affair had been over a long time ago. Or so they had thought. If the police were right then the affair had carried on while she'd been seeing him.

Alex had been preoccupied over the last few weeks, which she'd put down to wedding jitters, plus it was bound to bring up memories of Beth and what happened to her. When he'd first brought up the idea of a swim, she'd thought it was a big mistake, but she'd come round to understanding that it was a way for him to exorcise Beth's ghost. Had he been seeing Miranda all this time? Her own attention had been focused on the wedding and whether she'd manage to pull this off for Beth.

Her phone buzzed with a text. Felicity sighed. Her friends meant well but these constant messages were draining. The only person she wanted to talk to right now was Beth. But what if Beth had double-crossed her; could she have killed Alex? Her head pounded. Was Beth texting now? She picked up her phone. The text was from Miranda. Felicity glared at the screen, her heart thumping in her chest.

How did it go at the police station?

She would play along with Miranda's game. She was onto her now and so were the police.

Not good. They think he was murdered and I'm their prime suspect. I'm convinced I'm about to be arrested.

That's crazy.

Felicity grabbed her coat and ran upstairs. Letting Miranda think she was about to be charged might make her talk more freely.

'Caroline, I've got to go out.' Caroline came out of the bathroom holding her toothbrush. They hugged.

'Keep me posted,' Caroline said. 'I'll post the key back through the letter box.'

Felicity sat in her car and phoned Beth.

'We need to talk.'

'Already?'

'Yes, something's come up since I saw you. But not on the phone. Where are you?' A crashing sound was in the background.

'It's the wind. I'm here in Eastsea, on the beach.'

'You're here. What are you doing there?'

She hesitated. 'I wanted to see for myself where he died. Where are you?'

'At home. I was at the police station for hours.'

'That doesn't sound good.'

'I know.' Felicity sounded exhausted. 'I've got news. Can you meet me in the seating area on the cliff? It's sheltered up there. I'll be there in about twenty minutes. And Beth, be careful.'

She revved up the car and indicated. A car parked further down the road pulled out behind her.

FORTY-FOUR

'Beth?'

Beth jumped. The concrete shelter masked sound even without the wind whistling around it. Rosie was asleep again in her pushchair, wrapped up warm and with a contented look on her face. Beth could watch her for hours. She stood up at the sound of Felicity's voice. They hugged each other, holding the moment. Felicity spotted Rosie.

'She's so adorable.'

'I'm terrified for her. The police rang me earlier. They want me to come into the station tomorrow. I said I was at home, to give me more time. They called me Suzie Hill, so maybe they don't know about me.'

Felicity sighed. 'They asked me to go over what happened the day you went missing. I told them exactly what I told them last time.'

'Do you think they suspect?'

'They asked me about Suzie again, they were digging more, this time.'

'Oh no. They must know. I'll take the blame, but I'm terrified for Rosie. I can't be parted from her.'

'I said Suzie was an old friend from university. They don't give anything away. I thought they were going to keep me in overnight, but they haven't charged me with anything. It must be a tactic, to wear me down.'

'Don't let them. You haven't done anything.' As she said the words, doubt resurfaced, a wriggling worm that wouldn't keep still. She couldn't know for sure Felicity wasn't involved. She'd married Alex to get back at him, after all. Had he shown her his abusive side too? What if she'd taken it one step further?

'Beth?' She'd lapsed into thought, forgetting Felicity. 'You believe me, don't you?'

This was Felicity, who'd risked so much for her.

'Yes, of course I do.'

'There's been another development. The police told me who Alex's mistress was.'

Beth closed her eyes. 'Tell me.'

'It was Miranda.'

They sat in silence.

'Did you ever suspect it was Miranda?'

'I had no idea. I wondered about Sarah.'

'I knew it wasn't Sarah. I think he carried on seeing Miranda right up until his death.'

'No way.'

Beth got to her feet and looked out across the bay. It was a sheer drop below to the beach, down to the spot she'd sheltered in earlier.

She stared out to sea, processing this news. She'd liked Miranda, she was fun to be with, but she'd only ever seen her at swimming. She was younger than them, a vibrant woman with striking looks. She'd been right about him, when he made her feel so pathetic for suspecting him.

'It makes me feel less guilty about what we've done. Marriage obviously meant nothing to him,' Felicity said.

'Why would they tell you?'
'Because Miranda has confessed.'

FORTY-FIVE

PAST

Miranda sat in her car watching the house. The windscreen wipers were moving from side to side but the rain showed no sign of letting up. Two months had passed since Beth's death and Alex was still being cautious. Overly cautious. She switched the radio on. Two presenters were talking about how much they were looking forward to the summer, sick of the long spell of bad weather throughout the country. She switched the radio off. She was sick of waiting too, waiting for her new life to start. Her eyes followed the movement of the wipers, a headache forming behind her eyes. She couldn't see out and her side windows were steamed up. She wiped her hand over the window and peered at Alex's house. Had he spotted her sitting outside? It wasn't the first time she'd done it. She could win a memory game based on the various gnomes displayed in the house next door's garden, it had been that long.

Alex was taking this too far. Two months was a decent amount of time for him to grieve. She'd heard of plenty of people waiting less time to hook up again after a bereavement. It was natural; humans needed company. She sighed. Most of those people wouldn't have anything to hide; she understood the need for caution but the urge to resume their relationship was a physical ache for her. Surely he must feel the same?

He was reading her messages. Each one received two reassuring ticks shortly after delivery, but he never replied. No matter how much she reminded herself that he'd told her this would be the way they'd play it, anxiety was torturing her. She'd lost ten pounds since their last meeting. *Meeting.* That made it sound as if they were in some kind of business partnership. Obviously she didn't want to jeopardise his freedom, that's why he was doing this, but enough was enough. She was going in.

She checked her hair and makeup in the driver mirror. She'd spent ages getting ready, strategically applying concealer and highlighter to hide the pallor of her skin and bring out some colour. Alex was used to her being bright and perky. She reapplied her lip gloss, smacking her lips together. *Let's do this!* She pushed the car door and opened her umbrella before she got out when a familiar voice caused her to pause mid-movement. Her heart beat a little harder, recognising Alex's tone. She stood up, angling the umbrella to mask her face, while enabling her to see his front door where the voices were coming from. He was standing on his doorstep, sheltered in the porch, saying goodbye to a woman wearing a raincoat. She'd wait for the woman to leave before she went in – she wasn't that stupid; even if she didn't know the woman, she wouldn't go out of her way to be seen. They could still conduct their relationship in secret, if that's what Alex wanted. She reached back into the car to get her bag and when she stood up again she saw Alex had his arms around the woman and was kissing her passionately. She grabbed the car door to steady herself, her heart thumping. *What on earth?* Her hand shook as she attempted to manoeuvre the umbrella to hide her face as she slid back into the car seat, closing the door gently to avoid making a sound, although she'd rather have slammed it with rage. How dare he? While she was waiting to save his face he'd been getting it on with someone else. Had he forgotten what she could do to him? Rain dripped from her coat onto the seat and she watched through the drop-spattered windscreen as the woman closed the garden gate, turning back to wave before walking off. Miranda waited until Alex had closed the door before starting the ignition. She drove slowly, letting the windscreen wipers clear the screen and cruised along beside the woman, who was walking briskly down the street. As she drove past her, she glanced to the side to see what her competition looked like. The shock made her lose control of the steering wheel. The car swerved to the left and she wrenched the steering wheel back to straighten the car, and pressed her back against the seat to steady herself. Her heart was thudding. It was Felicity.

A car behind her honked its horn. She snapped out of her daze and pulled over to the side of the road, letting the frus-trated car owner behind her drive off. She ignored the driver, who was mouthing something at her. She turned the car round and drove back to Alex's, not bothering with the umbrella this time and slamming the car door as hard as she could. She held her finger on the bell until Alex opened the door. She pushed past him and went into the living room.

'What the hell are you doing?' He followed her into the room.

'Two months I've been waiting, do you know how hard it's been? Stupidly, I thought it might be hard for you too. How could you?' She pushed her hair from her face to stop it drip-ping down her front. So much for making herself look good for the occasion.

'I don't know what you're talking about.'

'Felicity.' She gesticulated towards the front door. 'I saw you with her just now. Felicity, of all people. On the doorstep where anyone could see you. You're supposed to be so worried about your reputation and how it looks, getting together with me straight away after your fiancée died but this is far worse. She's your colleague and she was Beth's friend. Meeting her secretly behind your back. You told me, remember. How angry it made you.'

'I'm sorry you had to see that, but it's not what it looks like. Think about it. Felicity could be dangerous. Beth was filling her with lies about me and I had to put her right, stop her taking Beth's side, making out I was abusive to her. Otherwise she might start asking questions. You, of all people, should understand how scared I was.' He looked at her and she held his gaze. Yes, she knew what he meant, and it gave her power. A drop of rain fell from her fringe and she wiped it away.

'Why don't you let me take your coat,' he said. 'I want you to understand. Do you want a drink?'

'Just water.' She sat on the sofa, patting her hair dry. He came back with a glass and handed it to her. She sipped at it, confused. He wasn't pushing her away, which was something. Or was it just because of what she knew?

'I'm going to be completely honest here. Felicity is a colleague and we've always had a good relationship at work. I've never seen her in a romantic way. When I took her out to dinner to talk through the situation with Beth, she'd dressed up and was flirting with me. I couldn't risk falling out with her. She's not unattractive.' He shrugged. 'But that's all it is. You know how hard my relationship with Beth was. I wasn't faithful to Beth, we'd fallen out of love. I don't want to make the same mistake again. Felicity knows the score. It's casual.'

'You must like her.'

He shrugged again. 'We've got a lot in common. I'm not in love with her. She's an intelligent woman, I'm sure she's fine with it.'

Miranda relaxed into the seat. The fear that he'd fallen for someone else had lifted; this she could work with.

'That makes more sense. I'm not saying it doesn't hurt, but

we're similar, you and me. Getting tied down isn't my scene either.' She crossed one leg over the other. 'I like my relationships casual too. And don't forget, I know you better than anyone.'

His eyes flickered to the fireplace, and she too was thinking of that night where he'd laid out his plans to her and she hadn't flinched. That spot on the rug was where they'd devoured one another afterwards. Their eyes met.

'I knew you'd understand. I don't like to be tied down. You know how discreet I am.' What a way to get back at Felicity.

She leaned back against the sofa and he watched her thoughtfully.

'I don't mind sharing,' she said, and his eyes lit up. *For a while.*

FORTY-SIX

PRESENT

Miranda waited for Felicity's reply.

Not good. They think he was murdered and I'm their prime suspect. I'm convinced I'm about to be arrested.

That's crazy.

Felicity was in her house. Somebody else had been in there earlier because somebody had pulled the curtains in the upstairs bedroom, before Felicity had returned. It must be Caroline. Or could it be Beth?

If Felicity was about to be arrested, then she had to catch her before she was taken into custody. But why would they let her go if they suspected her? Maybe they were tracking her too, but no other car or individual had been following her when she got back earlier.

A movement caught her eye. It was Felicity, again, wearing a jacket this time. She got into her car and sat there for a bit. Her hands were moving around, she was speaking to someone. Miranda kept her head down and waited a few minutes. She didn't want to accost her outside the house because whoever was inside might come out and she wanted Felicity to herself. She was driving off. Miranda switched the ignition on and followed her.

Seeing Felicity's car in front of her focused her thought on why she was doing this. The woman in the car ahead shouldn't be here; the marriage should never have taken place. She gripped the steering wheel as the scene from the wedding day flooded her mind as it had done so many times since. The small details of the scene she had left out when describing events to the police now filled in the cracks. Only Tania could have contradicted her, caused a problem with a slight variation in their statements, but what had she seen really – Miranda a bit drunk, a bit upset. It had happened countless times before.

They were changing under their robes, trying to be quick while shivering and giggling. The combination didn't work. Giggling made Tania lose her balance and hop awkwardly on the sand as her leg missed the leghole in her swimming costume, making Miranda laugh even harder.

'Are you sure this is a good idea?' That was Caroline, always irritating, spoiling their fun. She was wearing a white bathing cap with pink flowers on. Tania snorted when she saw it, which set her off again.

'Honestly, you two.'

Miranda had risked a glance at Alex, then almost lost her balance. He was drinking from the red flask.

'Alex,' she shouted, attempting to get to him but her feet sank into the sand. He turned and flashed her a grin, before running towards the sea.

He raised his hands to the sky, palms together as if in prayer, and dived into the approaching wave. He sliced through the sea. Felicity followed him into the water.

'Alex, no.'

'What's the matter?' A cold hand grabbed her arm and Tania was shaking her gently, a baffled look on her face.

Even if Miranda's feet hadn't sunk into the sand she wouldn't have been able to move. She stared out to sea, where she could no longer see Alex.

'You're so out of it,' Tania said, 'I don't think you should go in.'

Adrenalin kicked in; she pulled away and raced towards the sea, stumbling as she reached the water, landing on her knees. Alex had disappeared into the black void that was the sea.

Pull yourself together.

'Miranda?' Tania was at her side, her eyes asking questions. She stood up on wobbly legs. It had to be a mistake.

'Are you OK?' Tania was no longer laughing.

'Yes. I don't know what happened there. Come on.'

'If you're sure. We'll stick together.'

The cold didn't register for Miranda as she reached the water and waded forward. When it reached her thighs, she lowered herself under the water and swam a slow breaststroke. She was wrong, she had to be. She said a silent prayer.

Fat lot of use the prayer had been. She'd known as she scanned the horizon, willing Alex to return. She thought she'd seen him at one point, a figure swimming towards them; when the features had revealed themselves to be Felicity it had been a hard thump to the stomach.

Felicity shouldn't be here. She steered the car right as Felicity headed towards the coast. Was she going to the sailing club? Alex had spent hours there and she'd met him there herself on several occasions, but she'd never known Felicity to go there. They passed the club building. She had to be going to the beach. They were the only two vehicles on the coast road, save for the odd one coming from the other direction. She hung back, and when Felicity indicated right to turn into the car park near the old shelter where teenagers liked to hang out away from their parents, she parked out on the road. Felicity could only be going in one direction.

She switched the torch on her phone on and pocketed it, stashing the car keys in the other. The car park was lit by street-lights, but beyond that lay the cliff edge and the steep drop below to the beach where Alex died. Pain shot through her, as it did every time she thought about what happened to him. She clenched her fist around her keys, not caring that they dug into her fingers. Ahead, Felicity was walking towards the shelter.

Miranda's trainers made no noise but the wind was loud up here. Felicity disappeared behind the shelter. 'Beth' she heard her say. Miranda held her breath, listening, but she couldn't make out any part of the muffled conversation. Her heart thudded, sounding as loud as the wind to her. She inched around the side of the shelter and stood still. The voices had moved away slightly. She clenched her fists and inched forward, risking a look. Both women had their backs to her and as she stood there, she heard a small sound coming from her side. She glanced down and saw a child asleep in a pushchair. The girl! Alex's daughter. She swooped down and lifted her out.

FORTY-SEVEN

'Because Miranda has confessed.'

'What... to...?'

'She's confessed to being Alex's mistress.'

Miranda stood very still, listening to their conversation. She willed the child to stay quiet. Inch by inch she moved forward, until she was standing a few feet behind them, right next to the edge of the cliff. Down below she could hear the waves crashing against the rocky cliff side. She didn't dare look down.

Beth's scream pierced the air.

'Where's Rosie? She's gone.' Beth ran back to the shelter, so obviously empty and looking wildly around. Miranda stepped towards her.

'I've got her.'

'You. Give her to me.' Beth's voice sounded shrill due to the rising panic inside her.

'Expecting me to be shocked, are you? You almost pulled it off.'

'Stop this now, Miranda.' Felicity stepped forward.

'You're not in class now. Nobody tells me what to do.'

'I'm calling the police.'

Miranda waved Rosie towards the coast. 'Do that and she goes over the edge. How dare you keep Alex's child from him? You might as well have killed him yourself instead of getting her to do it.'

'Come away from the edge,' Felicity said.

'Shut up. Why haven't they arrested you?'

'I didn't kill Alex.'

'They've got it all wrong,' Beth said. 'Give her to me, please. Felicity hasn't done anything wrong.'

'Hasn't she? What do you know? I knew Felicity was no good for him way before I found out about you.'

'You're still in love with him.'

'Of course.' The words sound strangled. 'I never stopped.'

'Since...?'

'Since the first time we met. We had a break after you supposedly drowned, purely for appearances. Not that Felicity cared about that. We got back together and it's been going on ever since. He loved me, he never stopped, no matter that bloody Felicity muscled in on him. I was onto her, I knew she was fake. If I'd had a bit more time he would have seen what she was up to and then it would be just him and me. It should have been me marrying him that day, not you. I don't understand what he saw in you. But murder, I didn't see that.' She wiped her cheek.

'Felicity didn't murder him.'

'She might as well have done.'

As she spoke, she waved her arms in an agitated manner and Rosie swayed perilously close to the cliff edge. Beth screamed, waking her daughter, who let out a huge wail.

'Give her to me, please.'

'Why don't you come and get her.'

Beth moved towards Miranda, placing each foot carefully in front of the other.

'Beth, no, be careful!' Felicity warned. Beth was inching

closer to the edge of the cliff. Miranda held the swaying baby over the edge, the continuous crying piercing the air as Beth's stomach lurched, seeing her daughter suspended in the air.

'Please.'

'Stand there.' Miranda moved away from the edge and directed Beth closer to it. She wanted to terrify this woman who had spread lies about Alex, the man she loved and who should have been hers. How dare she threaten her? Everything she had feared was true; she was right about Felicity. Felicity should have died, not Alex. The rage that had been bubbling up inside her ever since Alex's body had washed up on the shore like a piece of old rubbish burst into her head. Beth whimpered. 'Sit down.' Beth complied, visibly shaking. Miranda stood over her, the arm that held Rosie wavering.

'You'll drop her,' Felicity said in a strangled voice. Miranda ignored her, and didn't take her eyes off Beth. It was as if she wasn't even present. She had to act now. Felicity curled her hand around the mobile in her pocket and squeezed the side button, to call the emergency services. If she kept the call open, surely help would be sent. She moved backwards, testing Miranda, but Miranda just carried on speaking to Beth.

'I want to know why you drove Alex to his death.'

Felicity turned and ran.

Beth looked dazed. 'You don't know what you're saying. I had nothing to do with it. Give her to me. Let me get up. You're scaring me.'

'Good. If it hadn't been for you and Felicity and your stupid plan none of this would have happened. I wouldn't have done it.'

'Done what?'

'Killed him.'

'What?'

'The tablets ground up in the tea were meant for Felicity, she was meant to die, not him.' Her voice sounded strangled. 'It was a terrible mistake. I picked the wrong flask to drug. How can I ever live with that?'

'You mean... you?'

'I had to stop her taking him from me. I got the wrong flask and I killed him. Do you know how that feels? And to find out you had his first child. It should have been me giving him children. You had to ruin that too.'

Beth's face was white and she looked dazed. A siren whined in the distance.

'Alex didn't love you by the way. He was trying to kill you. He hated you and wanted rid of you. We planned it together. Like I want to get rid of you now. How am I supposed to live knowing I killed him?'

Beth noticed a movement behind Miranda. She kept still, watched as two police officers crept towards her, one grabbing Rosie from her arms as the other grabbed Miranda from behind.

'Miranda Deacon, I'm arresting you on suspicion of...'

The words faded into the background as Beth was helped to her feet and then she was diving towards Rosie, whose crying stopped as she was pushed into her mother's arms. People were moving around her but all Beth could take in was the feel and smell of her daughter, safe in her embrace.

FORTY-EIGHT

The police officers burst onto the scene like angels sent to rescue her. The woman who knelt down beside her once Rosie was in her lap was talking softly and assessing her injuries. Beth refused to let go of her daughter. The tension that had been gripping her body relaxed and she burst into tears. Behind them Miranda was being handcuffed and led away, the police officer reading her her rights. Miranda was shouting.

'It's Beth, isn't it? I'm PC Button. Are you hurt anywhere?'

'No.'

'An ambulance is on its way and we'll get you checked out to make sure.'

'I heard a siren. Was that you?'

'It was.'

'How did you know we were here?'

'Felicity Maitland made a 999 call.'

'We'll get you seen by the paramedics and once you're signed off by them you will need to come to the station as a matter of urgency. We've got some questions we'd like you to answer.'

'OK.' Beth closed her eyes, light-headedness making her want to sleep. She was vaguely aware of an ambulance arriving.

The paramedics had cleaned her up and once she'd had some painkillers and a cup of tea she felt normal apart from a throbbing head. PC Button drove her to the police station, leaving her in an interview room while she went to find her colleague.

'What's happening to Miranda?'

'She's been charged with the murder of Alex Maitland. My colleague overheard her admitting it, which ties in with evidence found at the scene.'

Beth had seen the police officer running towards them while Miranda had been shouting at her and had almost fainted with fear.

'I will have to take you in for questioning,' Chloe said. It was almost a relief. Rosie was safe. Nothing else mattered.

'I want to tell you everything.'

FORTY-NINE

'Are you absolutely sure about this?' Beth asked. She stood on the doorstep holding Rosie's hand. Felicity looked behind them to where the removal van was parked.

'Bit late to change my mind now, isn't it?' She pulled Beth in for a hug, laughing. 'Of course I'm sure. You're sure too, aren't you, Rosie?'

She bent down towards the little girl, who clutched Beth's leg and attempted to hide. Beth stroked her hair.

'Stop pretending to be shy. You know Aunty Felicity.'

'Let's have a drink first before we unpack the van.'

Felicity made some tea. Rosie sat on the floor and played with her rabbit.

'His name's Jasper and he goes everywhere with her,' Beth said, noticing Felicity watching her.

'It's amazing isn't it, everything that's happened and she will have no idea. How much will you tell her?'

'Oh, everything, but not until she's old enough to understand. No secrets from now on.'

'I can't imagine what it was like having to reinvent yourself.'

'Don't even try. Being called Beth again is taking me some getting used to. I guess I'll quickly get used to it when I start my new job. The children call their primary teachers by their first names.'

'When do you start?'

'Not for two weeks. Rosie will be at the same school, they have a preschool attached. She'll probably hate having her mother there when she's older but it's going to be a relief being able to keep a close eye on her.'

'Does she mind moving?'

'Not at all, she's excited to be by the sea.'

'It won't be for long. The house sale will go through next week and then we can think about where we want to live. I can't believe we got there in the end.'

Beth stared out of the window, hit by a wave of sadness. It happened less frequently; the doctor had said she was suffering from a mild form of PTSD, the shock of the events of the past few years hitting her with the force of a tidal wave.

'I've got something to tell you,' Felicity said. 'I'm not sure how you'll react but in the spirit of having no more secrets I have to tell you. I went to visit Miranda yesterday.'

Beth put down her cup, shocked.

'How? Why?'

'She sent me a visiting order. It took me ages to decide whether to go, but curiosity won in the end, I was intrigued to know what she had to say.'

Beth picked her mug up.

'I need something stronger than tea to hear this. How was she?'

'She hasn't forgiven you. She wanted to know exactly what happened and I told her. I hope it will help her come to terms with what she did. I feel sorry for her, the saddest thing is she wanted Alex's child and she can't get over you having Rosie.'

'If she only serves half her sentence she may still have a child of her own.'

'Maybe. Shall we get this unpacking over with? Once that's done we can open the champagne I've bought to celebrate. I'm looking forward to living with you.'

FIFTY

MIRANDA

Did knowing everything help? Felicity hadn't spared her any of the details. How she'd helped Beth escape Alex and set up a new identity under the name of Suzie Hill. How Beth discovered she was pregnant just before she'd run away. Apparently, Felicity had seen bruises on Beth's skin, where Alex had allegedly hit her. Miranda had seen him get angry but the Alex she knew had never laid a finger on her.

Alex, the man she'd loved, the man she'd killed.

Serving time for what she'd done was only what she deserved. In court she'd been able to tell her truth. At least people knew she had never intended to kill him; that was important to her. She was being punished for the attempted murder of Felicity. She hadn't expected her to visit.

That night she slept for the first time since arriving here six months ago. Knowing everything had stopped the questions floating around in her head. Understanding that Felicity had married Alex purely to get back the money he'd stolen from Beth's aunt made it easier somehow; it wasn't a love story between them as she'd suspected and Alex died knowing Miranda loved him.

One day when she got out of here, she'd live a new life too. She planned to use her time in prison to improve her qualifications and work out what she wanted to do with her life. She'd be successful, buy her own flat. If she relied on herself, she only had herself to blame if she failed. She'd stay in Eastsea; Felicity had told her by the time she was released she and Beth would have moved out of the area. Away from the sea, which wasn't surprising.

Miranda went to sleep and dreamed of swimming in the sea but this time she swam through the waves and wasn't thrown back to shore.

FIFTY-ONE

PAST

Alex was humming away like he'd had a personality transformation overnight. Clearly he'd had a good night's sleep in the spare room. Not for the first time Beth marvelled at his ability to fall into a deep sleep the moment he lay down to rest, no matter what was going on in his life. She'd spent most of the night going over the plan she'd made with Felicity. She couldn't have done it without her. Felicity had sorted out the paperwork and arrangements making sure nothing was in Beth's name. Everything was watertight and it was the right time to go.

Beth rubbed her hip where the bruise was finally beginning to fade. The mental scars wouldn't go for a long time, if ever. Alex might be able to forget traumatic events in a flash but she certainly couldn't.

'We're early today,' she said as they drove down to the beach.

'I told you. I've got a meeting but I fancied a longer swim. This way I'll be sure to get back in time. I'll drop you back home first but I'll head straight off after.'

She nodded. Every nerve in her body was alive. She parked the car and the wind tugged at the door as she got out. She used extra force to slam it shut. She was trembling but not from the cold. What happened in the next hour would determine her life and it wouldn't take much to derail the plan.

She scanned the beach for any sign of Felicity. If she failed to turn up it would have to be postponed but Beth didn't think her nerves could stand it. A figure was walking towards them and she narrowed her eyes to see if it was her but as she got nearer this woman was far too tall.

'Are you looking for someone?' Alex asked.

'No, just trying to see what the water is like, as it's so windy. It looks pretty choppy.'

'We can't let a bit of choppiness put us off. As long as we're properly prepared.' He stopped at their usual stretch of rocks and put the bags down. 'Have your tea, make sure you're warm inside; that will keep you going.'

Alex handed her the flask and she held her hand steady. She turned her back to him and knelt down to pour her drink.

'Where's your cup?' she said.

'I don't want any. I had a coffee earlier while I was waiting for you.'

Her hands shook as she poured the tea in the cup. It looked normal and it smelled like tea, not that tea had much of a smell. She was trying to see if she hadn't been suspicious already, whether she would have known something wasn't right. She could feel Alex watching her and she held the cup to her mouth, pretending to drink. She rubbed the back of her hand against her mouth to make sure she didn't take in a single drop.

'Alex.' The voice came from nowhere and she jumped, spilling some tea. Felicity had arrived. With her back still to Alex, she poured the rest of the tea behind one of the rocks, before turning round and pretending to drink.

'Hello, Felicity,' Alex said. 'You're early today.'

'That tea was refreshing,' she said. 'Hi, Felicity.'

Felicity's eyes met hers briefly.

'I'm sorry to gatecrash, but none of the others can come this early and I have to get back for the meeting – that's why you're here no doubt too, Alex. I don't like to swim alone when it's windy, so I'd rather come in with you.'

'That's sensible,' Beth said.

Alex frowned. 'Beth and I were planning a longer swim today.'

'Fine by me,' Felicity said, taking her robe off and putting it next to theirs. 'Ooh it's cold. I'm going in. Are you ready?'

'Have you finished your tea, Beth?'

'Yes, I'm nice and warm now.'

The three of them headed to the shore. Alex was ahead. 'All OK?' Felicity whispered to Beth and she nodded.

'I've got this,' Felicity said, placing a hand on Beth's back. 'You know what to do?'

'Yes. Wait for me, Alex.' She ran to join him, ignoring the shock of cold from the water and plunging straight in. 'Race you.' She forged ahead swimming front crawl, soon out of her depth. She paused, waiting for Alex to catch up. Felicity was swimming alongside him. She trod water, shivering in the cold. As Alex drew level, she faked a huge yawn.

'Tired already?' he said.

She didn't answer, made a sleepy face at him.

'Shall we have a race?' Felicity asked.

'Are you sure you can live it down? You won't beat me,' Alex said.

'I wouldn't be so sure. Are you in, Beth?'

'No. That burst took it out of me. I'll watch.'

Beth had told Felicity that Alex would never refuse a challenge. The scenario was unfolding perfectly.

'See that red sign in the distance.' Felicity pointed along the coast. 'I'll race you there and back. You can be the judge, Beth.'

'Sure, I'll swim around here. My decision will be final though.'

'It's a foregone conclusion. Count us down, Beth.'

Beth froze. This was it.

'Come on.'

'OK, here we go, in three, two, one.'

They raced off neck and neck. Felicity was a fast swimmer but she didn't have time to stop and watch. She would imagine she was racing them too. She turned and launched herself forwards in the opposite direction, imagining Alex was beside her and she was soaring ahead of him. Her arms sliced through the water and she focused on her breathing. Images swam into her head of the vast seabed so far below her, and she tried not to dwell on how deep it was and what might be lurking underneath. It only took a couple of seconds to reach the line of rocks that separated this bay from the next. She glanced over her shoulder and could just about make out Alex and Felicity, who were still swimming in the opposite direction. It was hard to believe this would work and she would never see Alex again. She swam behind the rocks towards the next bay and trod water for a moment while she peeled her black bathing cap off to reveal a lime green one underneath. She let go of the black one and it bobbed away, back the way she'd come. She undid the strap on her watch and let it sail away from her too. She ducked under the water and set off at a fast pace towards the next bay, her destination. She'd never swum so far before and her pace was slowing. Not far to go now; she used her imagination to propel her body faster through the water. She visualised a shark, a film memory that always emerged whenever she went in the sea, the fin giving away the presence of a predator. She knew there wasn't an actual shark, but Alex was a threat to her. He was the one chasing after her and she was swimming for her life.

A LETTER FROM LESLEY

Thank you so much for reading *Her Perfect Revenge*. I hope you enjoyed reading it as much as I enjoyed writing it. To keep up to date with the latest news on my new releases, just click on the link below to sign up for a newsletter. I promise never to share your email with anyone else.

www.bookouture.com/lesley-sanderson

As with my first eight books, *The Orchid Girls*, *The Woman at 46 Heath Street*, *The Leaving Party*, *I Know You Lied*, *The Birthday Weekend*, *Every Little Lie*, *The Widow's Husband* and *The Mistress Next Door*, I hoped to create an evocative novel about obsession, secrets and the blurred lines between love and lies.

If you enjoyed *Her Perfect Revenge*, I would love it if you could write a short review. Getting reviews from readers who have enjoyed my writing is my favourite way to persuade other readers to pick up one of my books for the first time.

I'd also love to hear from you via social media: see the links below.

facebook.com/lsandersonbooks

twitter.com/LSandersonbooks

instagram.com/lesleysandersonauthor

ACKNOWLEDGMENTS

So many people have helped me along the way with *Her Perfect Revenge*.

Thanks to my lovely agent, Hayley Steed, and to everyone else at the fabulous Madeleine Milburn agency.

To Louise Beere, Ruth Heald, Rona Halsall and Vikki Patis for constant support with my writing.

Thanks to Susannah Hamilton and all the staff at Bookouture, who are a fabulous, friendly publisher to work with and I am proud to be one of your authors.

And to everyone else – all the other writers I've met along the way, too many to name but nonetheless important. I'm so happy to be one of such a friendly group of people.

To my family and friends old and new for believing in me, thank you.

And of course to Paul.

Milton Keynes UK
Ingram Content Group UK Ltd.
UKHW041859210923
429138UK00004B/90

9 781837 903429